THE
AMNESIA
PROJECT

PAYTON TODD

A WOOD DRAGON BOOK

Cover art: Callum Jagger
Inside design: Rochelle Mensidor

Published by:
Wood Dragon Books
Post Office Box 429
Mossbank, Saskatchewan, Canada S0H3G0
www.wooddragonbooks.com
Email: wooddragonbooks@gmail.com

ISBN:
978-1-990863264 - Paperback
978-1-990863257 - Hardcover
978-1-990863240 – eBook

DEDICATION

_____

For my family, friends, and teachers

ONE

The smell of rain. Soaked clothes and body heat. Strong arms clutch me close. Everything is silent but the pattering of rain on the roof and a nervous heart beat.

Ba-dum.

Ba-dum.

Ba-dum.

A single gunshot violently startles me.

I jolt awake, and sit bolt upright. My chest heaves but the smell of the rain and the feeling of wet, clingy clothes are gone. I press the heels of my palms to my eyes, watching the blobs dance on the back of my eyelids, and I take in a deep breath.

"Beta, it's time to wake up," the AI drones in a dull, feminine voice.

Yeah, well, I'm already up.

I look around the room. There's a small, black wood table on the wall facing the foot of the bed. My clothes for each day are delivered to me in the morning. Today, like yesterday and beyond, they sit folded into a perfect square on the left side of the table, closest to the door. The room feels so empty and lonely. Beside the table on the wall is a black screen littered with white words.

My operating file. A profile that tells me exactly who I am in case I forget. As if I would ever forget.

Kole Danvers. 17 years old. Beta 9X.

If I look close enough, I can see fragments of myself between the lettering. Feathery ash brown hair and almond-shaped eyes a hazel colour that's more brownish green than golden brown. Thin, long, soft pink lips, and hardly any eyelashes. No dimples in sight. Only hard lines down the cheekbones made overly dramatic by shadows.

I do a double take on the file. *Beta 9X.* Yesterday, it was simply *Beta.*

I've been assigned.

I dress quickly in the clothing set out for me. The same garb as yesterday and the day before that and every day stretching as far back as I can remember. Black athletic pants and a black, tightfitting short sleeved shirt. My fingers unconsciously run over the embroidered logo on my right breast pocket. The five-point star within the circle is branded on almost everything in sight. The logo belongs to the Pacific Acting Authority Council, or PAAC. It's a post-war military operation that trains small teams, called units, to neutralize possible threats before they can spiral out of control and start another war. And I've just been assigned to one of those units as of this morning.

I've never been plagued by so many emotions at one time. My mind races. I already miss the comfort and familiarity of my room, but am excited for this change.

The hallways of the compound are eggshell white. Florescent bar lights are embedded into the floor like trail markers. I don't stray from the blueish-hued path, afraid I'll mess this up before I even begin. The door I am searching for, the general's office, comes faster than I expected. *General Isiah Fallon* is engraved on the name plate. I knock on the wood timidly.

"Yes?"

I push the door. It opens silently and I step inside, keeping my hands folded behind my back respectfully.

"Well, hello there. Are you this exceptional new recruit I've been hearing so much about?" General Fallon grins, looking up from an array of papers neatly stacked on his desk. He's blonde, his hair just a bit longer than a buzz cut and slicked back. He's built strong, stocky and wide, with broad shoulders and large hands. Despite his size, nothing about him is all that intimidating. His energy is more calming than dominating and his eyes hold a steady patience within them.

"I wouldn't imagine so, Sir."

He studies me, his gray eyes sparkling in the cold light.

"Hm. What's your name, son?"

"Kole, Sir. Kole Danvers … Sir."

"You know what I make of a timid boy, Danvers?"

"No, Sir."

"A lion of a soldier. Walk with me."

The halls go on forever, a twisting labyrinth of drywall and pure technology. It would be all too easy to get lost, so I make it a point to pay attention.

"I take it you've seen your assignment?" General Fallon shatters the silence like brittle glass.

"Yessir."

"Ninth battalion of Unit X. They've always been my personal favourite." He winks before shoving open a pair of double doors into a room I'd never seen before. "I think it's time you meet them."

The space is circular, with six sparring platforms, arranged in a semi-circle. A stage with a large circular screen on the wall takes up the rest of the room. The room smells of salt, sweat and effort. Cries of discomfort, groaning, and mild yelling add to the feeling of energy that hums in the air. I locate the sounds as two people, take turns throwing punches or ducking out of the way.

"Over there." General Fallon points to a struggle between a training assistant dressed all in white and a girl, dressed all in black, with the blondest hair I've ever seen. It's practically white. Three others, two boys and a girl—all looking around the age of seventeen—sit cross-legged off to the side, not paying attention to the fight, but talking to each other instead. Fallon takes me by the shoulders and leads me over as the white-haired girl sweeps her opponent's feet from under him. The trainer lands hard on his back and stays down, grimacing and coughing. She knocked the air out of his lungs.

"Unit 9X," the General says and they all snap to attention. "This is Kole Danvers. Your new Beta."

"It's about time." A tall boy with a lazy walking style gives me a lopsided grin. He holds out his knuckles, reaching for a fist-bump. I notice the scars on his knuckles, little stars of split skin that never quite healed right. "Allister Shepard, Delta. It's nice to meet you, bro."

"Excuse Allister's informalities." The other boy offers me his hand. I take it. "Colin Dumont. Gamma."

The other girl, small and wispy with fine, copper hair, steps forwards with a kind smile. She seems meek and quiet. The nice kind.

"Hi. I'm the Omega. I'm Maisie Greyer."

"Hey."

Gamma. Delta. Omega. That's how PAAC runs things. The rankings are how they distribute power starting with Alpha, then Beta, Delta, Gamma, Omega. It's a funny thing really. PAAC draws a circle around their emblem to declare we are all equal, then writes the pecking order like it's a grocery list.

"You'll find it easy to earn a reputation, Danvers." General Fallon pats my shoulder with his catcher's mitt of a hand. "Your unit's already made PAAC history."

"Sir?"

"Your Alpha. First female Alpha in all of compound history," he says and I look up to the girl on the mats. She's peeling the tape off her knuckles, studying me.

"Y-you're the Alpha?"

"Don't worry," she says. Her voice surprises me. It's deep for a girl, but velvety and dark. She drops her gaze to finish off the tape. "Everyone's skeptical at first."

"No!" I blurt. "I think it's ... I think it's really great." She raises a brow. "Really great. Yeah."

"Uh huh."

Great.

The last thing I need is for the Alpha to hate me. This white-haired girl with the soul piercing eyes could make my life a living hell with the smallest flick of her baby finger. This hole I'm digging for myself is getting pretty deep.

"Maisie, Colin, Allister?"

"Sir?"

"Would you three be so kind as to show Kole to your common room? Get him settled in." General Fallon nods to the exit. "I'd like to speak to your Alpha for a moment."

"Yessir." Colin nods obediently and they usher me away. I steal one last look at the girl.

"Don't worry about Astrid." Allister nudges me with his elbow. "I think she likes you. I mean, she didn't punch you and that's always good."

"That's the standard?" I inquire.

"Yeah. You should've seen what she did to the 9C Alpha. Dude was in the hospital," Allister chuckles, grinning mischievously.

"Poor guy. Entirely his fault, though," Collin adds.

"What did he do?" I pry.

"He was being a jerk to Maisie," Allister says, sounding like he's told the story a thousand times.

"Oh ... So, her name's Astrid?"

"Astrid Cardinal," Colin confirms.

"Yeah, she's actually really nice once you get to know her," Maisie shrugs, speaking softly.

"Oh, yeah. She's the absolute best," Allister says with a grin that drips with sarcasm. "About as warm as a glacier. Snuggly as a jackhammer."

"She does her job. That's all that matters," Colin admits. I'm not sure if he's defending her or just looking for something to say.

"Suck up," Allister mutters under his breath so quietly I barely hear it myself, but it answers my question. The tension between the Delta and the Gamma is mild but noticeable, like a silent conflict no one wants to acknowledge. It makes sense, though. Colin probably thinks that he's smarter than Allister, but Allister is ranked higher, being a Delta. Gammas are chosen based on cognitive performance. They are like the brains of the operation while Deltas are usually weapons specialists. That in turn, leaves the Deltas and the Gammas fighting for equal recognition on the team for their practical, protective skills.

"Just don't look her dead in the eye and you'll be fine." Colin says and I can't tell if he is joking or not.

They lead me further down the hall, still following the lights in the floor, until we stop at a door. *UNIT 9X* is engraved on a shiny name plate. I can almost see my reflection in it.

"Here we are! Home, sweet, home!" Allister hands out another lopsided grin before placing his inner wrist under a scanner, turning it slowly. There's a chunky black bracelet clasped around his wrist.

"What is that?" I flick my head at it.

"I.D. tags." Colin holds up his wrist, showing me a matching bracelet. Maisie sports one, too. "It's like a clearance card. Put it under the scanner, if you have clearance for that specific room, the door opens. If you don't, you won't be allowed in."

"Oh." I frown. *What rooms could PAAC possibly want to lock us out of?*

"There aren't many." Maisie shakes her head like she read my mind and the light on the scanner turns green. Allister shoves the door open with gusto. "Rooms, that is. No dorm hopping, of course."

"That means you're stuck with our craziness." Allister bounds into the room. It's circular, no surprise, with inlets carved out of the walls and bunks nestled within.

"You poor thing," Colin snorts and points to a bunk, empty of personal touches and between a neatly made spread and a blanket versus pillow war zone. "That's you."

"Neighbors with Colin and Allister." Maisie grimaces.

Perfect.

"We'll leave you to get settled in. Supper is at seven." Allister slaps my shoulder good-heartedly.

"Sharp." Colin points at me with authority. "Seven sharp."

"Got it." I point back.

And then they close the door and I'm plunged into solitude once again. Only this time, it doesn't feel so empty.

TWO

I walk into the circular dining hall, at exactly six fifty-nine. My unit is already sitting at a table off to the side. They wave me over and I comply for two reasons; the fact that units aren't allowed to mix, but primarily, because I don't know anyone else.

"Six fifty-nine. Not bad, Danvers." Allister grins. I find myself grinning too, as I sit in the last chair left at the table between Astrid and Allister.

Right. The rankings.

We sit in a circle, but still in order. Astrid, myself, Allister, Colin, Maisie. Alpha, Beta, Delta, Gamma, Omega.

"This is for you." Astrid speaks so smoothly I almost miss it. She produces a black ID bracelet from the pocket in her grey sweatshirt. It is identical to the ones worn by the other members of the unit. I take it from her gingerly.

"Thanks." I hesitate.

You're digging yourself a hole, Danvers. Put the shovel down. My inner voice scolds me.

Good thing I can jump high.

Shut up. It hisses at me.

"So," I clear my throat. "When does ... training ... uh, start?"

Shut up. Shut up. Shut up.

"It should have started five years ago. At least for basic training. Specialized rank training starts whenever the council thinks we're ready." Astrid explains casually, narrowing her eyes at me. Before being assigned, I had done fitness tests and puzzles, but I always thought of those as games rather than training. The table is silent and I look down at the plate of food before me. Mashed potatoes. I hate mashed potatoes.

Thankfully, before the air could grow any thicker with awkwardness, attention is called to the podium on the stage at the front of the room. A woman with wide eyes and rusty-orange hair slicked back into a tight ponytail stands with her cherry red lips close to the microphone head.

"Hello? Hello, everyone? Up here, please! Yes, hi! Thank you!" She waves for everyone's attention and the noise quickly clears to silence. "Yes, hello! I am Colonel Everlade, the primary Gamma instructor and here are the co-generals of the operation with a little message. Please welcome our brave leaders—"

"Suck up." Allister leans to whisper in my ear. I stifle a laugh, choking on my water.

"Generals Ryker and Fallon!"

A chorus of heavy applause goes up like a wildfire and engulfs the room. I just add to the thunder, clapping along politely as two men climb to the podium. They stand together, sharing the space, but the man on the left, Ryker, steals my attention. His hair is shaved so close to the scalp that on first glance I thought he was bald. His eyes, brown like an espresso syrup, are narrow like the slit eyes of a venomous snake. His shoulders are square, large, and muscular, making Fallon look tiny by comparison.

This was a man who generated and consumed his own power, his own energy.

"Don't look him in the eye," Maisie hisses from across Astrid's folded hands and half-empty water glass.

"Why not?" I ask.

"Maisie's convinced he can read your mind. Boogey voodoo and all," Allister snorts.

"What?" I grin at the copper-haired girl. "Why?"

Her eyes widen and she shakes her head. "I've heard lots of stories about him from trainers."

"Rumors," Astrid corrects her with an amused glint in her eyes.

The pair on the stage dive into a speech; with Fallon doing all the talking and Ryker silently scowling as he scans the room, daring someone to interrupt. They make a good team.

"Thank you, Colonel Everlade, for that wonderful introduction, but, I'm sure everyone here already knows the drill," Fallon begins with a white-toothed smile. "Our units have all, finally, been completed. Missing puzzle pieces found and the order of the jigsaw restored. So ..." He brandishes his fingers like we are waiting for something spectacular. "In accordance to such perfection, our final examinations will soon commence."

A round of full-hearted cheering bursts to the ceiling and echoes back down again.

"Yes." Fallon laughs. "It is very exciting and I have full confidence that each and every one of you will do marvellously. The examinations will consist of two sequences."

A projector comes to life, splashing a picture on the perfect eggshell white wall. The image is split down the middle, a brain on the left side and a bubble-figure human stuck in a running pose on the right.

"The first, a cognitive evaluation to test strategy, reaction, logical thinking and problem solving." The brain pulsates orange hues as he speaks. "The second, a timed physical challenge designed to push your body's boundaries." The running man pulsates for a while until both images come to a halt. My own pulse quickens in excitement. "But, per usual annual examinations, failure is always a possibility. Mind you, possibility, not option. All units who come up with a total score of eighty-five percent will be cleared for active duty. Units who fall short will not make the cut and will be ... expelled from all further training and function."

"Can they do that?" I glance around the table.

"They can do whatever they want." Astrid looks me in the eye. A clear challenge to my ability to carry my weight on the team. I look back to the podium, but watch her in my peripheral vision as she shifts comfortably in her chair.

"Training will be conducted in units and in one-on-one format with the instructors. I implore you to train as hard and as often as possible. Being prepared is a weapon as sharp as any knife. I hope you all have a good evening, and remember although you be outranked, you are not unequal."

"Although we be outranked, we are not unequal." The gathered units echo like a thundering parrot, all together. Voices merge, combining to create something new. Something powerful. Something *united*. It feels empowering, strengthening and encouraging. The buzz of the room—pure, raw energy—is a hard and shocking kick compared to the dull solitude I was entangled with last night. This morning, even. And I like it. I realize just how

long I've craved this kind of inclusiveness. But apparently, if we score under eight-five percent, that can disappear as quickly as it formed.

The night is strange. New bed. New smells. New sounds. New shadows to imagine and build night monsters from. I hadn't realized that the bunks built into the walls had hidden dividers that slid in and out of place, separating the bunks from each other and the common area. They create a place of privacy. Separation. I sleep with my back to the closed divider and the covers pulled tight under my chin. The blanket is a silky sheet that would have been insufficient for a large room, but in close quarters like this heat builds and a thicker blanket would have been suffocating.

This dorm has upholstered furniture and a bathroom with a shower. A desk strewn with Colin's papers that we are forbidden to touch. Each member with their own personal space and a common area for socialization. It's small, but it's cozy. It's a home. It's *my* home.

I reach out, brushing my fingers, only two of five, on the solid wall facing me and sigh out of my nose. My space. My room, and even if it is the size of a broom closet, it gives me a sense of belonging. It feels like it's really mine and I'm not just borrowing the space. I love it.

THREE

Sunshine. Lemonade in a glass pitcher with matching cups on burlap coasters. A black wicker furniture set with that strange patio comfort, a plush surface and a hard backing. Yellow-petalled and brown-centered sunflowers in an antique vase sit as a centerpiece. My grandmother's old vase.

A little girl runs up, crawling onto the seat next to me. She holds out her index finger.

"Look! Look, Kole, Look!" She sounds like she's underwater. Her voice comes through in bubbling giggles. "Look!" A little red dot, a ladybug, crawls along her finger and climbs her knuckles. They must feel like mountains to the little insect.

"Where did you find him?" I ask, but I sound weird. Young. Like someone else is talking for me.

"Mommy's garden."

Mom.

I jolt awake to a heavy knocking on the divider slide. I open it to Allister grinning stupidly before firing a ball of crumpled clothes at my face.

"Rise and shine, sleeping beauty! We got work to do! Let's get your cushy behind to the training room for a proper butt whooping!"

"What?" I demand. "Why?"

"Initiation, bro. It's a thing. Just go with it," he says, grinning. I slide the door shut on him. He knocks again. I don't open it. "Colin, Astrid and Maisie are already in the training room and you're already late! Let's go!" he calls through the wall and I flop back onto the pillow with a groan.

Dressed and in the training room, I see my unit. Maisie and Colin stand with their elbows propped up on the platform. They're surrounded by other soldiers, grinning and waiting for a good show. Astrid stands ready on the platform, bouncing on the balls of her feet and stretching out her arms. Allister stands in the center of the ring, holding a permanent marker like it's a microphone. He helps me into the ring and slips on cloth knuckle covers over my shaky fingers.

"Ready?" he asks.

"No."

"Wrong answer." He claps my shoulder and gives me a shove forwards before diving into the role of hype man. "Challenger and champion! Master and commander! It's a breaking in! An initiation! Let's rumble!"

Astrid pulls her fists up, hiding her jaw and takes steady steps forward around the ring. Stalking, prowling. Rounding closer and closer until we're within swinging range.

"Swing!" she taunts. "Or are you afraid to throw the first punch?"

"I don't hit girls."

"That's your first mistake." She grins and feints right and darts to my left. She strikes while on the move and connects with a crafty kidney punch. I turn to face her, not wanting her to get behind me.

It's over when she's at my back. When I turn, I run into her fist and she delivers a hard blow to my sternum. I stagger backwards.

I watch in slow motion as she drops down into a crouch and sweeps my feet out from under me. My head cracks against the ring floor and I groan, seeing stars. I try to get back up, but fall again, my head spinning. Allister appears in my vision.

"The challenger newbie is down!"

"Not helping, man," I groan, trying to shove him away.

"Hey, dude, don't hate the players. Hate the game."

"I *do* hate the game," I grumble.

"Then you're set! Go get 'em, tiger!" He picks me up and pushes me back at the white-haired girl. I can see the amusement in her eyes. I shake myself off. Hands, shoulders, legs, head. I rotate at the hip and the top of my foot gets to the inside of her knee. When she buckles, I take advantage and kick at her shoulder. She puts an arm up to block it and rolls to her feet, her fists up yet again.

"Not bad." She nods, sizing me up for real now. "But not good enough."

"You're really bad at compliments," I pant.

She snorts a laugh. "Thanks."

I go at her again, trying her feinting trick. Unfortunately, it only works when your opponent doesn't see it coming. She stood, stiff as a board, and stuck out her arm, catching me across the collar bone and winding me. I hit the ground hard for the second time.

"Winner!" Allister hollers. Cheers from the crowd. I cough a little. The air feels like fire and I groan loudly.

Afterwards, I get in the shower to wash away the grime of the day. The water is scalding, but my muscles start to relax. The showerhead glints silver above me, only flecked by the odd dot of calcium. The heat and steam work with the pressure of the water jets to slowly uncoil my taut muscles, working out the knots like kneading bread. Although it feels wonderful, I know it's a short-lived reprieve— they'll be just as sore tomorrow morning.

"Sweet Jesus," I mutter, rolling my neck and shoulders.

I put my forehead against the tile, my mind reeling. Everything is happening so fast. It's day two already. I've been assigned, moved, beat over the head. I've met new people; people I would have never known existed. People who would have never known that *I* existed.

The water becomes more pleasant as I adjust to it. The dull ache ebbs away to nothing and I put my face to the stream. I hold my breath, then let it go. Feeling a new Kole take the old Kole's place, I smile.

FOUR

"Strategy. Exceptional strategy, follow through, and critical decision making." A woman paces the classroom stage, one hand on her hip and the other clutching a wire-thin pointer. The seats slope upwards like a college auditorium or a cinema theater. "These aspects create great soldiers of mind. Physical strength is important, but so is a sharp, ready mind. You can have all the ammunition in the world, but without the initiation from the gun to send the ammunition on its way? Pointless. Marry the two together and ... voila, perfect effort and exceptional performance every single time."

The woman, Logistics Professor Colonel Marriott, was a tough woman in clunky black boots, army pants and the standardized female high-necked uniform top. Her mousy brown hair was pulled into two thick braids framing the back of her neck. Her small eyes and flat nose made her unmistakable in any crowd.

"Training will consist of real time challenges in teams and solo settings. Some will be easy. Some will be difficult."

"But all shall be reward-eth," Allister whispers to me. I shake my head and grin, amused. It's his humor that gets me through Colonel Marriott's monotone speech. It's only the beginning of training, but being preached at by the Prof is already starting to get old.

"We'll begin small, as all great castles are begun with a single brick. Get yourselves into pairs. You'll find the chess boards in the right-hand cupboards." Colonel Marriott claps her hands together and Allister and I look at each other pointedly.

"Partners?" He raises a brow. I nod.

"I'll get the board."

———

"Where did you learn to play?" I ask, moving a pawn. The board is glass, the checkered squares clear or stained black. The playing pieces are made from heavy pieces of metal. Copper and silver.

"Can't remember." He waves the question away, moving a rook and trapping one of my valuable players. I frown. "What about you?"

A memory washes over me like a wave, tumbling and tossing. Choking, but cleansing at the same time.

"Good move, darling," Mom says with a warm smile. *"You're a very fast learner."* I drink in the praise like it's liquid gold. It is. In a way.

"Kole?" Allister waves a hand in front of my face. "Still there?"

"Uh, yeah."

"So ... where did you learn to play again?" he pries. I want to tell him, "My mom taught me," but the words get caught in my throat. For some reason, it seems wrong to share anything from my past. I frown harder, my gaze moving to Colonel Marriott who is watching us like a hawk from the platform.

"I ... I don't remember either," I say, swallowing hard. In what world do you have to lie about where or who taught you to play a game? Why is this wrong? Why is my first instinct to close that door? Is Allister lying, too?

Stop it. Just stop it. He's not lying.

I look around at the other players moving the metal characters across glass. Everyone is playing. *Do they remember where and when they learned?*

Maybe, maybe no one else remembers. Maybe I'm the only one.

"Your move, dude." Allister flicks his chin at the board. The metal meets my fingers and I make the final move of the game, despite all of Allister's brilliant play.

"Checkmate," I whisper.

"Dang, bro. Play again?" he pleads.

"Uh, yeah, sure. You set it up. I just ... have to go to the washroom."

"Okay."

I practically run there, jamming my wrist band under the scanner and sliding inside before the door is even fully open. My chest throbs with the ferocious beating of my heart and my hands shake as I splash water on my face. On my neck. I take a deep breath and stare at the eyes in the mirror. They look scared. Unsure. They remind me of a frightened deer.

"Get it together," I hiss at myself with venom. "You're fine. Don't be such a coward."

You're just stressed.

About what?

... Exams. That's it. Just stress. Stressed over exams. Stress makes people do crazy things, feel crazy things.

If you say so.

Shut up.

A mechanical sounding bell fires through the intercom, signalling the end of class. I put my head in my hands. It startles me and now I feel bad that Allister never got his second game of chess.

FIVE

The following days blur into a routine that bleeds into weeks. Every day is more or less the same. Wake up. Eat. Train. Eat. Attend Marriott's logistics class. Eat. Sleep. Wake up and do it all again.

And again.

And again.

Eventually, I start waking up before Allister even knocks on my divider.

Once or twice, I was the one knocking on his and using his line. "Rise and shine, sleeping beauty!" I'd call out, grinning.

He'd throw his pillow and try to stifle his own smile. "Get outa here, newbie," he would grumble, the sleep living in his voice making the sounds gruff and coarse.

Before breakfast, we would take to the punching bags, working up a little sweat. I could feel my body changing, the softness seeping away. The veins in my hands and neck became more prominent. My shoulders more squared, my jaw more defined. My collar bones were sharper. I felt entirely new, stronger. Better.

Day after day, I find myself training for longer, pushing myself harder, expecting more and more and more from my body. It is the most amazing thing I have ever experienced and I finally feel *myself*. I'd only been training for a few weeks, but it still felt good.

I feel like *Kole*. The Kole that should've been here a long time ago. Confident, strong Kole. A Kole that I was proud of.

Astrid found me alone in the training rooms as I pounded on a punching bag, watching it with satisfaction as it swayed on the chain.

"I have to admit." Her voice, silky and dark, comes from behind. It doesn't startle me anymore. I falter, turning to look at her. A wisp of a grin plays on her lips. "You've done good."

"I'm waiting." I grin.

"Waiting for what?"

"For the 'but.' It's not like you to just hand out a compliment." I smile when she smiles. She has a pretty smile, and the fact that I see it so seldom helps me know that it's sincere.

"Then, you know I really mean it," she says, pulling off her jacket. "Come on." She grabs the punching mitts, pulling herself up on the ring platform gracefully, the ring where she kicked my sorry ass a month ago, and puts the mitts on her hands. I follow.

"Oh, you're actually *helping* me now?" I raise my brows, following her.

"You're funny," she snorts. "I just don't want to get dropped. Helping out the weak link."

"Oh, I see. That's how it is?"

"Oh, that's how it is."

I take shots at the mitts. She adjusts, moving them, making fake jabs for me to block or duck. I work hard, trying to impress her by keeping in rhythm and not missing an opportunity to hit. Nor *getting* hit, either. She removes the mitts and hands them to me, telling me it's her turn. I stand with my hands up, feeling her fists through the padding but trying not to let it show that it makes my palms ache a bit.

"Can I ask you something?" I add my voice to the mix of laboured breathing and the sound of her knuckles on the punching mitts, breaking the tension. It shatters like a plate thrown on a cement floor. Awkwardly and in shards.

"Just did." She speaks with no trouble as she moves. Between her ducking and dodging, I see the flashes of a grin. I breathe a laugh.

"Okay, smart aleck."

"Watch yourself, Beta." She laughs. "I'm still the Alpha."

"Right, the first girl Alpha. How did you do it?" I ask. She pauses. A cluster of stray hairs has escaped her ponytail. I fight the urge to tuck it behind her ear.

"The same way anyone does anything. You want it bad enough, work for it. Work *hard*. It takes some luck, too, but … in the end it's all you." She says it so sincerely.

"So … what was the worst part?" I furrow my brow. She sniffs a little, looking at the floor and nodding her head a little, thinking it over. Her mind and her thoughts were like a tumbler to a raw gem, polishing them into a single, pure, connected thought.

"The loss," she says finally.

"Loss?"

She sighs deeply, shoulders and all. "Yeah. I had to give up a lot of things, cut out a lot of people. People who didn't really want me to succeed. Friends who weren't really friends … just looking to gain status by association. It hurt for a while, but it stopped eventually. Once I realized, you know, that they would've only held me back and everything." Her eyes are so chilling that a shiver runs through me. Their gunmetal grey to blue irises are stunning, holding and trapping me. The emotion in them lives silently, but not unseen. It's not quite pain, not a true hurt. More like a disappointment of sorts. A longing, nostalgia maybe. But in the mix of all this, regret is nowhere to be found. It's not a missing ingredient. It was never in the recipe in the first place. She doesn't regret a thing. And she shouldn't.

"Well, they were either really stupid or just really mean to stand in your way." I don't just say it to make her feel better. I already know she doesn't need me, or anyone else for that matter, to make her feel better. I say it because I can't imagine the kind of person who would choose to stand in her way.

"Yeah," she murmurs with a timid smile. "They really were."

"Stupid or mean?"

She laughs out loud, a real laugh. The kind that cleanses the soul. It sounds like a beautiful melody.

"Both." She chuckles.

The lights above us flicker. A little glitch in the otherwise perfect compound. A metaphor. Doesn't matter how hard we try, how far we go, there will always be something that falls out of place. A loose screw, or a weaker chain link. Nothing will ever be exact or perfect, and that's okay.

"What's it like?" I question, still staring at her. She glances at me, a little confused. "Working so hard. Having it all pay off."

"I don't know," she admits softly. "I'm not done yet."

SIX

Unexpectedly, one day all organized training was cancelled and the schedule was abandoned. Fallon said it was "a day of rest" before examination day.

Tomorrow's the day, then.

We sat in the 9X common room, sprawled out on the chairs, floor and sofa—all in perfect silence. I couldn't even hear the sound of anyone's breathing.

"Is everyone ready for tomorrow?" Maisie asks softly from her cross-legged spot on the floor. Her chin in her hands, elbows on the hardwood and a disassembled puzzle before her. I had already practiced that one. It's a giant squid. She's taking a long time despite having done this one before.

Just trying to find something to do. When people are stressed, they try to find something to do. Keep their hands busy.

She must be nervous.

We all are.

"We better be ready," Astrid answers, picking imaginary dirt from under her nails. "It's kind of a make-or-break moment."

"Yeah," Colin mumbles. "No pressure."

"I'm sure we'll do fine," I interject. "Besides, how many units actually fail?"

"I heard a story that a few years ago, only five out of twenty-six made the cut." Astrid shoots me a look.

"... Oh ..." Maisie looks back down at her puzzle.

"Who told you that?" I ask.

"Fallon," replied Astrid

"Ah, right then." I nod.

We plunge into an awkward silence.

"Kole's right, guys." Maisie sits up. "We have to think positive or we've failed already." Colin scoffs and Allister shoots him a glare. I take a long sip of the water from the glass sitting next to me.

"I agree," Allister adds. "Whatever happens tomorrow, good or bad, we're still a team."

"Our best is all we can do." We all look at Astrid for the final word. She is the Alpha, after all. She nods through a sigh. "Let's do this."

SEVEN

"Good morning, Units A to Z and welcome to the ninth annual examination day!" Fallon beckons for a hearty but nervous applause. The energy in the room is intense, crackling and threatening to bubble over. The severity of my emotions gradually increases, going from nervous jitters to full-out panic. I take a shaky breath, just trying to calm myself.

Calm down. Chill out. This is normal.

"We will begin with the mental examination after a few brief words from our partners on the military defense council." He smiles. "Roll the clip!"

The circular screen above the podium comes to life, first with PAAC's circle and star emblem and then a man's barely smiling face. He wears professional military clothing and looks of high rank. He has no facial hair, but on his head, a salt and pepper collection is groomed to shining perfection. He is the image of neatness, cleanliness, and self-respect.

"Hello, soldiers." He speaks through the room's booming audio system. "I wish you all the best of luck in this year's testing. I have the utmost faith in every single one of you and know you will do exceptional work. Good luck." As quickly as he appeared, he was gone again but his message was like the starting bell to a high stakes horse race.

Staff come and usher us away, Unit by Unit starting at A. The wait just to be called is excruciating. PAAC organizes the different units by letter and number, the letter noting which of the twenty-six possibilities of the alphabet the unit stands as, the number being the iteration of that particular letter. Unit 9X, my unit, is the ninth version of unit X. Once our unit is called, we are taken to yet another waiting room and then tested individually, separated by our ranks, from lowest to highest.

"Maisie Greyer."

"Colin Dumont."

A little while later. "Allister Shepard." Then finally. "Kole Danvers." I stand up awkwardly and make my way to the door, but not before Astrid's voice stops me, silky and dark.

"Hey, Kole?"

"Yeah?" I turn. She stares me in the face, then her expression softens.

"Good luck," she says. I hesitate.

Say something you idiot!

"... You too," I mumble.

She smiles a little before returning her gaze to the floor and I leave the room, silently cursing myself.

"Welcome, Kole Danvers, Beta 9X. Please be seated and wait for further instruction." That familiar emotionless AI voice of a robotic woman speaks as soon as the door closes behind me. The voice sounds like knives scraping on rocks, worming its way into my brain. I take a seat on the only chair in the room, assuming that's what the AI lady meant rather than the floor. The chair is on a platform two steps high and has a lengthy back, silver supports and black cushions. It faces a screen with a white PAAC logo on a black background.

"Prepare for examination in three ..."

The lights go out and the emblem sears itself further into my vision.

"Two ..."

The chair rises slightly. I notice two little red lights blink to life from the sides of the screen. I'm being recorded.

"One. Welcome, Kole Danvers, to your cognitive examination. Let us begin."

––––––––––

Coming out of the exam room was like being poked in the eyeballs with hot forks. The lighting difference between rooms makes me blink quickly so my eyes can adjust. The relief of being done washes over me like a pleasant spring rainfall, serene and peaceful. But the inner peace lasts only until my inner voice begins to speak.

Halfway done. Don't get ahead of yourself. And you haven't even seen your scores yet. They could be awful.

Thank you. I really needed that added confidence.

You're welcome.

I wander the hallways. The thought that I could've absolutely bombed that test descends like a ten-pound weight on my shoulders. The weight increases to fifty pounds as I think about how my possible failure would affect the rest of the team. What if it's my fault that the unit gets expelled? And they would know. With one glance at the score sheets, they would know that it was me who screwed everything up. No. I can't fail. Not now. Not when my entire unit is depending on me to succeed. Depending on me to do one specific thing—and that is not to fail.

"Hey! Kole! There you are!" Maisie leads the unit towards me from down the hall. They are a very welcome distraction from the war raging inside my head.

"Yeah, I just got out." I pull a grin. I'm surprised at how sincere it feels.

"No, you didn't," Maisie smiles. "It's been thirty minutes."

I frown, but she must be right or else Astrid would still be in testing instead of with the group.

"We thought you got lost, man!" Allister chuckles. "C'mon, they're serving ice cream in the cafeteria as a treat for our hard work."

"I'm there." I nod, eyes wide. Together as a unit, we walk down the hall. I try my best to cut the mental rope tying me to my testing round and leave my doubts behind, but my knife isn't sharp enough and my worries drag behind me defiantly.

After lunch, they split us up again. One at a time, in a seemingly random order, we walk down a windowless hall and through a door that leads to a room with a glass partition that serves to separate the test subject from the assessment area. A stab of nervousness slices through my gut like a hot knife through butter. I try my best to settle myself and fight down my lunch that's trying hard to make a second appearance.

It isn't the obstacle course that's concerning me. It is the seated spectators, some red faced and shiny with sweat, others staring right at me in calm, tight-lipped ways. I scan them, searching for faces. Ryker and Fallon flank each side. Fallon gives me a sporty thumbs up.

Breathe. Breathe. Just breathe. Don't panic.

Too late.

"Kole Danvers. Beta 9X."

The glass doors start to slide and I wait for them to open completely before taking even a single step forward. I roll my shoulders, hearing a little pop which makes me grimace. The course looks simple enough, but I know I shouldn't underestimate it. Fallon and Ryker designed it with overly confident kids in mind. Hence the live audience. I swallow hard and close my eyes, taking in another deep breath until my chest feels ready to explode.

"Stand at the line."

So, I stand at the line, the toes of my shoes almost touching it, but not quite. I take another breath.

"Building simulation opponent." A hologram of a genderless human form appears beside me—cubistic, in an orange hue. "The opponent is not your real rival. The clock is. Complete the course in under ten minutes and you will pass. Fail to do so and your overall score will be impacted immensely."

"Got it," I answer, even though I know no one can hear me.

"Ready yourself. On the count of three. One."

I take a breath and try to prepare. My muscles tense like springs begging to give their burst of life.

"Two."

My heart is already pounding. I'm ready.

"Three."

I am ready.

I jolt to life at the sound of a buzzer and burst into the race. I feel alive, awake, powerful as I take to the course. I tackle the first obstacle in time with the hologram and its fiery orange glow. The second challenge—a series of elevated tiles, getting higher and higher and ending at a rope to swing across to another platform—makes me feel like I am flying. I reach out to grab the rope, but hesitate and come to a stop. The hologram doesn't make the same stupid mistake and continues at full speed.

Of course, it does. It's an AI feature.

I grab the rope, swing, and hit the other side, all the while chastising myself for stopping at all. I have a lot of ground to cover in a short amount of time.

The next obstacle is a long set of monkey bars similar to what you would find in a school playground. Crossing the obstacle, swinging from bar to bar, will take time. Time that I don't have. Colonel Marriott's voice comes to my head in paraphrased verses.

"... Marry strategy and physicality ..."

I run at it, grabbing onto the first rung. Instead of continuing on with upper body strength alone, rung after rung and blister and blister, I pull myself through the gap and balance, running over the bars. I almost grin to myself, pleased with my tactics.

Not yet. Celebrate later.

I finish the obstacle, landing hard on my feet. I am a comfortable distance ahead of the orange rival. I jump over the hurdles that come next, feeling awkward and splayed out. Next, I army-crawl under a cargo net and push on. I make it through obstacle after obstacle. I am starting to feel worn and burned out, but before I know it, I stand at the finish line.

It's over.

I bend over with my hands on my knees. My heart is beating out of my chest and I can barely hear the AI announcing my time over the roaring of my pulse in my eardrums. I pant, wiping the sweat off my forehead with my shirt before finally standing up straight and looking at the clock.

7:42.

I look to the spectator booth and catch Astrid's gaze. She looks serious but gives me a little nod. It's funny how that one little gesture makes the world spin a little faster. The room plunges into high definition as the last of my adrenaline pumps like fuel to a race car engine. I allow myself to smile before they usher me through a door and into the viewing area. As I reach for the door, I fight the urge to turn around and give the hologram my favourite finger.

———

That night, the illuminated screen in the cafeteria steals everyone's attention. It's not like many people are actually eating—nerves are horrible on the appetite. One word glows. It reads *"RESULTS"* in large, uppercase block letters. The atmosphere turns lethal with energy. Fallon appears like a ghost at the podium and we clap politely.

"Well done, everyone! We have an abnormally high success rate this year, so, bravo!" I can feel Allister's elbow in my side. I bat it away as soon as it starts getting painful. "I could stand here and preach to you forever, but let's move it along. Give me ... the Omega scores."

Instinctively, I reach out and put a hand on Maisie's as she watches the screen with wide eyes.

No. 9: Maisie Greyer. Total: 89%.

"Give me Gamma!"

No. 9: Colin Dumont. Total: 95%

"Delta!"

No. 9: Allister Shepard. Total: 90%

No way would Colin not use his higher score against Allister. Allister would wave it off, pretending it didn't bother him. I was determined not to get involved in their competitive game.

"Beta!" Fallon calls out and my breath catches in my throat. It sits in the back like a frog, or an itch from a cold.

No. 9: Kole Danvers. Total: 96%.

A bubble of relieved laughter forces past my teeth and I relax. I made it. I did it. I smile wider at the thought.

"And finally, Alpha scores."

No. 9: Astrid Cardinal. Total: 99%.

One percent off a perfect score and her facial expression doesn't soften in the slightest. Fallon leaves the stage, but someone intercepting him catches my eye. It's General Ryker. He's trying to persuade Fallon of something with exaggerated hand motions and an urgent look to his snake-like face. When he looks directly at me and points, my blood chills. Fallon looks at me, too, before sending Ryker on his way. Fallon approaches the table.

"Well done, 9X, well done," he sings in a praise, but it's like he's stalling. "Impressive scores all around."

"Thank you, General," Colin pipes up like an obedient puppy, drinking in his praise like fine wine.

"Kole," he says when he makes it to me. "Can I have a word with you?"

"Sure," I say, trying to hide my apprehensiveness. "Is something wrong, General?" I push in my chair when I stand. He claps a hand to my shoulder, steering me towards the door.

"I hope not."

———

"I don't understand." I narrow my eyes. "How was my test inconclusive?"

"We're not sure."

"Then how did I get a final score?"

"I overrode the error to get your result, but the system found an error regardless. We can't let it go unexplored. At the time, we did not know what the computer picked up on or deemed to be an error, but we will be looking into it." He sighs deeply through his nose.

"I'm still confused. What's going on?" I furrow my brow.

"That's a very good question, Kole, and one day, I will have answers for you." Fallon sighs again, lacing his giant hands together. "But for the time being, Kole, I need to know if at any time you felt strange or out of place?"

"Strange, Sir?"

"Like you were ... someone else. Someone you are not, yes?"

Oh. The memories. That's what he wants. It's less of a confession, more of an investigation.

Maybe you're crazy. Paranoid. Maybe they're just trying to help. Emotional counselling or something.

Yeah? You think?

No. You're under a searchlight. Don't get cocky.

"No, Sir." I lie through my teeth. It's becoming a horrible habit. "I don't recall anything like that."

"Very good, Kole, very good. I'm positive that it's just an error in our systems. Something on our part. A coding issue or a bug, maybe. Your original score stands and there's a door to your left. Thank you for your time."

"Yes, Sir. Thank you, Sir," I say, leaving with the sick feeling that he didn't believe a word I said. I put a hand on the door and freeze. I turn back to the General. "Sir?"

"Yes, Kole?"

"What would happen if I did ..."

What? Remember? Careful.

"If I did feel ... strange?"

Fallon draws in a slow breath, shifting in place as I hang off his every word.

"I think ..." he says finally, drawing out the words like a smoker sucking every ounce of buzz from a drag, "we would have to discuss that at the time of occurrence. What do you think?"

"Of course, Sir. I agree." I blurt and leave quickly, feeling his eyes on my back as I exit.

EIGHT

"I thought for sure I was gonna fail."

"You did not! Look at the score you got!" The conversation is already excited when I walk in. My unit sits on the couch, chairs, and floor of the 9X common room without a care in the world. How I wish I could do the same. I flop into an empty chair and feel all the stress crash down on my shoulders at once. Allister nods his head at me in greeting.

"Don't celebrate yet," Astrid says, a knowing smile playing on her lips. "We still have specialized training. I've heard it's absolutely grueling."

"What's specialized training?" I ask, entering the conversation.

"You train with your rank, learning to do what your rank was created for," Allister answers. "Delta, Delta. Omega, Omega. Beta, Beta. That kind of thing."

"Yay," Colin voices. "New friends." Maisie slaps him playfully. He just smiles.

"So, big man, what did the General want?" Allister takes a heavy swig of a dark coloured juice that smells like raspberries and cranberries combined. Sweet. Too sweet for me.

"Just checking in." I shake my head and look at the array of dominos on the floor. Maisie arranges them, standing them up like towers before knocking them over in a cascading, rippling effect of clatters and light thuds.

"Looks like someone's the boss man's favourite," Colin snorts, but I don't hear him. Not really.

The dominos are huge in my tiny hands and I am more interested in making castles with them than playing the actual game. I could make entire cities. I could make an empire with domino blocks. And the best part is knocking them all down and building it again from scratch.

"What do you have there, kiddo?" A voice. A man's voice. I hold up the dominos with a wide smile, tongue darting in and out of the hole made from a missing front tooth. He picks me up and sets me on his lap. His sweater is knitted, colours that felt symbolic. Greens and reds. Snow fell in independent and uniquely crystalized flakes outside the window. I can still see the sledding tracks through the living room window from our adventures the day before.

"You know what the best part about this time of year is, kiddo?" the man asks, his lips close to my head now. "Hmm?" I just hold up my dominos. He chuckles, deep and throaty. Echoing from his gut. "No, it ain't dominos. It ain't the gifts or the food, either. It's the feeling. The air. Close your eyes, kiddo. Tell me when you feel it."

I don't understand what he means, but I close my eyes and wait for something spectacular. I wait for as long as I can and I finally get it. The overwhelming feeling of safety and comfort. Love and joy. Something I'd never forget. Then the sweet scent of something so achingly familiar.

"David! Kole!" Mom calls us from the kitchen. "I made hot chocolate. Come get some!"

"Right, Danvers?" Allister's elbow jolts me back to reality, although the feeling lingers and the smell of hot chocolate is warm in my nose.

"Sorry?"

"Colin says that he's excited to learn knew things. Allister says he just hopes there's a few hot girls in his class. What do you think?" Astrid asks, with the pointed raise of a brow and I hesitate like a deer caught in headlights.

Aw, crap.

NINE

In exactly a week, the specialized training started. I stood in a tight semi-circle with twenty-six other Betas, boys and girls, all complete strangers. The instructor, General Isaiah Fallon, stood at the open mouth of the semi-circle.

"The Beta's job is to back up the Alpha. To convince and persuade the other members who may not be fully on board. But, of course, if it is a truly terrible idea, ask your Alpha, politely, to rethink their course of action. Listen to your instincts. They are more powerful than you know. Your job is to trust, follow, and lead by example. You are second in command and very important." Fallon pauses and then says, "Teamwork is an asset, so let's form groups of three and get to work."

I was paired with a girl with espresso-brown hair, even darker eyes, and warm-toned skin. She said her name was Myrka Del Gatto, Beta 9F. She was nice. I liked her. The second was a pale, orange-haired and freckle-faced boy named Peter Tarek, Beta 9G. Myrka was kind and Peter was boisterous. Something about the combination allowed us to work smoothly together. And, I had to admit, a break from the usual 9X crowd wasn't such a horrible things. A few fresh faces kept thing interesting and not as predictable. As we worked together, my two fellow Betas became more than distractions, they became friends.

The challenge presented to each trio was to establish a sort of hierarchy in a peaceful way, which sounds simple until everyone wants to be the boss. That was just the beginning. We ran through mission scenarios, each taking a turn at playing a different rank. Fallon stressed that we needed to know what it was like to be in the shoes of our fellow team members. To feel what they feel, power-wise. It didn't make sense to me. Why would we be focusing on any rank other than our own? But I didn't ask my questions out loud.

Myrka, Peter, and I become close, not as close as 9X, but close enough. It wasn't until after we had worked together for several weeks that I discovered I wasn't the only one Fallon questioned about feeling strange.

"I can't control it," Peter whispers as we wait in line for a challenge. "The memories, I mean. They just ... happen."

"I have more dreams than flashbacks." Myrka says, chewing on her thumb nail.

"How long have you guys had them?" I furrow my brow.

"Only a few months, maybe. Not very long."

"And you're always really young in the memories? Like ... I don't know, five, maybe?"

"If I had to guess," Myrka says, keeping her voice low. I bite the inside of my cheek, chewing on thought. I look around, anxiously.

"What?" Peter shrugs at me.

"I don't think we should tell anyone else about this." I lower my voice to just barely a whisper.

"I had the same feeling," Myrka agrees.

"What? Why?" Peter demands. "You don't understand the amount of cred we could get for something like this! Being the only kids with memories inside of PAAC? We'd be freaking legends!"

I shake my head. "Peter, listen to me. After the exam results, Ryker was talking to Fallon and they brought me in for questioning. They asked me—"

"If you felt strange or out of place?" Myrka asks the floor. I nod at her, wide eyed. "Yeah. They asked me that, too."

"I think they're looking for kids like us," I hiss.

"Who?" Peter snorts. "Fallon? Dude wouldn't hurt a fly."

"Not him. Ryker."

"It makes sense." Myrka nods vigorously. "Ryker went to Fallon and Fallon seemed annoyed with Ryker already. You can tell they don't like each other by the way they interact. I just don't understand why Ryker doesn't act on his own. He has the same authority as Fallon, doesn't he?"

"Yeah, okay. Maybe." Peter shrugs again. "But what would Ryker want with us? What could he possibly do to us with the council breathing down his neck every second?"

"I have no idea, but I really don't want to imagine."

I make them swear that they wouldn't tell anyone. That they would keep it to themselves. I have no idea what Ryker will do if he finds out about the memories.

We went for weeks staying clean with zipped lips and hushed tones. We didn't get a single sideways glance from anyone in the entire compound. I felt like we had jumped the system.

But our pact didn't last as long as I'd hoped.

One morning I woke to a pounding on the common room door. I moved to open it, as every one was still asleep. It was Myrka and she looked extremely distressed. Her hair was dishevelled and she was breathing heavily like she had ran across the entire compound.

"Myrka?"

"Kole." She pants. "Something's wrong. Peter talked and I tried to stop him, but he already said too much and—"

"Where is he?"

"I don't know. I can't find him. I don't know what to do, what if something really awful happened?"

"Hey. Hey, calm down," I say. Her words babble past her lips like water from a fountain. At this point, she's simply talking for the sake of talking. "What else do you know?"

"Ah, Fallon is giving an address in five minutes. You guys must have slept through the announcement."

"Where?"

"The cafeteria."

I surge out of the door like flood water rushing through the gates of a dam and grab her hand, barefoot and still in my pyjamas. We come into the cafeteria just as Fallon taps the microphone to life. He looks crestfallen. The audience of the round room stares back at him, a little confused.

"Good morning, everyone. Sad news today, I'm afraid." In my peripheral vision, I see Myrka put a hand to her mouth. "The Beta from Unit 9G, Peter Tarek, has been charged and convicted of espionage."

"What?" I blurt at the ridiculousness. Good thing it was noisy, so no one but Myrka really heard me.

"I know, I know." Fallon tries to hold the peace. "I assure you that he has been expelled and properly taken care of, but if anyone has any further knowledge on the matter, I implore you to step forward. Thank you."

"What do we do?" Myrka squeaks. I narrow my eyes, watching Fallon moving through the crowd.

"Stay here." I let go of her hand and force through the crowd, en route for the man.

"Excuse me, Sir? Sir? General Fallon!" I reach him finally and he turns to me. "Sir, I have a few questions."

"About the spy, surely?"

"About *Peter*, yes, Sir," I emphasize, making sure to use my friend's real name. Not to just call him *The Spy*, although I'm sure the dramatic flare it has would've excited Peter. Fallon looks around like he's checking for something. Or someone.

"Of course, Kole. You have every right to know. Please, come with me."

TEN

"Now, soldiers are prohibited caffeine, so don't tell anyone, eh?" Fallon jests, setting a steaming mug of sharp smelling black liquid in front of me.

"Your secret's safe with me, Sir," I say with less humor than intended.

"I understand you and Beta 9G were particularly close."

"Peter, Sir."

"Sorry?"

"His name is Peter. Peter Tarek."

"Oh, of course. Excuse me." He puts a hand to his chest, not in the way that a sarcastic person would mock sincerity, but in a way that makes him seem like he's truly mortified at his own insensitivity. "I'm so sorry. It's easier for me, you see, if I just pretend there is no emotional stock or value. It's better on the heart, I find."

Is it? Is it better on the heart, or better on the conscience?

"It's okay. Sir, I have to ask—"

"You want to know where he is, hmm?" He raises a brow and I nod hopefully. He nods back. "Exactly where he is, I have no idea. We excised him from the program and that is the extent of my involvement. I have not been informed what has happened to your friend beyond that decision. The system security is very hush hush."

"But you're the General."

"One of, but yes."

"But he *is* okay?" I pry. "Right?" He hesitates. I grow desperate. "*Right?*"

"Presumably. Frankly, PAAC has cut off all communications with the boy. We have no data, no intel. No sources on his current state."

"How do you—" I start to shout in anger then I remember who I'm talking too. Someone with years, decades even, of more experience and seniority than me. I can't fight him. Or I can. I can fight him and lose. So, I bite my tongue and look around the office. Circular, white with a stocky desk and two chairs in the very center. The logo glares at me from behind Fallon's blond head. I swallow hard.

"What were the details on his expulsion?"

"Espionage."

"Yes, but ... anything else?"

Fallon blinks, staring at me. Studying me like I'm a taxidermy piece in a glass case. Analyzing. Searching. He probably sees right through me and that's a terrifying thought.

"I'm afraid I'm not allowed to disclose such details. You can go now."

Wrong answer.

I get up to leave, but before I can, he stops me again. "Oh, and Kole?"

"Yes, Sir?"

"Be careful who you trust, yeah? Salt and sugar seem the same until you put them in your tea." He gives me a smile. I leave without another word, leaving him in his chair and the coffee on the desk, untouched.

But which one are you, Fallon? Salt or sugar?

That's a cup I don't really want to drink from.

ELEVEN

The unit is cleared for active duty. This means that not only are we continuing our specialized training sessions, we are starting to run minor operations. Fallon calls them "warm-up missions." I try my best not to think about Peter's situation and the role Fallon or Ryker played in his expulsion— that was a challenge within itself.

Our first mission comes only two short days after General Fallon smuggled me coffee and told me not to trust anyone. The same day Ryker must have been snooping through the examination recordings. How else would he have discovered that my file was supposedly faulty? Red flags cloud my vision.

The mission is to rescue a group of young children from a refugee camp an hour's flight off compound.

"They know you're coming," our coordinator explains. "PAAC has been providing them with aid for a while now. This is just the next step in their recovery."

It must have been true because nothing exciting or dangerous happened. The children were waiting for us on the edge of their tent city and within three hours the 9X team was back in the training room. It was a perfectly executed mission. For those three hours, my mind was in the moment, but once I returned to the compound, my mind returned to Peter. About the shady spy allegations. Peter Tarek? A spy? Not only would he have made a terrible spy, I refuse to believe it. But I still needed to know the truth—and that could only come from Ryker or Fallon.

I wait for rest of my unit to fall asleep, listening for their breathing patterns before slipping Colin's Gamma lab key card off the desk and advancing down the hallway. I swipe the card and slide inside the computer lab before the door even has a chance to fully open. I don't sit, but type furiously at the keyboard. I'm not sure what I am looking for, so I look for everything. Anything. Anything at all. A code or a word that could've possibly been related to what happened. But it's like reading a blank map with my eyes shut to a destination that doesn't even exist. I scan aimlessly until stumbling on gold.

File 2X9. Sub-branch File 2X.

Dismissals.

I furrow my brow, clicking to open the file. When it loads, then opens, my heart drops into my stomach so fast I think I'm going to be sick. Files, hundreds and hundreds of files, all arranged by rank and unit. I scan down, scrolling through all the names before my eyes find Peter's file. I pause and just stare at it for a few minutes before clicking on it. It's a picture of him smiling with all his critical information, a PAAC seal and a glaring red slash across the page that reads *TERMINATED.*

I swallow hard, surfing the rest of the files under the dismissals folder and finding them all, chillingly, the same. Terminated file after terminated file. It takes a minute for me to realize that these were people, pictures of functioning, living, breathing, loving humans. Real people. Children. Not even adults. These were *kids*.

All with the word *TERMINATED* stamped in red over their names and faces.

I scroll to the bottom, a sick feeling spreading to every cell in my body. I passed the Vs. Then the Ws. I get to the bottom of the Xs when a name jumps out.

His name was Jackson. Jackson Alexander. He was a year older than me. His picture—two sparkling wide eyes of deep blue and hair, long and unkempt, but still with a rugged, badass movie-star charm. He would have been someone people liked. One of those people who generate their own gravitational pull, someone you're drawn too. Someone you would be desperate to make like you, but you wouldn't have to try very hard because he was such a good person, he would decide to be friends with everyone unless given a reason not to.

"Danvers. What are you doing in here?" A venomous growl comes from the door. I turn, scrambling to close the screen. Ryker hides like Dracula in the shadows, and there's no telling how long the bloodsucker has been standing there.

"Colin ... asked me to get something for him."

Liar. Liar. Liar.

Shut Up. You're going to get yourself caught.

And throwing Colin under the bus? Nice touch.

"Is he not competent enough to get it himself?" Ryker narrows his already slit-shaped eyes until they look like he's closed them entirely. I'm on a tightrope and he's preparing to cut the line. I swallow hard, looking down and trying to play it meek.

I'm the victim.

I'm the victim.

"No, Sir. I just wanted to be helpful."

I'm the victim.

"Hmm. Desperation is infectious, Danvers. I'd watch your step, boy," he says, walking closer in threatening and rhythmically slow steps. I'd be a fool if I didn't think it wasn't deliberate. He gets close, too close for comfort. Right in my face, just to make a point. "I know what you are, Danvers," he hisses.

I'm the victim.

"I know how your mind works. Remember this next time you think the rules don't apply to you. The next time you think you want to play the hero to impress your little friends. I could ruin you, Danvers. You are on thin ice, boy." He talks almost as slow as he walks, quietly and intimidating. "You are not the only one in danger. Your Alpha has a long way to fall, a whole lot farther than you." He straightens as my chest tightens and mind races with anxiety. "Get out of my sight before I decide that tonight is not the night for mercy."

"Yes, Sir. I'm sorry, Sir," I mutter quickly before hurrying out of the room. I white knuckle the lanyard on the access key as I travel swiftly down the hall with the words of the general still ringing in my ears. The looks of Jackson Alexander still seared into my vision.

Jackson Alexander.

Former Beta 9X.

TWELVE

"Why didn't you tell me?" I demand. They all look at me like I'm insane. Maybe I am. "Why didn't you tell me I'm just a back-up? A *replacement?*"

"What are you talking about?" Maisie asks, getting upset.

"Don't act like you don't know." I spit. "I saw the files. Jackson Alexander? You did a pretty good job of hiding it."

"Kole, stop it." Astrid snarls at me with just as much venom as I use to glare at her. "We have no idea what you're talking about."

"Liar," I hiss softly and her eyes narrow. For a moment, I think she's going to hit me before Allister puts himself between us, defusing the ticking bomb.

"Everyone just calm down, alright? Chill out," the taller boy reasons, but Astrid still looks like she wants my head on a spike. My anger is still bubbling, threatening to boil over.

Why didn't I know?

Why didn't they tell me?

Why would they lie to me?

Why are they lying to me?

"Jackson Alexander. Beta 9X," I growl dangerously. "How long were you going to hide him from me?"

"I don't know what you're talking about!" Astrid barks. "How many times do I have to say it for you to believe me?"

"You can't say it enough!" I clench my fist. "There are files in the system proving he was here! Proving he had my spot until something happened and I was called up and told I was special!"

"Yeah?" She nods condescendingly and that just winds me tighter. "Yeah? He was a person? He was here? Okay, Sherlock, where is he now?"

"I ... I don't know."

"You don't know?"

"No, I—"

"Oh, you don't know, Mr. Holmes? You don't know where he is?" She pushes Allister out of the way, opening the gate for aggression and getting really close to me. So close I can smell the clean scent of her shampoo. She looks up at me and I try not to wither under her kill-shot gaze. "Admit it," she growls.

"Admit what?"

"That you're just a jealous, scared, directionless little boy. You're a child. When the time comes, you'll run. You'll run and throw a fit, just like you are now. Admit that you are no different than he was!"

"Oh." I nod. "So, you do remember him."

"I remember everything," she snarls, her voice shaking. "Case closed, Mr. Holmes. The guilty got away, but the bad guy is still here." She grabs her coat from the chair and leaves, slamming the door behind her so hard it echoes and a picture falls from the wall. I start for the door, but Allister's hand settles on my arm. He looks stern. More stern than I've ever seen him.

"Leave her be, man," he advises. "She needs some space and you need time to write up a real good apology." Then, they all leave, closing the door behind them.

I don't see how it's my fault. I asked them who Jackson Alexander was and she lied about something she clearly knew. Why would she do that? Who really was he?

What was he to her?

Stop it. It doesn't matter who he was. What he was. Whatever. You messed up, Kole.

Did I, though?

Yes. You did. Dug yourself a real hole that you can't jump out of this time.

Whatever.

Don't pretend like you don't care. We both know you do. You care enough for it to hurt.

It doesn't hurt. I'm just mad.

Okay. Keep telling yourself that.

———————

I don't go to dinner. I don't want to see her. I know that's childish, but at this point, space is best. I come out of my bunk that night and notice the divider to Astrid's space is yawning wide open, her bunk empty. The window in the common room is open, too. It protrudes from the slope of the roof just like an attic window in an old house. The screen has been taken off and is set against the baseboards.

I stick my head out into the night air. She sits on the slope of the roof about a metre, maybe two, away from the open window. Her hair is down, being tossed around in the night wind, catching and absorbing the rays of the silver moon. She looks like a ghost. I stuff my hands in my armpits. Now, I just feel petty.

"Hey," I call. She just sits there. She doesn't answer. She doesn't even acknowledge I'm there. "Hey, Astrid? Can you look at me please?"

She throws me a lazy glance. Her cheeks are red from the bite of the breeze. She doesn't look mad anymore. It's more of an exhausted gaze mixed with lingering annoyance.

"Listen," I start. "I'm sorry. Allister told me to apologize, I'm going be honest about that, but I am sorry. Although ... I also think that's a two-way street." She looks back out over the roof, watching nothing and everything at the same time. I bite my lip before moving closer, taking a seat beside her.

"Who was he?" I ask softly. She swipes stray strands of hair off her face and looks down at her hands. They shake.

"He was, uh, my best friend. The Alpha and the Beta are always supposed to get along for the sake of the group, but ..." She shakes her head. "We were friends because we wanted to be. Not because PAAC told us we had to be. That it was for the good of the unit. Something like that."

I supress a grin. She can only hide her distaste for PAAC for so long until the cup overflows. She may enjoy the structure and the opportunity to advance, but she doesn't like the suppression one bit.

"Was he our age?" I pry, hungry for details. "How long has he been gone?"

"No, he was a year older than us," she sniffs. "He was a year behind in his training. He would be eighteen right now. He's been gone for about a year."

"What happened? If it's okay for me to ask."

"Same thing that happened with your friend, Peter. Just, one day, he was gone and they called him a spy."

I frown. Is that standard protocol? Espionage conviction and termination? It has to be something more than that. It just has to be.

But what if it's not.

"So," I lead in, trying to be as gentle as I can. Aggression never works with her, as I've so recently discovered. "Why didn't you tell me?" She draws in a breath, frowning hard in the dark.

"I didn't want to make you feel like you were in second place. That you had some ... golden standard to live up to because you wouldn't have had the confidence we needed from a Beta to get cleared for active duty."

"And you know about those. Standards."

"Yeah." She makes a face somewhere between a grimace and a smirk. "Yeah, I do. I know all about them. Gold standards, double standards. Glass ceilings." She snickers a little, shaking her head. She looks over at me, serious now. "Kole, I'm sorry."

"It's okay."

"No. No, it's not. I ... I just try not to think about anything that makes me lose focus. Anything that would distract me, but that doesn't mean I can rip a hole in anyone who asks honest questions."

Her apology sounds like honey, but I don't really want it anymore. Now it just feels like a point to be made. A trophy. It feels childish. We don't say anything else, falling into silence like it's the most comforting thing in the world. And it is. For now.

THIRTEEN

"They're called holographic goggles. State of the art technology developed by some very brilliant minds at headquarters," states Professor Victor Barnes, pacing back and forth in front of the class. Eccentric would be the perfect word to describe him. His tufts of graying hair stick out like the fuzz of a hatchling. It reminds me of the first feathers of a tiny owlet. His hands move constantly, always doing something. Clicking the button of a pen or picking something up just to put it back down again. His eyes, a dull green, are wild. Darting back and forth like he'd stuck his fingers in an electrical socket one too many times.

"And what are these?" Colin picks something up off the table strewn with gear and gadgets.

"... Binoculars."

"Nothing special about them? Heat vision? Night vision, maybe?"

"They help you see ... but far away." Barnes pushes his coke-bottle glasses farther up his nose to the bridge. They act as his own personal set of binoculars.

"How much caffeine do you think this guy's on?" Allister whispers as Professor Barnes launches into a lecture about the many uses of ordinary, non-specialized binoculars.

"At least four cups." Astrid appears on my left.

"Creamer? He looks like a pumpkin spice kind of dude."

"Nah, straight black coffee for maximum effect." She grins good heartedly. Professor Barnes puts his hands together, fidgeting with the brass ring around his index finger.

"The mission is relatively simple. It's simply a locate and secure operation. It's a basic set-up."

"Details?" Astrid asks, picking select things from the table, knowing exactly what she needs already.

"Foreign intelligence is dropping off a package at the airport, but it's military entrance only. Unit 9X was chosen based on training results to complete the operation." Barnes pushes up his glasses once again.

"What are we picking up?" Allister furrows his brow. "I don't wanna mule anything illegal."

"No, no. It's nothing harmful."

"What is it, though?"

"Influenza B vaccine."

"Is there an outbreak?"

"Just in case."

"Right."

The gear on the table is impressive, including the holographic goggles. They looked like a pair of Pit-Viper sunglasses. Once you put them on, the holographic picture appears with features like night vision and heat tracking. We each get a pair and are all grinning like idiots with them on.

"I wonder if these things have an X-Ray feature." Allister grins, looking at everything through the tech with his smile growing wider by the second.

Professor Barnes catches me while I am putting in my earpiece, trying to get it to connect to the correct signal wave. He has a white envelope in his busy hands.

"Here." He hands it to me. "Give this to the captain of the stock plane. It's the discussed currency."

"Okay," I answer, trying not to be rude. "Thanks, but shouldn't the Alpha handle this?" He blinks once, a blank expression on his face before speaking.

"You're not ... I thought ..."

"No, I'm Beta." I smile kindly.

"Interesting." He murmurs with narrowed eyes, takes the envelope back and makes his way across the room to where Astrid stands. I frown at his back as he goes. I shake my head slightly and continue to gear up.

The military airport was too close to arrange air transport, so we drove. Two hours on highway and gravel roads in a boxy, darkly camouflaged vehicle. Allister insists on driving and settles in behind the wheel.

"Seriously, guys." He tells us as we load up. "I'm a great driver. You're looking at the future Indie 500 champ right here. I mean, c'mon."

The first thing I did was fasten my seatbelt. The second thing was I wished I'd brought a helmet.

"So," Colin says over the growl of the engine and rushing of wind. "We'll be meeting up with German scientist Henrik Osvauld and his security party. Oh, and Allister?"

"Yeah, bro?"

"These are grown men; you can't take them in a fight."

"I bet I could." He waggles his eyebrows in the rear-view mirror. "I bet I could take five all at once."

"No. You can't."

"You doubt me, my friend. You seriously underestimate me, bro."

"Let's just avoid any dramatic confrontation, okay?" Astrid interjects from the passenger seat, although I can tell she's just as amused by their banter as I am. "Colin, what else do we need to know?"

"Uh ... Astrid has the currency?"

"Got it."

"I think that's everything." He pauses. "Oh, wait. I lied. We are not to open or tamper with the package at all. That was like ... rule number one."

"So, how do you forget it if it was rule number one?" Allister looks back at him.

"Hey, eyes on the road, kamikaze, or you'll be demoted to passenger," Colin threatens but with a grin starting to spread across his face. The engine groans as Allister presses down on the gas pedal, spurring the metal beast faster.

FOURTEEN

"That," Allister says. "Is a big box."

The German crew unload a giant wooden crate while Astrid converses with the intellegience operatives, white envelope in hand.

"He seems tense," Maisie whispers to me as we tie down the crate with towing lines to secure it in the back of the vehicle.

"Who?"

"That one." She points across the tarmac to a tall, gangly man in black dress pants, shiny shoes, and a dark maroon button-up dress shirt with the sleeves rolled up neatly to the elbows. He wanders around, glancing at everything playing out before him with his hands stuffed in his pants pockets. I can see the golden glint of an expensive watch in the afternoon light.

"Who do you think he is?"

"Probably Dr. Osvauld. I mean, everyone else is in combat uniform or pilot's whites. It must be him." Maisie throws her head in the man's direction, watching him with a peculiar gaze, absorbing every detail. She must be more in tune to the situation than I had originally thought.

"Maybe we should go say 'hello,'" I suggest, securing the last of the lines. The crate won't be going anywhere, but Allister is driving again so I shouldn't speak so soon. Maisie and I make our way across the tarmac. The eyes of the German flight crew follow us the entire way, not even turning away once we reached their location. I don't think it's because the flight crew doesn't trust us, although I'm sure they don't. It seems more like they are watching us. Seeing how we react.

"Hello, Dr. Osvauld." I extend my hand for him to shake. His palms were rough and calloused. I wouldn't have expected that from someone who worked in a lab. He has little chips and knicks on the backs of his hands and his nails are cracked and long, as if he hasn't cut them in a while.

"Yes, this is me. And you?" He confirms, speaking in a thick German accent, making me concentrate on every single word that rumbles past his lips.

"I'm Kole Danvers and this is Maisie Greyer."

"Ah, PAAC soldiers?"

"Yes, Sir."

"Very good. Very good. Tell your generals that I hope this will come in aid for your ... little problem." The doctor says with a knowing wink. I try not to frown in confusion

What little problem?

Probably the non-existent influenza B outbreak.

Ah. That problem.

"Yes, Sir. I will tell them." I nod, withdrawing my hand.

"You people do good work over there. Ground breaking work, yes? Very impressive, indeed," Osvauld says. Something about him doesn't sit right with me. I scan his face and notice a few odd markings. Tiny scars on his lips, below and above. More on his ear lobes and the top arches of his eyebrows. Evidence of piercings? A slit through his left eyebrow hastily filled in with makeup just a shade too light. The way he carries himself, like he was really someone else in real life. Playing a role, like this encounter is nothing more than an eighth-grade stage play. Like his lines were written and rehearsed. He seemed nervous and unsure of himself. Everything about him just seemed ... off. Even Maisie had noticed it. She hadn't said a word since we'd approached him.

"Well, thank you, doctor." I take the compliment politely. "PAAC prides itself on its accomplishments, even the small ones."

"And promises more?" He pops a single brow.

"I hope so, Sir."

"Ah, very good." He claps a hand to my shoulder before moving to board the plane as a bodyguard beckons to him. It's time to go.

The curtains close on the final act.

"Very good indeed," he declares. In ten minutes, the German plane takes Dr. Osvauld and his platoon of security into the sky, homeward bound. We get into our transport and drive off with a new, very heavy, boxy travel partner. Astrid has claimed her throne in shotgun again, leaving Maisie, Colin, and I to the back. There is no conversation in the back seats as both Colin and Maisie nod off within fifteen minutes of travel.

"How much do you think PAAC dished out for our little prize here?" Allister asks, inspiring a topic for conversation. Talking for the sake of talking and not doing anything in silence. I'm glad not to sit in that silence.

"A pretty penny," Astrid snorts. "The envelope had some weight to it."

"Health is worth a lot of dough." Allister frowns.

The road changes from gravel to pavement and the ride becomes smoother. I run my fingernails down the grooves in the material of the seatbelt and back up again. The sun is just going down, splashing all kinds of colours on the sky. Ombre purple to pink to orange to yellow. A golden masterpiece of light. Only when it fades to a star speckled black, can we see the headlights sitting on the side of the old road. I frown as the mood in the vehicle plummets.

"Guys." I reach over to get Maisie's and Colin's attention. They're already peering out of the hazy windows. Our headlights illuminate a rig in front of us, a truck with jacked up monster-truck tires and a vulgar paint job. The driver gets out, followed by more passengers, one from each seat. They stand, five in a line, waiting for us.

"Drive past," Astrid says calmly. "They won't do anything."

Allister presses the gas and we immediately find out Astrid's theory is wrong. The thunderous clap of glass penetrated and shattering make my ears ring and the Alpha tries to shield her face from the shards as they rain down on her.

"Watch out!" Allister shouts, cranking the wheel in a frantic panic. We fishtail to a stop, spitting up gravel and dust like a fountain. My attention goes to Astrid, her face is cut in a couple places, evidenced by beaded filament trails of blood.

"Astrid," I call. "Astrid, are you okay?"

"I'm fine. Pass me my gun." She turns and points to the weapon in the rack next to me. I see a giant gash in her shoulder, right side with muscle exposed, the rest of her arm bathed in copper scented, scarlet waves.

"Astrid ..."

"Gun. Now. I'm fine," she orders. Her eyes are raw and alive. She's ready to fight.

They approach her door first, but soon flank both Astrid and Allister's sides of the vehicle. She just looks forwards, calm etched into every line of her face. Her left hand clutches the gun, finger hovering over the trigger, the muzzle jammed under her thigh. Her other hand crawls for the door handle.

"Shoulda stopped, pretty girl." The driver grins, exposing a mouthful of rotting teeth. "Hm? Window replacements ain't cheap these days, sweetheart."

Astrid's fingers make it to the door handle, lacing it. I kick a gun over to Colin and give him an affirming nod, quickly picking one up myself. The clock ticks in my mind, second after second, waiting for something to act like a starting bell.

We wait.

We wait for Astrid's first move.

Tick. Tock. Tick. Tock.

Tick.

Tock.

And it comes quickly.

She and Allister exchange a knowing glance as the men flanking either side of the vehicle come closer. Astrid clucks her tongue once. Twice. And on the third, all hell breaks loose. Astrid and Allister open their doors with as much force as possible. The doors slam into the brutes, fast and hard and they crumple under the impact. Astrid jumps out over the groaning body on the ground, gun at the ready. Allister punches a button to open the back hatch and follows suit. We slip out the back before it's fully open, standing to face the other three. They grin stupidly with matching chipped and rotting smiles, like this highjack will be a breeze.

"Don't come any closer," Colin warns. "We are trained soldiers."

"I bet you are, squirt." One comes closer and knocks the gun out of the Gamma's hand in one swift movement. His eyes narrow and Colin swallows hard. "Really. I bet you are." The other two get an amused look in their eye and I can hear the struggle behind us between Allister, Astrid and the other two rogues.

"Follow my lead," I hiss, slowly raising my hands. "We don't want any trouble," I call out, louder than I have to.

"What are you doing?" Maisie jabs me in the ribs, pointedly. I take a step away, not wanting another hit from my own team.

"Just play along," I urge and she reluctantly follows. Colin's fingers reach for the navy black sky, too.

"Really. We don't want any trouble," I say again, trying to fill the restless silence. We hold our positions of surrender and they relax a little more. They come closer at a faster speed than they would have if I was still acting defensively. When one reaches for my wrist to wrestle it behind my back, I swing. I clock him in the side of the head with the hilt of the gun and he careens off to my left. The other two whirl on me and I get pushed up against the open floor of the vehicle. I reach back, grabbing something cool and hard to the touch and swing it like a baseball bat before pulling my knees to my chest and thrusting out, catching the closest one in the chest. He drops down, winded. I tighten my grip on the tool, an iron rod with impressive heft and used for who knows what.

On one knee, the attacker is panting heavily. I give him another good wack with my tool and he falls, face to the dirt and doesn't get back up.

A single gunshot pierces the air and I freeze.

One rogue has a hold of Maisie by the back of the collar of her shirt. The muzzle of his pistol is aimed for the sky, like he's using the stars and the moon for target practice. A trail of blood is making its way down his face. I grit my teeth and clench my fists. He brings down the gun and presses it into the side of Maisie's neck, burning her with the muzzle heat. She cries out and squirms as much as she dares, tears appearing in her eyes.

But they don't fall.

"Stop that!" I shout angrily. "Stop it!"

"Can it, Freakshow!" he barks. Maisie gasps with relief when his gun hand drops. I can see the red welt in the glow of the headlight. He takes her by the neck instead, but never takes his finger from the trigger. Astrid and Allister skid to a halt beside me. The other attackers stand close to the man and Maisie, grinning at us.

It's like the world is frozen in time, but once the ice melts, Hell's fire will rain down.

"Alright," the rogue says, licking the droplets of blood from his rapidly swelling lip. "Now that I have your attention. What's in the crate?"

"Nothing you would be interested in." Astrid throws out her voice like a sharpened weapon. It cuts the air.

"How can you be so sure?" he snarls, venom dripping from every twisted word. Maisie whimpers slightly and I can practically hear her praying for this night to end. For this to just be over.

"Unless you work in an immunization clinic, you don't care about these." Allister puts his hands up, taking a step forward and trying to be disarming. I can barely concentrate on what he's saying over the rush of adrenaline surging through me. It's hard to focus, and right now, that's extremely dangerous.

"Vaccines?" The rogue nods to the crate.

"That's right."

"Influenza B," Astrid chimes in.

He doesn't believe us. I can see it. It's written all over his face.

"Bull," he snarls after a brief pause. "Do I look like an idiot to you?"

"Well," Allister begins, his eyes trailing from the man's unkempt hair down to his rumpled stain shirt and torn jeans. "I wouldn't be heading for fashion week if I were you, buddy." I bite the inside of my cheek, waiting for the fireworks. That's obviously not what he wanted to hear, even if it was the truth. The man's eye twitches before he tightens his grip on Maisie's throat.

"Open it!" he shouts.

"Hey, hey! Just calm down!" I call out, putting a hand out towards him.

"Open it or I'll shoot!"

"Alright! Okay! I'll open it. Just calm down, bro. I'll open it."

"Hurry up!"

"Let's stay calm, now. I'm opening it!"

It wasn't a single heartbeat later when the helicopter appeared. The chopper touched down, ruffling a sea of prairie grasses as teams of officers poured from the open sides. They surged forward in organized waves, rushing the rogues. A team of two brought the attackers to their knees after short and futile struggles, securing our Omega and detaining the crazed man who had a hold on her. Most surprising of all, was Fallon emerging from the helicopter, looking very distressed and very much not himself.

"Are you all alright?" he asked, putting a hand on each of our shoulders for a brief moment like he was checking if we were real or not. When he reaches for Astrid, she takes a step back and makes sure to keep her injured arm hidden behind Colin standing next to her.

"Astrid's hurt, Sir," Allister confesses, as we all know she wouldn't have. Her glare confirms my suspicions. Fallon looks her over, despite her protesting.

"Yes, that's quite the gash. It will no doubt require stitches," Fallon declares on inspection. "And antiseptic. We'll have to clean it before any infection sets in. Come along, 9X. Back to the compound."

FIFTEEN

"How did you find us?" The sharp scent of antisceptic that infects the medic's wing hurts my nose. Fallon and I stand behind a glass divider as a field nurse pours hydrogen peroxide over Astrid's battle wounds. The gash spits pink bubbles like a science fair volcano.

"I was watching the clock as it grew later and began to suspect something. Of course, the brain always assumes the worst," he answers softly, arms crossed over his chest, watching the window.

"But ... how?" I press. "How exactly did you find us?"

A pause.

"We use that road often."

Fallon left me after that. He expressed something about checking in on the other unit members and let the door swing shut behind him. I enter the medic station behind the glass where the Alpha is.

"Hey," Astrid greets me, looking up at me and away from her arm as the nurse starts threading her skin back together. There is a little silver dish full of splinters of glass and little strings of pink flesh. Her arm is wet with peroxide and crusted with the leftover congealed blood. She has a gash on her forehead that will probably need stitches, too.

"You okay?"

"Never better." She sighs, scratching a collection of craggy maroon off her forearm with a fingernail. She chips it away like paint. "How are the others?"

"They're all good." I don't really know. I'm just trying to make her feel better. She reaches out, grabbing a spool of gauze as another cut makes its crimson appearance as she picks at her arm. She sighs again, the tips of her fingers shiny and red with her own blood. She touches her thumb and index finger together, watching with an unreadable expression.

"Talk to me." I pull up a foldable chair.

A tear winds its way down my face, paving the way for others should they choose to follow. I sit on the kitchen counter, my heels against the rough cabinet doors, the varnish long gone and faded. I sniff a little and don't dare look at the war wounds from falling from the back of my two-wheeled aluminum steed and tumbling into the gravel.

"Ouchy." Mom dabs at my skinned knee with a cool, damp cloth.

"Ouchy." I sniff in agreement, wiping my nose with my sleeve.

"You know, buddy, you're pretty tough," Mom says, looking at me through her black-framed glasses with wide, warm, and loving eyes. My fear melts like ice cream on a summer's day.

"Yeah. I'm real tough." I nod, agreeing again. She chuckles slightly, straightening and setting the cool cloth to the side. She cups my face in her hands, planting a gentle kiss on my forehead.

"You gonna be okay, buddy?"

"I'll be okay."

———————

The memory fades like a fast-moving fog, billowing away and just out of reach.

"I'll be okay." Astrid grins. At least I got her to smile, even if it was just a little one.

"Hey, losers. Check this out." A familiar voice says through the loud speaker and I turn to see Allister with his finger on the button for the sound system. A goofy grin takes up a good half of his face. Astrid and I laugh out loud and it feels good. Scratch that, it feels absolutely freaking amazing.

I'll be okay.

We'll be okay.

———————

Myrka and I continue Beta training just as partners rather than adding another to our dynamic.

She has really pretty eyes, I thought one day as she took strikes at the target mitts, making the palms of my hands ache a little.

Yeah, sure, but Astrid's are prettier.

It always came back to her. Every wispy train of thought that crossed the expressway that was my brain. And once it started rolling, it was hard to slow and impossible to stop. I was stuck, and I refused to believe that Allister was right. Even though I know he was.

"I heard about your last mission."

"What?" I ask, snapping from thought. Myrka grins.

"Your last mission?" she clues. "Did you really get stopped by highway pirates? Did they slash the tires and gut the whole vehicle from top to bottom like everyone said they did?"

"What?" I grin at the ridiculousness. Someone's spinning tales like a spider spins a web. "Who said that, Myrka?"

"Well, I heard it from the 9A Beta. He says it was really wild." Her eyes grow wide, reminding me of the way a child looks on Christmas morning. "Was he right?" I glance around the room and grin, shaking my head slightly.

"Beta 9A knows how to tell a good story, doesn't he?"

"I guess he does," she says sheepishly.

"I had another memory," I blurt. "That night. It was just a short one, but still." She studies me with wide eyes.

"What was it?"

"My mom. She was helping me clean a cut I had gotten in a bicycle accident," I explain. It feels good to be able say it out loud. To get it out. I would talk to Astrid about it, but that would be putting myself, and her, in danger. I think back to Peter. Would they do the same to me if they found out I have memories, too?

"Oh. I haven't had one in a while." Myrka sighs, almost somberly.

"I think they're triggered by my surroundings. Astrid was hurt and the nurses were taking care of her wounds—and then I had the memory of my mom," I explain.

"That makes sense. But Kole," Myrka looks at me seriously. "Be careful who you tell."

———

The days start and end with training. I can't help but think back to when I was still, somewhat, on my own. No sense of any real purpose or responsibility. No unit, no title. All the same, no *family*. Exchanging white walls for more white walls seemed great at the time, but at least I recognized the stranger in the mirror then. Now, when I glance at my reflection, I see fatigue etched into a hard jaw line. A permanent frown and stress acne. The constant grind and toll of training and missions are designed to break us. Fallon and Ryker are trying to see just how resilient their soldiers really are. I am growing tired of it.

Before long, I find myself standing in the hall in front of the door to the common room, wrist under the scanner. The light turns green and the door cracks. A single shove finishes the job. My heavy booted footsteps echo off the walls in the empty space. I wish the walls weren't so eggshell. So ... whitewashed. Dull. Lifeless. I'd even take a cream-coloured palette at this point.

Just something different.

Even the furniture inside is standard black in the standard arrangement in this standard room. The space is almost as tired as I am.

Jaded and tired and frayed.

But I'm okay. I'll be okay.

All the bunk dividers are yawning open. Everyone's bed is made perfectly but Allister's, as usual. The conflict between neat and messy keeps things interesting, but not enough to make any real difference. He is walking chaos, his hair always dishevelled, bed always messy. He lives outside the box but still within the lines. I didn't think that was possible until meeting him.

I pass Astrid's bunk, moving slowly like a ghost in a hall. There's a necklace on her blanket. A silver chain and a crucifix pendant. The metal is still warm when I touch it. She has papers tacked on her walls. Photos, mantras, and quotes.

To conquer the chaos, you have to surrender.

Fear is courage's first form.

Overcome what you must.

They all sound the same. You can gather a lot about someone by their mantras, apparently, because none of them surprise me in the slightest.

I sit, noticing a drawing of what must be a sunflower. A straight, blocky stem the colour of lime and the petals with darker outlines than coloured centers. The petals are in a pattern; orange, yellow, orange. It's in crayon, a few steps above scribbled. The paper is yellowed and rough, showing its age through clipped and torn corners and little droplets where water was spilt on it. A name at the bottom written in childish scrawl in black wax. *Adelyn.*

Who's Adelyn?

The door opens and I jump to my feet, thinking about how suspicious I must look right now. The white-haired Astrid narrows her eyes at me, angling her head.

"Kole," she says, flatly. "What are you doing?"

"Just ..." A blotch on her skin catches attention. It's faint, a yellowing spot the size of my palm or maybe a little bigger just below her left eye. There is another on her shoulder. More on her arms.

Bruises.

It's not like they're uncommon. Training permits the skin to tinge, but not like this. There are too many and they are far too big and deep of colour. My stomach crawls in horror.

"What happened?"

Her hand flicks to her cheek. She knows it's there.

"Training," she mutters and I cock my head. Her eyes harden, freezing over like Hell never will.

"Astrid," I say softly, trying to disarm her. She shakes her head and moves across the room. I back out of the way and she reaches into her bunk, pulling on a sweater.

"You wouldn't understand," she insists.

"So then help me to."

"No."

"Why not?"

"Because—"

"You trust me, right?" I take her elbows, not sure if it's the right move or not. She doesn't fight me off, but opens her mouth, wanting to say something. Then she seals her lips and looks to the floor.

"Yes, I trust you," she whispers. I watch the ghosts dance in her eyes.

"Then tell me what happened," I whisper back. "Please. I want to help you." She looks up at me and I see something shocking. Fear. Real fear. Deer on the road at night staring down speeding headlights kind of fear. I start to second guess whether I actually want to know what happened or not.

"I didn't give them anything." Her voice breaks. I follow a first instinct, wrapping my arms around and keeping her close. Keeping her safe. She smells sweet and smoky. A tough, but still lady-like scent and her hair is softer than it looks.

"What did they want?" I swallow hard, blinking harder.

"Information."

"Information?"

"On you. They asked me if you seemed strange or ... or confused. Kole, why are they so desperate for information on you?" She's shaking. "What did you do?"

"I'm not sure."

"About which part?"

"All of it." I sigh. "But it's okay. I'll deal with it. It's over now."

"Are you stupid?" she snaps, pushing me away and reverting back to the old leather-hearted Astrid. "It's just beginning. Ryker and Fallon aren't just going to ... what? Give up? I don't think so. They're going to keep pushing and pushing and pushing until they get what they want. This is never going to end until they are satisfied." She pauses for a deafening moment. "Unless we end it first."

———————

A half-hour later, Astrid and I walk side by side, en route to Ryker. At the moment, he is in a very important council meeting joined by partners world-wide. Exactly the group of people we need to confront.

But one thing still sits on the edge of my brain.

"Who's Adelyn?"

"What?"

"Adelyn? She signed that drawing on your wall."

"The sunflower?"

"Yeah. Who is she?"

"I don't know."

"Seriously—"

"I actually don't remember *her*." Astrid shrugs. "Just remember finding the drawing in a pocket somewhere."

"And you kept it. Why?" I furrow my brow. We stop at the doors and she tosses me a pained smile that doesn't quite reach her eyes.

"It's fun to pretend," she tells me. "Shall we?" Then, she pushes open the double doors and the entire assembly of men and women both on screen and in the flesh fall silent. She walks in slowly, like a huntress stalking her prey. Her head high and her finger on the pulse of the room. She's controlling them and all I can do is follow her lead.

"What is this?" An unfamiliar mocha-skinned man asks, becoming impatient with our theatrics. "Fallon? What is this?"

"A minor disturbance, General Zhang. Forgive us." Fallon apologizes, in the most graceful way possible, to fix the mistake. A mistake he had nothing to do with, but trying to take the fall for us anyway.

I glance around the room. Ryker is missing. Fallon has left his chair and is walking towards Astrid. She watches him approach and I see her fists tighten.

"Stop," she says and the council does, indeed, stop. "I have something to say."

"We don't have time for this!" The man, General Zhang, growls through the screen.

"I, for one, would like to hear what the girl has to say." Fallon narrows his eyes at her. "Besides, General Zhang, what else do we have to discuss? Please, Alpha. Grace us."

I watch the intensity in the room grow like a blood red flower on time lapse. Astrid makes the first move like she's playing a game of chess in Professor Marriott's classroom. She sidesteps and brushes past Fallon and takes a spot in the center of the room.

"I hope you're recording this." She clears her throat. "Hello, Council. I am Astrid Cardinal, Alpha 9X. But I wish I wasn't. Your systems are broken and your minds are corrupt. There are secret agendas and plans being formed and set in motion without you even knowing. You are falling prey to hubris, and to that man," she points with a straight arm at Fallon, "who is serving you as bait on a silver platter. He has secret intentions—"

Fallon's hand dives into his pocket and a surge of security officers storm the room and rush at Astrid. They grab her, wrestling her down while she thrashes and struggles like she's fighting to the death.

"Hey!" I yell, trying to fight my way to her, but they hold me back. In a fleeting chance taken with purpose, Astrid is loose and hurling herself at Fallon. She puts her balled fist to good use, punching him square in the nose with a sickening crack before the security can get her under control. The scarlet of the man's blood is the last thing I see before they force us from the room.

SIXTEEN

Astrid and I sit in a windowless room with two chairs facing a door. It was just us. It felt childish, like a sort of time-out. I had no idea how much time had passed between us being restrained and Allister coming to collect us.

"Well, well, well. Look what the cat dragged in." The boy walks in, arms crossed like a father scolding his children. "Thanks, boys," he tells the guards behind him, "I got it from here."

"Allister," Astrid breathes.

"You two dummies are left alone for five minutes and you go rogue soldier? What's worse is you went without me. You got a hell of a lot of explaining to do."

"It's good to see you too, Allister," I grin sarcastically.

"Don't start with that, bro. I'm supposed to be mad at you."

"Oh." I grin. "Sorry."

He sighs, putting his hands on his hips and then beckons. "Well? You want out of this hole or not?"

Allister held the bad cop persona until we had returned to the dorm, then he wanted a complete play by play. I was happy to tell the story.

"Holy crap! You punched Fallon? In the face?" Allister exclaims and Astrid pulls up her strawberry knuckles as proof. Allister holds up a hand for a high-five. "Yeah! Get it, girlfriend!" That makes her smile. I really like it when she smiles.

"It was pretty cool," I say. Now she's smiling at me and I feel like I'm under a spotlight.

"Okay, so what now?" Allister raises a brow. "What's the plan?"

At that we fall into silence. Astrid and I toss each other a mutual glance.

"There is a plan, right?" Allister pries. "Or is it more like 'jump in with both feet and just go for it' type of thing? Gut instincts only."

"There's a plan," Astrid insists.

"About ... ten percent?" I interject.

"Five percent," she corrects me.

"Five percent of a plan. So, there *will be* a plan. Eventually," I say through a grimace.

Allister blinks once and sits back. "Oh, good. I thought we were in trouble for a minute," he scoffs. "Five percent. What even qualifies as five percent of a plan? The *idea* of forming a plan? Five percent. Jesus, you two *are* crazy." He pauses. "But I want in."

"It'll be dangerous." I narrow my eyes.

"I hope so," he growls.

"We'd be traitors even if we pulled it off."

"Wonderful."

"We might even die."

"I eat death for breakfast with a side of glory. And maybe a tall glass of butt kicking if I'm thirsty."

Astrid clears her throat and stands up, leaving whilst shaking her head. Allister looks affronted.

"Where are you going?"

"To find you two some spare brain cells. Jesus, I can't believe you lasted *this* long. And *this*? *This* isn't even that long."

———————

The idea of being a rebel and raging against the machine was thrilling, but the reality bit harder than the dream could compensate for. Astrid and I were confined to solitary dwellings for the better part of a week for breaking code. I guess it wasn't a serious enough offence to be terminated for. Cushy jail. Still jail, just called something softer. Calling it a punishment or a consequence makes it sound like we are two toddlers who scribbled on the walls with markers. A time-out of sorts, just a longer one.

I still felt like a hero when it was over, though.

Walking into the packed cafeteria with a new own-the-world gait drew gazes from every corner, side and slant of the room— from unit members and professors alike. I slide in next to Maisie and Allister reaches out across the table for a fist bump.

"Hey, Jailbird. How was the clink?" He grins.

"Can't complain really."

"Kole," Colin hisses tersely.

"What?" I demand.

"That was supposed to be a punishment. You know, head down 'Yes Sir, never again, Sir.'"

I shrug, looking around. I don't really care, I'm just happy to be out.

"Where's Astrid?"

"She's not out yet," Maisie says quietly and I frown.

"What do you mean? Our sentence is up."

"*Your* sentence is up. She's still in confinement and until they let her out, we can't run any missions or rack up any credit. Thanks for that, by the way. Do you know how hard it is to function without the top two ranks in a unit?" Colin looks me in the eyes as he speaks, looking annoyed.

"Uh ..."

"That's a trick question. It wasn't hard at all," Colin says bitterly, taking a long drink of his water. I know what he's trying to say, his eyes alone speak a million miles faster than his mouth ever could. He thinks this is all my fault. He thinks this is all because of me. My actions. My irresponsibility.

Maybe it was, maybe it wasn't.

Whatever it was, it was *fun*.

SEVENTEEN

The rain always smells clean. It is a refreshing, breezy scent. The clouds gather on the horizon as the winds force them closer, pushing and shoving them on their way.

Then it begins.

A thunder clap booms and jagged bolts of lightning arch through the dark, like zags of yellow magic dancing between a wizard's fingers. Sometimes the storms are dry, not a single tear shed by the clouds. Not a single droplet falls from the sky. Other times, they soak everything.

I watch the droplets of rain water slide down the dirty glass of the window pane, creating streaks of clean and clear just barely distorted by the grime. The droplets race until they all combine in the end. The screens on the outside of the windows are being pushed and pulled by the gusts in a game of tug-of-war. The same wind moans through the gutters, rattling the hardware and pulls on the doors, making the hinges creak.

But this time, there is no joy in the chaos. There is no love in the storm. There is no refreshing smell. This time, it is like a deadly wave cresting on the high seas before smashing ships to splinters. There is only intensity. There is only fear. The clouds turn a sickly, haunting dark grey and turn in the sky like a finger was stirring the air from above. It *grows into a funnel, the winds harsh and strong enough to throw things about. Branches break from trees and crash to the ground, taking leaf and limb with them on their descent.*

"Come on, Kole. Let's go downstairs. It's time to hide," Mom says, reaching her hand out to me from the threshold of the stairs. She's waiting for me. I frown.

"Hide?"

"That's right."

"But ..."

"Kole." Mom uses her stern voice. She never uses her stern voice with me. Ever. "Let's go. Now."

"But why do we have to hide?" I ask. "Aren't we supposed to face our fears?" Mom just stares at me for a moment, wracking her brain for a way to respond.

Finally, she takes a knee in front of me and brushes her fingers over my bangs, flattening them. The static in the air seals them to my forehead. It tingles a little bit.

"Oh, honey," she croons. "Baby, it's good to face your fears and it's good to be brave, but sometimes we are afraid for a very good reason."

"Are you afraid right now, Mom?"

"... Yes, darling. I am afraid. But I know it's safe in the basement where the storm and the wind can't get us."

"I don't want you to be afraid, Mom."

"I don't want to be afraid either, sweetheart."

"Let's go downstairs. Then you won't be afraid, right Mom?"

"Right."

Okay. I almost answer out loud.

The memories, because they are too vivid to call dreams and too peaceful to call nightmares, are becoming stronger now. More frequent. Some seem relevant to the current situation, others seem sporadic and out of place. But still, I'm grateful for every last one. I know they are real. They must be. My hallucinatory family can't just be a figment of my imagination. They seem too real for that. My mother and father. My little sister. The family dog.

Too *alive*.

———————

I had just settled down after the hallucination, when I was notified over the intercom that Ryker wanted to see me in his office. Before I left my room, I prayed for the first time in a long time.

"So," he says, lacing his fingers together while his oily voice worms past his teeth. "You're a rebel now? A renegade?"

"No, Sir. A poor decision. That's all."

He narrows his eyes. "Do you take me for a fool, Kole Danvers? Maybe someone who is easily tricked?"

"I—"

"Maybe someone who doesn't know who you really are? What you are really capable of. Someone who misinterprets you? Doesn't understand you?"

"Sir, I—"

"A word of advice, Danvers. Me to you and free of charge. You. Are. All. The. Same." He hisses, spit flying from his mouth like confetti twirling through the air at a parade. "Nothing sets you apart other than your dumb and annoying little habit of being a recurring pain in my backside."

"I don't mean to be difficult, Sir. Really, I don't."

"No, no. Of course, you don't. No one ever does. That is, until they want to. Until they mean to. Until they, for some unbeknownst reason, *need* to," Ryker growls. He reminds me of a shark, smelling blood in the water before attacking. Only going after already wounded prey like the coward he is. His snake eyes open wider than I've ever seen, waiting for my reaction. For the first time, I really get a look at their chilling pupils, focused and menacing.

But still, I don't give him the satisfaction.

"And you would know a lot about purposely trying to be difficult. Wouldn't you?" I murmur.

He looks taken aback for a moment. How would anyone ever dare to talk back? To say something other than "Yes, Sir," "Sorry, Sir," "You're right and I'm wrong, Sir." To have a spine.

"What did you say?" Now he narrows his eyes, looking like he's staring right into a hot sun's glare. I watch him tremble in his own anger.

"I meant, Sir. You would know a lot about being an intentional bother, *Sir.*"

"Get out," he snaps. "Right now. Get out, you worthless child! Get out!" he shouts, spinning into a storm of rage.

I turned my back to him and his empty, immature insults. When I leave, I leave in silence and with the sweet taste of victory under my tongue. I know what he can do, but at the same time, I know he won't do anything. He could damage me, remove me, terminate me. But at this moment? I couldn't care less, I won.

I won.

I won.

I won.

David against Goliath. Jack against the giant living in the clouds on the beanstalk.

They won, too.

The tortoise instead of the hare. The little engine.

They did, too.

Add me to the list of underdogs. I walk the halls with a new confidence. A lightness nothing quite like anything I've ever felt before and that I never want to go away.

I won.

EIGHTEEN

We have a mission.

"You ready, man?"

"Born ready." I grin. Allister slaps my back.

"Alright. Let's go, then."

While our Alpha was in lock-up, we were training but not running any missions. Usually training gets scheduled around our missions, but now that Astrid was sprung, officially off her sentence, we had work to do.

"Do any other units do this? Missions, I mean?" I ask with a light frown.

Allister shrugs, digging through a storage bin of old body harness supplies used for rappelling. "It's based on performance, so we are called up first. Take the workload as a compliment. We are obviously the best. Maybe the favourite." We comb through the bins of supplies in the garage while the rest of the unit is preparing and loading a vehicle for transport.

"Oh, obviously." I roll my eyes as dramatically as possible. Allister doesn't see it though, because his head in buried in the storage bin. Good thing, too. My comment probably would've warranted a good smack upside the head.

I need the conversation more than I want to admit. When the conversation lulls into a silence, I become anxious. The last mission we ran as a solo group was when we were accosted by the highway pirates. How pleased they would be if they knew that they shook me up like a firefly in a jar. Made me glow with nerves. I'm lit up like a candle, burning with anxiety; fear from that night still resides within me.

Thinking about the highjack makes my stomach lurch. But despite the butterflies in my stomach, wildly dancing like they're at a massive, out-of-control hoe-down, I know one thing: I handled it. To the best of my abilities, I handled the situation, which is what my training is all about. Keeping the peace. Preserving the peace. Sharing that peace.

"Alright, bro?" Allister picks his face out of the storage bin to see me lost in the space of thought.

"Yeah. I'm good."

"Good, because Marbles is coming our way." Marbles. Allister's nickname for the eccentric Professor Barnes. The scatterbrained man picks his stumbling way towards us, walking like his shoes are ten sizes too big. His coke bottle glasses and greasy hair are almost iconic at this point.

"Boys." He greets us politely, shaking with that over-caffeinated, wild, on-the-edge look to his eye. He looks to Allister. "Would you mind giving us some privacy? I'd like to speak to ..."

"Kole, Sir. My name is Kole."

"Yes. I'd like to speak to Kole. Alone. Please."

"Sure thing, Professor," Allister agrees before shooting me a look. I'm pretty bad at reading facial expressions, but I think this one loosely translated to "Good luck with Nuts."

"Did you need something, Professor?" I try to spur him on, trying to wrap this up as quickly as possible. I still have a mission to complete and a unit waiting for me.

"I'd like to share information with you. Something I found rather ... peculiar."

"Peculiar, Sir?"

"Odd. Interesting or out of the norm."

"I know what it means, Sir." I press on. He wrings his hands in a very Professor Barnes type of way.

"Yes, of course. I thought you would, being such a clever mind—"

"Professor, please. I have to go soon." I try to urge him on before his yarn begins to unravel from both ends.

"Right. Right!" He puts two fingers to the center of his forehead. "I don't exactly know how to word this. It's troubling, you see."

"I really have to go, Professor. Really," I urge, looking back at my unit loading the transport. Astrid stares at me with piercing eyes from behind the wheel. I hold up five fingers for five minutes. She holds up three in return.

"Professor, really—"

"You were meant to be an Alpha," he blurts.

"What?" I ask, exasperated and feeling the blood rush from my face. "What are you talking about?"

"Your original file. It says you're an Alpha. The file was deleted and replaced with the one which you operate under now, but that's not the initial point." He spins on.

Terminated.

"How do *you* know?" I narrow my eyes. Barnes' face goes slack. He knows he's said too much. He watches me with a curious expression, cocking his head to the side. In this moment, I wonder just how big of a mistake I've made. Now the wack job of a professor knows I know. He knows I know one of PAAC's darkest secrets. And I know I'm in trouble. More trouble than ever before.

If I were playing chess, Professor Marriott would have called my admittance to knowing more than I should a rookie's mistake. An amateur move. A doomed sacrifice with no real end benefit. A play wasted on nothing but to prolong one's failure.

It's unfortunate that this is a little more important than a game of chess.

"I'm sorry." I apologize, but it sounds more like a question. I back up towards the transport, a confused look etched into my face. "I have to go now."

"Be careful, Kole," Professor Barnes warns and I run the rest of the way to the transport, head spinning with these new puzzles to solve.

"What did Nuts want?" Maisie giggles when I finally get into my seat, strapping myself in.

"I'll tell you later."

Astrid looks back at me in the rear-view mirror. I lift my brows.

Later.

She nods, confirming.

Later.

NINETEEN

"Are you sure that's what he said? Exactly?" Astrid stands, arms crossed, two fingers straddling her lips. If I didn't know better, the position would have made me think she was a hardcore smoker.

"He specifically said 'you were meant to be an Alpha.'" I shrug, running a hand through my hair.

"Yeah, but he also forgot your name." Allister purses his lips. "Maybe he mistook you for someone else."

"I don't think so." I shake my head. "When we went to get the vaccine crate—"

"When we met the pirates."

"Yeah. He came up to me with the envelope that had all the currency. He thought I was the Alpha, then looked super confused when I told him I wasn't."

"I saw that," Astrid concurs. "That was weird."

"Maybe this is why!"

"But why would they change your status? It makes no sense," Colin adds from his desk, his chin in his hand and his elbow on the table.

"Maybe they made a mistake?" Maisie winces a little.

"No. They only make mistakes when they're trying to cover up for something. This isn't a mistake." I cross my arms, then uncross them because it makes me feel like a pouting child. "They did something," I insist. "They changed it on purpose."

"Yes, but Kole," Astrid insists, "they've done a lot of things. But they always seem to have a reason for it. What reason would they have to make you an Alpha, then go back and change their minds?"

"I don't know," I mutter lightly. "Maybe I did something or messed something up."

"Or maybe it's just a glitch in the system." Colin rubs his forehead like the conversation is hurting his brain. "Technology isn't perfect, you know."

"Or maybe Professor Barnes applied one too many caffeine patches and went off the deep end, like, officially. I wouldn't put it past him, honestly." Allister forces out a laugh while Astrid gives me a troubled look. I'm not sure what she believes. I can't read her this time.

"But," Astrid continues, "for all we actually know, it could be true. We don't have much evidence for either side, an error or deliberate action, true or not true—PAAC isn't exactly known for its transparency."

"True." Allister dips his head to the right.

———

The next morning at breakfast, Fallon and Ryker take the stage as a pair to inform us of Professor Barnes' unexpected resignation.

"We are as shocked as you are," Fallon addresses the silent crowd, but I wasn't shocked at all. PAAC has a nasty habit of carving out the secret spillers and eliminating the loose tongues. Not to mention forging on without remorse or second thoughts. "So, let's all raise a toast to a fantastic teacher and a wonderful colleague who decided to leave us far too soon. To Professor Barnes!"

"*Professor Barnes!*" The crowd cheers and I watch the poison in Ryker's eyes. He makes eye contact with me. I don't look away until he does.

"Ten bucks says good 'ole Marbles didn't resign on his own." Allister nudges me with his elbow.

"I wouldn't take that bet," I say and take a long drink of water. Water is supposed to melt witches, but what does it do to devils? Probably nothing.

I'll have to find something stronger, then.

———————

The compound has box upon box of stored decorations, all in white to match the colour of PAAC's star within a circle logo. I get an eyeful of the sparkling baubles as I organize each string of lights in the entire ornate archives. The decorations are only used for special proceedings and apparently this party is going to be a big deal. Astrid has volunteered our unit to decorate the cafeteria and I think about her unfavorably with every strand I untangle.

"What's going down again?" Allister groans as we both lift a table. It is heavier than it looks.

"It's a celebration," Astrid explains from her perch up the rungs of a ladder. Colin hands her ornaments to hang from the arches over the doorways.

"Never would have guessed." I strain with my end of the table.

"I wasn't finished, smart guy." She grins, reaching to hang another bulb. "It's like an anniversary for PAAC."

"Oh, I see. A perfect reason to break out all the fancy decorations and rearrange them over and over." Allister sighs. "An anniversary! Perfect!"

As the date for the party comes closer, the mood in all the units lifts. It isn't just the thought of not having classes or training for a day, it is the celebration itself that people are excited about. To both Allister and my surprise, Colin is the first one with a date to the ball.

"Sarah Mansfield," he says, glowing with pride. Allister, Maisie, Colin, and I sit in the common room. Astrid is out training. She said PAAC's anniversary is no excuse to be lazy. I happily disagree.

"Gamma 9C?" I raise my brows.

"Yup."

"Good work, Buddy," Allister says, clapping him on the back.

"I think that's really sweet," Maisie agrees. "What about you Allister? Who are you going with?"

"Well, despite the fact that I'm being absolutely swarmed by chicks every time I step out that door, I'm going alone."

"Alone?" I grin, waiting for the classic Allister punch line.

"Yeah. That way I can dance with everybody and not make anyone mad at me. Not even a little bit." Allister shrugs. I grin a little wider.

"I think Kole should go with Astrid." Maisie sits with one leg draped over the other, looking and talking like an old-style heiress gossiping over afternoon tea.

"Everyone has something to say, don't they?" I scoff.

"Well, don't leave room for conversation, dude." Allister puts his hands up, giving me no slack whatsoever.

"People will always talk about something, Kole. I find it best just not to listen to the noise," Maisie says with a confident nod. I glance at her and she just smiles.

"Amen!" Allister shouts.

The days are winding down, but in those quickly disappearing hours, I find myself thinking. I catch myself many times thinking about Professor Barnes, which evolves into thoughts of Peter Tarek. I haven't heard his name in a while and my memories of him were becoming cloudy. It is so hard to dust off the cobwebs; it is almost like he never existed at all. Like he was just a figment of my imagination. The thought plays with my mind a little too much for my liking.

And Jackson Alexander.

"You are meant to be Alpha."

Maybe that was why. Maybe the two are connected. Maybe I was just thrown into Beta position because they had no one else. Maybe I was going to be an Alpha, then the morning of, this other 9X got taken out and they used me as a bridge to fill the gap. That thought is oddly flattering but also disappointing at the same time. I could've been a great Alpha, if only I'd gotten the chance to prove myself before they decided who I was. Before they *told* me who I was. Who I am now.

Who I was *going* to be.

Having no room for discovery, no chance to find your purpose on your own, leaches the colour from life. It leaves things dull and bland like the white walls of the compound. No decoration, no originality, no nothing.

———

Except for the occasional mission, the days are the same. The up-and-coming dance anniversary is the only spice in recent times besides missions and training.

There wasn't a great deal of personal preparation required. Other than a shower, a stick of deodorant and a fine-toothed hair comb, I didn't have much to work with. We were made to wear our best formal PAAC uniforms, meaning a tight-fitting shirt, army pants and chunky combat boots—all in the monochromatic pattern of black, black and black. In other words, the uniforms we wore every day. The girls tried to change their hair, pulling it in different kinds of ponytails and braids while still staying within the dress code. Other than that, the only formal thing about the formal event was the setting, and that was after the professors re-did our decorating job.

Coming into the room and seeing how the professors had re-arranged the tables and the decorations, Allister and I just shrugged. We hadn't spent that long setting up the decorations and it's not like we really poured our creative heart and soul into it anyway. I do have to admit, it did look better their way.

The event started exactly how I thought it would; girls on one side and boys on the other. After a while it went to mingling, only a few brave souls actually dancing. Colin had Sarah Mansfield on the dance floor any of the rest of us even had the chance to ask someone. Then, before I knew it, I was sitting alone at our table. Maisie and Allister had run off dancing and chitchatting together.

"Hey, stranger," someone says warmly. Myrka Del Gatto smiles down at me. "Can I sit?"

"Yeah," I reply.

"I haven't seen you in a while. How've you been?" She cocks her head and her matte black hair, done in both a ponytail and a braid, falls over her shoulder.

"Busy," I breathe, half scoffing. "The compound keeps me running."

"I was gonna leave a complaint." Myrka smiles good heartedly. "Leave some adventure for the rest of us, why don't you?"

I grin at the floor. She picks up on the dip in conversation and leans in.

"She's waiting for you to ask her, you know," Myrka whispers with a sly little smirk on her rose-pink lips.

"She is?" I look around, trying to find her in the crowd.

"Mm hm. Don't let her down," Myrka says finally and gets up, walking away. I finally spot her, sitting with a bunch of type-A looking guys. I imagine they're the other Alphas. Astrid's eyes meet mine and my stomach comes alive with butterflies for a moment. I move, going straight to her. When I get to the table, she says something that I don't quite catch.

"I'm sorry," I say, leaning in to hear her better. "Did you say you wanted to dance?"

"No. I said you look fat in those pants," she jests. I blink. I know it's meant to be a joke but her delivery was very blunt and dry. "I'm kidding, I'd love to dance."

"Technically, I didn't ask you yet." I grin. She glows.

"Fine, then. I'll ask. Do *you* want to dance?" She gives me a playful look and I grin a little harder.

"Love to."

"Okay then." She smiles and gets up. I take her hand and we move to the dance floor.

"Who taught you to dance?" I ask, trying to break the silence and fill the space. Not that I had a problem staring her in the eyes for the length of the song and not saying a single word, but it *was* getting slightly awkward.

"... Jackson." She flushes red, looking away. "But whoever is in charge of this music? We are going to have words. This is a pathetic effort."

I grin at her just because she's pretty.

"What?" She snickers.

"Nothing."

Everything.

The bunk, my bunk, with the thin sheets is the only place where I can find silence. I'm still on cloud nine and nothing even happened. I feel complete. The joy on her face and the energy in the room was like the last two pieces in a thousand-piece puzzle. I listen to the silence as I close my eyes, trying to stifle my excitement. I don't remember falling asleep.

TWENTY

"... not a creature was stirring, not even a mouse." We read the story every single Christmas Eve. It is just as exciting as the first time I heard the words. I watch Mom from my bed, the flannel sheets and the blanket with cowboy stitching pulled right up to my nose.

The story continues as it did every year before and as it will every year to follow, Mom's voice bouncing off every nook and cranny of the room. The walls are a kind of brownish red, wall stickers of horses and cows arranged next to the shelf with the Woody from Toy Story figure Santa brought me the previous year. It felt fitting to have him on display this time of year. The western, ranch life and Old West theme wouldn't last very long. This phase would give way to astronauts and space, then hockey teams like the Oilers and Golden Knights. After that, the white walls of the PAAC facility.

But there's something missing. The bridge from here to there, then to now, has been washed away by a storm of amnesia. A storm of time.

Or maybe, something a little bit stronger.

———

A sharp jab to the gut, one that I can feel, tells me it's not a game. He moves fast and I can't read him. A fake left, fake right and when I think the hit is coming from the left, it comes from the right. I struggle just to stay on my feet. Well, until I get mad, then I'm here to play.

He takes a little step, ready to punch, so I step into it. I grab his forearm and redirect the power somewhere I am not. I twist his wrist, tweaking it a little and pulling it behind me before I bring the sole of my boots down in the back of his knee. He goes down on a knee, but doesn't stay that way for long. He stretches forwards, slipping out of my grip and tripping me up with his feet. I lose balance and his fist comes out of nowhere, slamming into my sternum like a small truck and sends me careening off.

The ringing in my ears is murder and I shake my head to clear it. It's like glass marbles are rolling around in my skull. I can't focus.

"Don't let your anger get the best of you, Beta. It'll cloud your judgment. Turn your world into a fishbowl."

I hear someone talking, but it's like I'm underwater or something.

"C'mon, man."

"You got this."

"Pull yourself together, Danvers! Fight!"

"FIGHT!"

I bring myself upwards and throw myself at him, locking my hands around his neck and hitting him in the gut with my knee cap. When he staggers a bit, I change it up. I grab onto his shirt collar and drive punches all the way home. Punch after punch, hit after hit, until it's over.

A buzzer sounds and the opponent dissolves into orange pixels and the lights turn on with a glare.

"Not bad, eh?" The Russian accent sounds like stones scraping stones, or nails on a chalk board. The pudgy Professor Romanov, the eccentric Professor Barnes' replacement, saunters forwards, beer belly jiggling. I wipe the sweat from my brow, taking the VR goggles off my face.

"It hurts," I note.

"Eh, pain is nothing, yes? Be thankful for pain. That's what Mama used to say. 'Be thankful for pain, Niklaus. Pain is the doorway to strength,'" he rambles, almost one hundred percent for his own ears.

"I'd take Barnes back right about now," I pant. Astrid grins and hands me a little face cloth and I mop up my sweat. "You did good. Well, for Beta."

"Don't even start with me." I shake my head at her playfully. Romanov continues his downward spiral of soliloquy.

"The simulation will teach you ..." Something, something. Pain, pain, pain.

"Excuse me? Professor Romanov?" Colin raises his hand no higher than his shoulder.

"Yes! A question! What is it?"

"How does it work?" The Gamma furrows his brow, ever and always in the eternal pursuit of knowledge. "The simulation, I mean."

"Wonderful question, Carson!"

"Colin."

"Colin! Yes, right! The simulation works on the same frequencies as your standard colour television, only in a four-dimensional aspect, giving it length, height, depth *and* weight. Which gives it substance. You ever make those pin-hole, uh, kaleidoscopes in science class, eh?"

"No."

"Well, it's just like that, eh? Just like that but with more pain," Professor Romanov explains, his eyes lighting up at his favourite word—*pain*. Fitting for a weapons and combat specialist. "The simulation," he continues, "will provide the necessary training, without that training being at the expense of any human resource. It is revolutionary technology. Saves both time and energy. But it is experimental, of course."

"Experimental?" Allister raises a brow. "How 'experimental' are we talking here, Doc?"

"Eh, a prototype. A model experimental, but it obviously works fine, no? Kolby—"

"Kole."

"I am getting closer all the time. I will know all your names, eventually. But Kole is okay, see? So, no, I have no worries." Romanov pushes up the sleeves of his grey cable knit sweater to his elbow and shrugs.

"What happens to someone if it malfunctions while they're in the simulation?" Maisie wrings her hands, watching the machine with an uneasy light in her eye. Romanov takes a few uncontrollable bursts of laughter, breathy and disjointed.

"Now that, that would be *bad*." He chuckles. "Imagine; electrocution. Bubbling eyes and burning skin." He mimics a strangled face, then laughs again before walking off, still laughing.

"He's literally a psychopath," I remark after he's well out of earshot.

"He's definitely something else," Colin snorts. We take a moment to laugh at the old Russian's expense. The machine behind us whirs away, radiating heat like an old PC computer with a broken fan. I can feel the heat even standing a few metres away. The machine looks ominous and otherworldly, like something from the future.

"This is revolutionary technology!" exclaims the professor.

The crowd disperses and most of the onlooking units shamble off to find something else to do. I look to the side, upwards to a glass shielded compartment for spectators. Fallon and Ryker, stand together at the glass. They watch with unreadable frowns. I glare up at them. After Fallon exits, Ryker takes a step closer, finding me and staring me in the eye. My spine bristles and I stand a little straighter. Ryker narrows his eyes before turning to follow Fallon, always under his command.

"Jesus." Astrid puts a hand on my shoulder, looking up at the glass, now empty. "What was that about?"

"Old beef," I say.

"Ah. I should have known. The hero versus evil?" She grins at me, poking at my chest. I smile at the floor, letting her take her shots. "Iron will against iron will?"

"Alright, alright," I jest. She punches my arm with force.

"Guys. Guys." Allister wrenches my shoulder to get my attention. "Wanna do something fun?"

"What's this fun you speak of?" Astrid smiles wider.

"Funny. I'm serious though."

"Where?" I inquire, flicking my chin at him.

"Training room."

"What's happening?" Astrid asks, her smile turning sly and mischevious.

"We, my friends," he grins stupidly and pops his eyebrows boisterously, "are going to a party.

The lights flashing blue, purple, red and yellow hang like beads of energy off the strings hung wall to wall. The music is so loud that the air vibrates with the heavy bass, the sound reverberating and echoing off every solid object. The people, our fellow soldiers, dance and yell, laughing and cheering as the beat drops in the song and the lights sync to the tempo.

"I didn't think this would be allowed!" Maisie shouts over the thump of the music.

"It's not exactly encouraged." Colin grimaces, hands to his ears to block the noise.

"No one cares!" Allister exclaims, never looking more at home in his entire life. His eyes are wild and alive, drinking in everything in sight. I can tell he's more than loving this. "The Generals one and two don't care, the Profs are just glad they don't have to babysit and Ethan Hartfield from 9Y has the best playlist in the compound."

"Omega Ethan Hartfield?" Maisie's eyes light up. I give her an amused look. It's no secret that our Omega has a little crush on this Hartfield.

"That's the one. Let's get a drink." Allister drapes an arm over Maisie's shoulder and takes Colin by the scruff of the neck, trying to find the drinks in the throngs of dancing teenagers.

"Drink?" Astrid asks.

"Alcoholic?" I reply.

"I don't think so. Everyone who looks drunk is acting, unless someone spiked the punch bowl with isopropyl stolen from the lab," Astrid says flatly, then freezes thinking about the alcoholic possibility.

"Yeah, I'll go with water for now," I decide.

"Me, too."

The training room has no tables, so Astrid and I sit on the ledge of a sparring platform and watch the madness before us. People acting ridiculously, but never losing their smile even if they topple over. It's strange to see, really. All these tight-lipped, straight line, disciplined soldiers flailing about and making fools of themselves. And all for what? Attention?

"I think it's beautiful," Astrid says, breaking my thought like shattering glass.

"What?"

"The chaos. I think it's beautiful."

"Really?" I chuckle. "This is disastrous."

"No, it's not. Not really." She shakes her white-blonde head. "It's just different than what we're used to. The colour and the light, the music. No one has to march in a perfect line. No one has any real mission to complete. It's just so ... perfect."

A beat of silence.

"Have you ever thought about what it would be like if we weren't—"

"Kole and Astrid?"

"Yeah," I say, looking over at her.

She sighs deeply through her nose. "All day, every day."

"Mm. Same."

"I don't think we're unlucky, though," she admits with a shrug. "It's not bad being Astrid and Kole."

I take a moment to think about that before leaning in and pressing my lips softly to hers.

TWENTY-ONE

The scream comes in the middle of the night. A shrieking, piercing scream that echoes like murder up and down the halls.

Get up.

I spring bolt upright, rip away the covers, slam open the bunk divider and the door to the dorm. With my unit close on my heels, I run full speed down the hallway, instinctively following the horrid sound. The screaming is coming from the simulation room and my stomach trades spots with my heart as I shove open the door. A circle of people are gathered around something I can only see in my imagination. Something I fear to see in real life.

A girl with amber hair and pale skin, beside herself with grief or rage, is struggling against someone holding her back. She screams and thrashes, clawing to get free and through the crowd.

"I'm sorry!" she howls, her guttural tones ringing through the air. "I'm *sorry!*"

I break through the edge of the crowd and see the scene for the first time. A girl with espresso skin and long, braided black hair lies on the ground, the simulation VR goggles still strapped to her head. Bolts of blue electricity leap from the goggles to random spots on her face. The air smells of burnt hair and charred skin.

The girl is dead.

"Kole." Myrka appears, swimming through the crowd. "Kole, what—" She pauses. "Oh my God!"

"It was the tech!" someone cries out. "The machine! It killed her!"

"Make way!" The booming Russian accent comes floating over the commotion, almost cutting it out entirely. "Move! Out of the way!"

"Professor Romanov!" I call, as he crouches by the victim. I come to his side as he eases the goggles off her face, revealing her eyes rolled back so far you can only see the whites. A racoon mask of skin, burnt and crisp, rings her eye sockets. "What happened?"

"Not now," he grunts, pointlessly checking for a pulse. He won't find anything. She's way beyond saving. She's already gone. The amber-haired girl continues to thrash and wail in the background. I find it hard to ignore that kind of pain and suffering.

"But, Professor—"

"I said 'Not. Now.' Boyo." He looks up briefly, with a nod to the crying girl. "Will somebody please contain her! Alpha C, do it now." The boy holding her back tightens his grip as the Russian digs in his pocket, pulling out a single syringe filled with a clear liquid. He goes to the struggling girl and jabs the needle point into her neck, warranting a sharp cry from her lips and presses the plunger. She goes limp almost immediately. The rest of the room falls under a blanket of silence. No one moves. No one even blinks. Except for Romanov.

"No one," Romanov points to his simulator. "No one is permitted to use this machine until we find the problem, understand? Now, everyone back to your dorms. Now."

"Professor—"

"*Now!*" he seethes and I have no choice but to obey. I put my head down and follow the flow of traffic out the simulation room doors and into the hallway. The walkway is jammed with soldiers hustling to get to their dorms. My mind is spinning. Lines cross, thoughts intertwine and nothing makes sense.

"I'm not surprised," Colin says almost passively, coming up on my flank.

"What do you mean?" I try not to snap. Tension over the situation hangs in the air like a heavy fog and the hallway quiets as units peel off. Soon, we are drowning in silence but for our own noise, as we come up to the 9X door.

"Romanov said it was just a prototype a few days ago," Colin explains. "It's faulty."

"Yeah, but no one expected it to actually kill anyone." I glare at the door ahead. PAAC was supposed to be sure. Accurate and efficient. The professors and council members aren't supposed to make mistakes, especially not of this gravity.

A hand falls lightly on my shoulder, holding me back from entering the open dorm door. Colin doesn't wait, going ahead without me. I turn to see Maisie's sad, misting eyes moving from the floor to my face.

"You okay?" I ask, having nothing else to say. Maybe more like not knowing what else she needs to hear.

"I *knew* her." She wipes the slow tears, just now daring to fall. "Her name was Siobhan Myers. Omega 9S. I trained with her. She was quiet like me. She was *special.*"

"I'm really sorry, Mais. Really."

"No." She shakes her head like I missed the point completely. Maybe I did. "No. Listen to me. She was *special.*"

"What do you mean?"

"She could remember things. She'd tell me stores from when she was small. About her parents and her siblings. She had a twin. She remembered things, Kole. Just like you."

TWENTY-TWO

"Myers?"

"Yeah. Siobhan Myers."

"Oh wait, I think I ... yeah. I got her." Colin and I search through the unclassified files using the computer on his desk.

"Right there." I point to the screen. "Now search for all the soldiers with the last name Myers."

The tedious searching and endless scrolling through every Myers in PAAC history led to a large collection. A ruthless headache grows behind my eyes.

We get to the bottom of the list. Third from the last file is labelled *Delta 9B*.

"There. There he is," I blurt, tapping the screen with my fingernail. Colin clicks on it and the 9B file opens with a plethora of information.

"His name is Jordan. Jordan Myers," Colin informs me. I sit back and cross my arms. They held two siblings, never letting them meet. If Siobhan had never been able to remember that she had a twin, she would have never known. But she did remember . She remembered him, just not where he was.

Does he remember too?

Don't get ahead of yourself, Kole. You're in enough trouble as it is.

No, I'm not. I'm fine.

It's not your business, Kole.

Oh, but it is. It is in every way.

"C'mon," I say, standing as I make up my mind. "Let's go for a walk."

Jordan was the one to open the door. His long hair, done in chunky braids that fall across his face whenever he moves, matches the picture exactly.

"Can I help you?"

"Yeah, actually. We wanted to know if you knew anything about the simulation thing?" I question, trying to play dumb and be as blunt as possible.

"I wasn't there."

"Did you hear about it?"

"Not really. I heard some girl died, but that's about it." He scratches his eyebrow with a thumb nail, looking like he has something better to do.

"Do you know who it was?"

"An Omega, I think? Not really sure." He sighs. "Anything else?" he asks. It's then I know for sure that he doesn't want to talk to me anymore.

"No, I'm good. Thanks," I say, my heart sinking a bit.

"Any time, man." He shuts the door. I look to Colin, who was silent the entire time.

"Jordan?" I nod to the door speaking quietly. "That was her brother. He didn't even know she was his sister and now he'll never be able to talk to her, face to face.

He didn't even know.

TWENTY-THREE

"The human body, on average, holds about five litres of blood. Blood is the fuel of the body. It's a highway for glucose and oxygen and they are vital for survival." Wound and injury survivalist, Professor Elliot Kingston, paces on his little teaching stage. A slideshow presentation plays through the blue rays of the projector beside him.

"Now, blood loss is a killer. If you get stabbed, the knife is no longer the problem. It's the aftermath that kills you. In the case of severe bleeding, applying pressure is now your best friend." He paces a little more, hands folded diplomatically behind his back. His close-cropped hair is so short, it is almost non-existent. His skin is a warm brown and his eyes, an almond shape, are so dark they just look black.

"The pressure points; femoral artery for stopping bleeding from the legs and the brachial artery for stopping bleeding from the arms and hands. When applying pressure, aim for these certain spots."

The class practices putting pressure on arteries, making clumsy attempts as tourniquets and wrappings. Professor Kingston floats from table to table as we work with dense rubber limbs the colour of an orange crayon. He either passes on with an approving nod and smile, or spends five minutes showing the proper technique. He's climbing the list of my favourite professors, and fast.

"Good work, Kole. Try to create as much pressure and tension as possible. Looks great," he informs me, before carrying on to the next table. For me, the hours spent learning about anatomy didn't drag or crawl, I found the subject fascinating overall. The spiderweb network of veins and arteries in the human body—the extensive highways for blood and oxygen, essential nutrients and sugars—was the essence of life.

"In the loss of a limb, " Professor Kingston continues, clicking through new slides of his presentation, "the major arteries will contract back into the muscle, but only if the limb is completely severed. For this example, let's say it was a clean slice all the way through. The limb is completely detached from the body. Now, what is the first thing we do?"

"Assess the situation," the class rumbles like a choir of sleep-deprived husks.

"Very good," Kingston continues. "Now, should the ... let's say ... arm, be completely severed as we discussed, the—"

"Psst."

"—brachial artery will already be compressed. This does not stop all bleeding. This is an extremely dangerous and dire situation."

"Psst. Kole."

"Find the closest spot to the heart as possible that you can tie off. But remember when you—"

"Psst. Kole! Hey!"

"What?" I try to hide my irritation. Colin blinks at me from across the round table. No one else is paying attention, they are all focused on the bloody images on the screen. Colin flicks a neatly folded piece of lined paper expertly into my cupped hands. I give him a look somewhere in the crosshairs between stern and confused. The paper crinkles loudly under my fingers as I try, and fail, to unfold it silently. Written in blue pen in Colin's neat, practiced handwriting, are seven words. Seven words, that until recent events would have meant absolutely nothing to me. Seven words that sent instant shivers up my back like someone's fingers were dancing on my spine.

There is something you need to see.

———————

I can only see the rough outline of Colin's slim figure ahead of me. It is the middle of the night, and the daytime hallway lighting has been toned down, the dimmed fluorescent tubes bathing everything in an eerie glow. The white walls are now a shadowy black, a daunting dark soupiness. It feels like the beginning of a horror film where I, the victim, am being led to my demise. I can hear dramatic music playing in my head in rhythm with my soft footsteps.

"Where are we going?" I ask for what seems the thousandth time.

"You'll see," he answers, also for what seems the thousandth time.

"Can't you just tell me? It's, like, three in the morning." Colin had dragged me out of my warm bed hours after slipping me the note. It must be secret if Colin is travelling under the cover of dark. He hates the dark.

"Wait and see. It's hard to explain."

Which was a lie.

He pushes open the doors, bringing us into a lab I didn't know about. The room is bathed in green light. In the back of the room, ringed by tables and equipment and backed by cabinets full of chemicals and other scientific matter, is a stage. On this stage is a large cylinder, glowing an iridescent green. It is full of a membrane-like mucus, bubbles moving at a snail's pace, fighting to get to the top. When I moved closer, I find the air around it disturbingly warm. Warmer than any other part of the room.

"What is it?" I ask, not having to speak very loudly. Colin comes to my flank in silence.

"We call it an incubation chamber."

"We?"

"Yeah." He winces. "General Fallon came to me with a project and, well ... here it is. I wanted to show somebody about it. It felt weird not to, you know? Greatness was meant to be shared."

"What's—" As I start to take a step closer, something slams against the inside of the glass, rattling the entire chamber." I jump back. It looked like a hand. A human hand. "What was that?"

"You do know the definition of 'incubation,' right? That's our project. We call it *H-Con7870*, or *Patrick*, if we're speaking informally," Colin explains, beaming with pride as I look on in disgust. "Fallon says it's the future of military defense as we know it. A new breed of soldier specifically designed to complete tasks based on H-Con7870's unique genetic coding. H-Con7870 breaks down into Hydrogen Carbon Number 7,870."

"Is it ... human?"

"Oh, no. Of course not. We made synthetic DNA based on other models that PAAC has acquired over the years. Under the correct circumstances, we've been able to speed up the maturation process. It's actually really cool, and this is just the prototype. All the next generation models will be extremely advanced. It will be like comparing a human to an ape."

A red flag waves in my face like the checkered material at a racetrack.

"You're going to make more?" I ask, my eyes growing wide.

"Well, yeah," Colin confirms, as if I had asked a silly question with an obvious answer. "The future can't just rest on the back of one man. It's kind of a group effort."

"What will that look like?"

"Well, each soldier will be genetically modified for specific tasks. A spy. A fighter. A leader. Whatever PAAC thinks it needs, we'll make." Colin sighs.

"Humanoid weapons?" I ask. "What if you can't control them?"

"It will be no different than having you running around." Colin glares at me with a sour face. He obviously meant it, but I strongly disagree. I can be controlled, contained. It's not like I'm hurting people. I'm not as wild or feral as he makes me sound.

I didn't know he felt this way. I'm not sure how to respond.

"Well, I ... uh." I clear my throat as the face floats close enough to the glass for me to make out its features. It's distinctly male with a wide nose and a broad forehead. Its eyes are closed peacefully, almost like it's sleeping, and I am grateful for that. "I'm going to go."

"It's unsettling. I know," Colin begins. "But once it's out, or born as General Fallon likes to say, it's going to be revolutionary." The air about him is infused with pride. He keeps saying that this is the future, but how can fake life be the future? How can test tube humans and programmed algorithms be what's in store? Once they can create life, what will they do next?

Where will they stop?

Who will stop them if they don't stop themselves?

"Sorry, Colin. I can't stay here," I groan, a sick feeling in my gut. I turn around, putting the slow bubbling sounds to my back. The light makes my shadow look grotesquely long. I follow it out the door quickly, swinging the door shut behind me.

I'm glad I didn't stay, but I don't think I'll be able to sleep either. And I don't.

I lay awake in my bunk; eyes wide. Every time I close them, the image of the H-Con7870's mucus-laden face looming slowly through the murk replays repeatedly. What did they call him? Patrick? Such a human name for such an unhuman thing. It was alien. It was strange. It was completely unnatural.

It was wrong.

The sounds of the night buzz around me. The occasional footstep in the hallway and the odd, louder-than-average snore from Allister's bunk. He always leaves the compartment door yawning wide open.

... This is just a prototype.

A copy for everything PAAC thinks it needs.

Does he not see the danger in that? If PAAC has everything it needs, all the manpower and none of the resistance, they will be unstoppable. Imagine a total knockout force prowling over a world that's already shattered like glass. Does he not realize he just engineered his own replacement? He created a living super computer. Fallon isn't going to have a use for Colin's human brain once he gets his hands on the power generated by H-Con. Fallon isn't going to have a use for anything living once this thing leaves its mucus tank.

And when did Colin find the time to work on it? He must have been burning the midnight oil while we were asleep. Sneaking out at dark, a page out of my playbook. I'm not sure if I should be alarmed or not.

I turn over, not wanting to think about anything else for the rest of the night.

TWENTY-FOUR

I knock on the door and the response is almost instantaneous.

"Who is it?"

"It's me. Kole, Sir," I say, my face close enough to the oak door that I can smell the wood finish.

"Of course, come in," he replies. When I crack the door, the pudgy Russian is sitting at his desk, leafing through papers. Untouched manila file folders sit stacked on the corner like the leaning tower of Pisa. A collection of candy wrappers litters the floor around the garbage can.

"Sir," I venture slowly. "Do you have a minute?"

"I have all the minutes in the world, my boy. It's up to me whether to spend them on things that truly matter or—" He motions to the war zone of a desk. "Things that bring me no joy whatsoever."

"They look like important papers to me, Sir," I say, sliding into the pleather chair opposite of him.

"Important, yes. Worth my time? Not so much." He grins. "What can I do for you?"

"I have a few questions." I frown. He nods like I've already asked them.

"You want to know about the simulation tragedy, eh?"

"Uh, yes. Yes, Sir, I do."

"Drop the 'Sir.' No General in this room, eh?"

"Okay ... Professor." I comply awkwardly.

"Almost, but better." He dips his head. "Now, this accident, eh? Terrible."

"Yes. What happened?"

"I saw you in the front row, yes? You know what happened." He straightens the papers on his desk and stacks them on some others.

"But, technologically? What happened to the simulation?" I pry a little, digging my heals in.

"Truth be told, we don't exactly know." He sighs heavily, sitting back. Examination of the machine suggested no problems. There was nothing wrong with it."

"All due respect, Professor, but that is obviously a lie," I retort.

"That's what I said." Romanov grins at me in the way two similar people would agree on something.

"You didn't investigate yourself?" I frown.

"I was not permitted to. Something to do with my being an entry level professor position. Really makes me feel like a part of the team. Especially when I'm not invited to the staff parties."

That makes me smile. This man in all his stereotypical Russian gruffness makes fun of the compound management almost as much as I do.

Or maybe he's looking for a way in.

You have serious problems.

I have serious doubts.

Just calm down, Kole. Seriously.

"But don't feel bad for Romanov, no," he carries on, playing out the bit. "I don't want to go to their parties anyways. They gossip like teenage girls."

"Really?" I laugh out loud.

"Oh, yes," Romanov says, making a dramatic face, eyes wide and lips pursed. "Always going on about who did this or who said this. It's exhausting really. For once I'd just like to talk about the weather! But no. They like to gossip and I leave because there is no worse way to waste my time." He picks up one of his many manila file folders. "I'd rather do the paperwork." He shakes his head at the desk. I'm still amused by the thought of General Ryker sipping tea or champagne, depending on the time of day, and getting his fill of hot gossip.

"Do your friends gossip much, Kole?"

"They're not really the type." I shrug. It's hard to imagine the stone-faced Astrid getting dirt on others just for fun.

"Ah." He nods, looking at me with new, kind eyes. "This is a crazy world we live in, Kole. Absolutely raving mad."

"Yes, it is," I say to the floor, not having heard anything truer today.

"But you know what I think it the best part of this ... this complete madness? This insanity?"

"What's that, Professor?"

"I think the best part is the lesson. The things that struggle and failure can teach us are so valuable. Absolutely priceless. That, that is what I think makes this all worth it. What makes it meaningful. What makes it precious and beautiful."

"That's very insightful, Professor," I comment, smiling, not knowing that he could be wise like that. I guess I shouldn't have doubted him. I spent another twenty minutes with him, talking, laughing, and listening to him pour out life quotes like he was reading from a poet's personal diary. It was time well spent.

I was standing, my arm outstretched for the brass door handle. That's when Professor Romanov tells me something very typical of himself.

"It's hard to wash the blood from your hands, eh?" he says. "It stains so dark. Once you touch it, you can't get rid of it. Like glitter. That stuff is relentless." I stare at him. He has to be the only man I know who can relate blood and glitter while sounding just a little bit crazy. I was beginning to like Professor Romanov more and more.

The smell of the training room is one you don't easily forget. No matter how many coffee grounds you snort, the stench is there to stay. The pungent, deep nostril burn gets you every time you walk through the doors. Air fresheners, aerosol or gel cones, couldn't put a dent in it.

Allister, Astrid, Maisie, and I went to put in some hours on the platform. Colin said he would've come, but he had some Gamma training to catch up on. I know the real truth. He is going to work on Patrick.

"Parry," Maisie instructs me.

"Bottom left inside. Switch," Astrid rattles to Allister.

We are in teams, coach and player style. Allister had spoken faster, scoring Astrid on his team. I know neither of them will take it easy on me. Luckily, we're the only ones left in the training room, so it's not like I have anything to prove to an audience.

"Evade. Left. Left. Now right," Astrid coaches at lightspeed and Allister has no problem keeping up with the commands.

"Come on, man. You wanna dance? Wanna dance, bro? Two-step? Let's dance." Allister pokes and jests at me.

"Allister. Don't talk to the opponent." Astrid grins. I flash her a look and Allister takes his moment of opportunity, folding me at the gut with a cheap shot. Astrid grins some more and gifts me with a little wink.

"Yes, Boss," Allister says, only partially joking.

"Sorry, Kole." Maisie winces from the ropes.

"It's okay. I'm taking it easy on him anyway," I groan, straightening.

"Oh?" Allister plunges into a ridiculous show of made-up karate moves. "Taking it easy on me, eh? Well come on, then. Let's dance for real."

"Deke right. Left, right. Snap kick," Astrid barks from the side lines, gripping onto the ropes like she's watching a professional boxing match. Allister moves like lightning, swift and smooth.

"Forearm. Block gut," Maisie instructs and turns out to be right. Allister's knuckles connect with the fleshy muscle of my forearm with a satisfying thump. The sound of a solid block. We spend time getting into the fun and the camaraderie of the match. Just having a laugh or two, a good and true belly laugh is healthy for the soul. In light of recent times, the general easiness around my friends is important to me. It's worth more than the hero stories or the glory or the rankings that this place is built on. Everything Romanov had said in his office is all finally coming into perspective.

TWENTY-FIVE

"The Tournament of Valor. A promise of glory. Of heroism. An opportunity to fight for respect. To earn your place. To earn your name." The deep bass tone of the recorded message plays from the speakers in the cafeteria. "A series of challenging tasks designed to weed the good from the greatest; the strong from the strongest. The rules are simple: no sabotage, no cheating, and no giving up. Remember, although you be outranked, you are not unequal. Thank you and good luck."

"*Although we be outranked, we are not unequal.*" The collected audience calls back like an echo, even though we know the voice from the recorded message can't hear us.

"So ... what do we do in this mighty tournament?" Allister whispers roughly. Astrid shushes him aggressively, but has a hint of amusement living in her eyes.

"Hold your tongue and maybe we'll find out."

"The tournament will last twenty-six days." Professor Romanov's heavy Russian accent skates over all the background noise with ease. "Twenty-six days for twenty-six levels or rounds. After each level, one unit will be eliminated. Understand? Yes? Good. Oh, and your prize?" He pauses. "Your prize is glory."

From then on, the air holds a new energy. The compound is alive with friendly competitiveness and healthy rivalries. The halls buzz with playful smack talk that always ends in laughter from both parties.

The entire compound is just waiting for that green light. Waiting for *Go*. For day one of twenty-six.

"I wonder what the challenges will be," Maisie thinks aloud with eyes as wide as saucers. "Maybe puzzles or riddles ... or something like that."

"Nah." Allister shakes his head. "I bet it'll be something *super* James Bond. Total 007. Infiltrating the White House or crossing an alligator-infested river—something daring and dangerous and super awesome like that."

"Ooh," Maisie's eyes grow wider.

"And jetpacks," Allister continues, getting that dreamy look in his eye he always gets when he talks about stunts or James Bond.

"Can't forget the jetpacks." Astrid grins to me, off to the side.

"For us or for the alligators?" Maisie giggles.

"Both." I snicker. "Then we can race."

"Don't joke about that." Allister points a finger at all of us. "That's some cool stuff right there. Alligators wearing jetpacks? Sign me up."

"Oh, please. You'd be scared stiff."

"That's not the point."

"What actually is the point? Tell me again?" Astrid fakes a confused look. It's impressively believable.

"Alligators and jetpacks are super cool." Allister looks affronted. He says it like it should be obvious. "Where have you been for the past two minutes?"

"Braincell City," she snorts and Allister gives her two of my favourite fingers. The lightness gives me positive energy. It's better than self-confidence. Gives me that buzz that holds deep in your gut and squeezes at your heart. That sweet feeling you don't want to lose but you know is impossible to hold on to. When grey clouds fall over skies and the sun can't punch its bright face through, it will be a memory of these moments of teasing and joking about jetpacks, alligators and James Bond that will hold the light of positivity.

I smile wider and wider as the moment carries on.

The days go on, but now that I know the secret, things aren't so bad. Smile every once and a while. Engage in only the things that bring you joy unless it's necessary to do otherwise. Romanov's insight was more useful than I'd have thought.

Professor Romanov has the most interesting lessons in the compound. Not even Kingston can touch his originality. I credit most of that originality to his violent personality and love of the colour red. His slideshows or video presentations almost always contained gory images or dismembered body parts.

He presents with his classic maniacal smile and explains the weapons most likely to have been used in each scenario. "Knives, eh? An axe maybe. Okay, next slide. Oh, this was definitely a chainsaw. One hundred and ten percent, this was done with a chainsaw. Hands down. Next slide." He reads and comments on the presentation, only asking for questions at the end. No one ever has any questions.

Romanov and Kingston are quite different. Romanov teaches us how to inflict the injuries and Kingston teaches us how to heal them.

Between Romanov's chainsaw depictions and the excitement over this new, glorious Tournament of Valor, the days never cease to be interesting. *Dull* is non-existent. Training has become harder and more frequent, but I won't complain. The changes to my body are all worth it; hard lines and defined muscle make me feel just a little more accomplished. I've grown and not just physically. Since I was assigned, I've grown smarter and sharper with every challenge; able to go longer, fight smarter, strike and parry harder, and run faster. All while the professors watch me bloom into exactly what they want me to be.

Just a product of the system, trained, polished and battle ready.

It's kind of strange, knowing your strength and being able to see it. Watch your progress. To work for it, and better yet, achieve it. To be where I am but still have all the strings, all the connections to where I started. Some days, I feel I'm no different and other days I feel like I've traveled galaxies in leaps and bounds.

My bonds and my friendships have strengthened too. Battling through arguments, being brave enough to admit that I am wrong every once and a while. Learning I can be the bad guy in certain situations. Every time I'm arguing with Astrid, it's only a matter of time before she out-wits me. The white-haired girl is still a complete mystery to me, even after all this time. It's like she has this titanium barrier around her with no breaches.

That doesn't mean she never smiles or laughs. I find myself laughing more with her than with the others lately and that includes Allister, the King of Clowns. There's something about her that's so natural; it eases all tension in any room. She makes secure places feel safer. She's a force, a storm to silence all others, a silent strength. She possesses a mental stillness. She thinks only in conclusive thoughts that are well put together, confident ... and almost always right. I can't say the same, as my mind seems to run itself and the best I can hope for is just to hold on, to stay in the saddle.

—————————

The weeks dwindle as do the number of teams. It didn't become real to me that we could actually win the whole thing until there were only eight units left in the competition. We stand together in the training room, each unit huddled around a small table, similar to one you would put beside a bed. A black velvet bag with yellow ropes rests on each surface.

"The challenge is simple," Romanov drones robotically, as he has before every challenge. He looks miserable. I'm pretty sure he was assigned the task of overseeing the tournament because no one else wanted to do it. No doubt he would rather be in front of a class, teaching. "Get to the table, untie all the knots to open the bag and solve the puzzle inside. Only rule is, you must go one at a time. If you think you can't untangle any of the knots, trade spots. Everyone must take a turn or your unit will be disqualified. Last one to finish is knocked out of the tournament so work fast. Are you ready?"

"Allister," Astrid says. "You first."

"I'm on it," he says, ducking into a running pose and looking like the Flash. I notice Maisie shaking her head comically from the corner of my eye. I grin at her.

"Three, two, one and go." Romanov counts down, sounding very underwhelmed. The eight units launch into action. Allister channels his inner superhero and leaps at the table, knocking into it because he was so excited. He works furiously at the knots with us yelling encouragement at his back.

"Come on! Come on!"

"You got it!"

"You got this. You can do it!"

"Come on!"

Allister slams a hand on the table. "Trade out, trade out," he barks, really getting competitive. Colin takes his spot, ripping away at the rope's knots quickly. I watch the tail end grow longer and longer with every knot undone. I can't help but smile and match the excited shouting from all corners of the room. My turn comes and I get down through the three last knots and open the bag, dumping the puzzle pieces on the table for the girls. We had decided to let Astrid and Maisie tackle the puzzle itself because they are far better at that kind of thing than we boys are. Especially Maisie. Puzzles and riddles are her thing.

Astrid takes the first crack, so we can get everyone's hands on the challenge. Maisie jumps in and goes to work, fitting in wooden block after wooden block and shifting around. She tries new angles and works relentlessly, her face a blank slate of calm. A unit in front of us cheers, putting their arms in the air. Then another team finishes on the other side of the room. She doesn't acknowledge them, and soon, we cheer next, with our hands up in the air.

"Hey, hey!" Allister grins, putting an arm around the girls' shoulders. "Third place ain't bad. Ain't bad at all. Good work, Mais."

"Thanks."

"You did good," I say to Astrid. She shrugs lightly.

"Maisie won it for us."

"We worked together," she insists. We all laugh. Allister gives one more loud whoop, filling up the entire room with his noise before we log in our success and are given the go ahead to just sit and watch the rest of the challenge play out.

And then just like that, there are only two of us left. Unit 9X and Unit 9D. The professors gather us in the simulation center where they ran our physical examinations. We stand in huddles and wait. Romanov appears and the other units watch from the seats behind the glass. The obstacle course stands in front of us.

"Unit 9D and Unit 9X, our final units left in the tournament of Valour. We've seen them do very, very well with all the challenges. Give them some love!" He beckons for louder cheers and the crowd roars. "The last challenge is for the Alphas. That quote, the team is only as strong as the weakest link? I personally think that is utter bull. I think the leader makes the team strong, eh? Well, let's see how strong your leaders are. I want Alphas 9D and 9X on the starting line. Let's race."

We pat Astrid on the back as she rolls her shoulders and steps out, her toes just before the painted line on the floor. She looks over at her opponent, who watches her with an unreadable expression. I smile when she offers her hand for him to shake.

Romanov's cheerful call for clapping from the crowd has disappeared, replaced by an instructive tone. "Like the rest of the rules, no sabotage and no giving up. You must past that finish line even if you lose. Pass it for yourself and for your unit. No quitting, no crying." He speaks like he's reading from a drill manual. "Alright. Get ready."

Astrid tenses up like a spring, waiting to be set free. Waiting to explode into action.

"Go."

And she does. She bursts forwards and tackles the first obstacle in exact time and pace with the other Alpha. She matches him, making it look easy. They run over the rope bridges, launch themselves over hurdles, and muscle through hanging obstacles. When it comes time to make a jump before the sprint to the finish, Astrid summons all her strength and channels it, launching herself about two feet farther than Alpha 9D. She bolts through the end like a deer, taking the win while the rest of us, watching from the starting line, cheer like lunatics. She looks back and when she smiles, wide and for real, you know she's feeling the win.

The fabric of the suit is matte black and itchy. Matched with sleek polished shoes, a white shirt and a maroon red tie, the entire outfit is stuffy and uncomfortable. My hair is gelled back and formal. I smell like a can of hairspray and feel like a plastic Ken doll. It is an odd feeling. Allister and Colin are in the same boat, but I think they're enjoying it just a little bit more. Colin leans forwards in the mirror to better part his hair and Allister swivels back and forth to look at himself from every angle. I smile and shake my head, not saying a word.

Just let them enjoy it while they can.

"You guys ready yet?" Astrid knocks on the bathroom door. "Seriously, and they say girls take forever to get dressed."

"We're good." I grin at the guys as they have their eyes glued to the mirror. Astrid and Maisie open the door, ready to go and pry

Colin and Allister away from the mirror. Maisie wears a light teal dress that makes her skin glow and her hair look like fire. Astrid's hair is done up in an intricate Viking braid; she told me about it earlier, but I couldn't picture it until now. She's in a pale, lavender dress, her eyes a steely grey and more piercing than usual. I try not to stare but it's hard.

"You look nice," I tell her. She gives me a little smile. I notice the faint shimmer of lip gloss on Maisie's mouth and a darkness to her eyelids. Astrid has none of that. I guess she drew the line at makeup. In the corner, Maisie glows, obviously loving every second of it.

"Dang. We look fine." Allister grins his wide, lopsided grin and looks around at all of us.

"So, this is the target." Astrid holds up a printed picture of a business man shaking hands with another man in a suit. A proud smile on his face and a gold watch on his wrist. The print came from the information packet Fallon had given us when he assigned us to this mission, to bring in the man for questioning. "Sebastián Russo. Weapons dealer. He's flying in from his home in Tuscany, Italy specially for this posh awards ceremony. He's using the event to get to multiple buyers at once. Apparently, he does this every year—usually at a high-powered IT event like this where researchers, buyers, sellers and investors all come together. It is a good foil for business beneath the business. For now, we don't care about the buyers. We're after the supplier. Russo." She jiggles the picture a little bit.

"Anything else we need to know about?"

"We need to make friends when we get there. Engage with the public. Blend in." She sighs, scratching her hairline briefly before continuing. The hairspray is already getting to her. "Mingle. Talk. Laugh. We have to appear friendly and peaceful before we come in with the hammer. This is extremely important so Russo doesn't get spooked and call security as soon as we arrive."

"How do we get to Russo? Once we make our appearance."

"We've intercepted a few messages that he's going to meet with the first buyer." She pulls out another photo, this one blurrier than the last, of a man in a trench coat walking on the white crosswalk of a street. "Petro Koval of Kiev, Ukraine. They will be meeting in an upstairs conference room. Number 24, at exactly 8:15 P.M. We need to be up there and waiting before Koval."

"What's the positions?" Colin asks.

"I want Allister, Maisie, and Colin upstairs at the ready. Kole and I will take downstairs and if anything goes sideways, we'll flush Russo and Koval your way," Astrid instructs, looking at the ground then looking at the photos. "It's going to be loud and crowded. It's going to be fast. We're going to have a lot of civilians, a lot of possible collateral damage. Let's go after Russo, but first priority is minimalized causalities. If I think the numbers could get too high, I'll call off the entire mission."

"Astrid, we can't promise that." Allister shakes his head and frowns. Astrid swallows hard. Every firefight Unit 9X has been in so far has ended in blood, either for us or for the guys we're against. I understand where she's coming from. She doesn't want her mission to be the lynchpin that causes a cascade of pain for hundreds of people. She doesn't want that on her hands, but more importantly, on her conscience.

"I didn't ask you to promise," she answers softly, nodding a little. "Just to try."

"We will." Colin nods, putting a hand on Allister's shoulder. I expect him to shrug it off, but he doesn't. Maybe we've grown more than I thought.

"Alright. Let's get moving," Astrid says finally, starting the mission.

The building is lit up like a beacon in the center of the city. Red carpets are rolled out from the entrance to where a few news reporters crane their necks and angle cameras for a better shot. We drive quickly by the entrance, park a block away, avoiding recognition of the PAAC logo slashed across the paint. Before leaving the transport, we gear up with small concealable pistols and ear pieces. After a quick walk, our feet hit the red-carpeted entry and we walk in. The bouncers and doorman control the lines of public figures and I mull over my cover—my part to play, my alter-ego, designed to blend in with the crowd and protect my real identity.

My cover is Sam Jenning, the adopted son of the CEO of the IT giant, Legendary Tech Industries. American.

That's who you are tonight. Sam Jenning.

That's who you have to be.

You can do this.

I get to the line, and finally, after listening to Astrid deliver her lines as Anastasia Levi, an heiress on family business from Moscow, in a flawless Russian accent picked up from Professor Romanov, it was my turn.

"Name?"

"Jenning." I flick my head, getting into character. Astrid lurks by the door frame, champagne flute already in hand, making sure we all get a clear entrance. I try not to look at her, just the bouncer. "Sam Jenning."

"I'm sorry. Who?"

"Sam Jenning?" I swallow hard, panicking. "Ever heard of Legendary Tech Industries?"

"... No. I haven't."

Astrid makes a motion.

Bold. You have to make a bold move.

"You will." I pat his arm and breeze through the doorframe. He doesn't stop me and I regroup at Astrid's point. She nods approvingly, watching the others like a hawk in case anything goes wrong, silently coaching them from the sidelines. I watch her watch them. She is doing her job flawlessly.

The entry hall of the building is dominated by polished marble pillars holding up rings of balconies spiraling upwards. The main meeting room is styled as a Roman temple with purple velvet drapery, potted plants with large green leaves, and side tables with ornate vases of white ghost orchids, lilies of the valley, and deep purple amaryllises. Little statues of gold and silver elephants peek out amongst the greenery. Russo has a grandiose side and a taste for showmanship; an event of this opulence served his purpose and aligned with his ego.

It's such a beautiful place to do something so terrible.

"Alright. Kole, move to the main room and keep your eyes peeled for Russo and Koval. Allister, Maisie, Colin, take your positions upstairs. Stay hidden until go time," Astrid tells us, reminding us to check our earpieces. She uses the clear model, manufactured and designed by a Gamma to be less detectible. Less noticeable. That's exactly what we're going for.

I move through the crowd, testing my earpiece by scratching at my lobe. I get past the clutch of people crowded around the doorway and enter the main room with its dome shaped painted ceiling. The intricate depictions of angels remind me of photos I have seen of the Sistine Chapel; decorative balconies edge the second floor, leading to other hidden hallways. More art, spanning the art periods from Leonardo da Vinci's Mona Lisa to Pablo Picasso's Blue Room, line the walls, a museum of visual culture. One hundred round tables with pearl white tablecloths are lit by Victorian era chandeliers, the warm light creating shadows on the accompanying cushioned chairs. At the front of the room, on a stage with a single microphone, a woman with sun-kissed dark skin, striking in a golden yellow dress, sings like an angel. Crisp, clear notes ring out in a language I don't understand. Italian, or French maybe. Still ... gorgeous and classical.

Men and woman in stunning attire mill around, some standing and chatting with easy smiles and glittering glasses of champagne, others sitting and talking quietly in corners. The air is clean and light, a formal social event attached to a day of business. Most are here simply to enjoy themselves.

You're about to wake them up. Open their eyes.

No. Not all of them. Just Sebastián's.

Right. No unnecessary collateral damage. No civilian casualties.

Exactly.

Seeing him for the first time makes me freeze on the spot and shiver like I caught a cold breeze. Sebastián stands in the very center of the room, surrounded by pretty women in tight dresses, wearing big flashy jewelry, and dark, intense makeup like masks around their eyes, making them look sharp and deadly.

"I have eyes on him," I whisper into my earpiece. "He's dead ahead."

"Status?" Astrid responds.

"Mingling. He seems happy. Oblivious."

"Keep it that way."

"Ten four," I reply and turn so as not to stare and give myself away.

The awards dinner celebrating the philanthropy of IT millionaires not only had drawn the players from the high-powered IT event, it had also attracted the beautiful and important people of the city. To these people, with their dress up costumes and designer shoes, this was saving the world. This was how they did their part. How they make themselves a name.

As the well-dressed find their seats, the ritual begins and crystal statuettes are given away, one by one. I don't listen to the ceremony; I'm focused on something else. I pick a seat at the table directly behind Russo and stare at the back of his head, daring him to move.

"Astrid. Floor position?" I ask into the ear piece when a chorus of clapping and cheering will drown me out.

"To your right."

I throw a quick glance to the right and see her lavender dress standing by the wall, her half empty glass of champagne on the high-top table beside her. She grants me a little nod. I return my gaze back to the stage and Russo.

"Koval just pulled up. Outside, just entered the building." Maisie says through the ear piece. I frown, looking at my watch. It's only 8:00.

"He's early."

"Move when Russo does. Not before. We wait on him. Maisie, did you notice any kind of identification? Anything to look for in case we lose him in the crowd?" Astrid responds promptly under the cover of another round of clapping.

"Or Russo gets to him first and business goes bad?" Allister suggests grimly.

"He has a ring on his right hand, middle finger. It's quite large. No stone, just a band."

"Copy," I say, watching Russo more intently. Observing the way he sits, easily with his legs crossed and one shoulder lower than the other with a hand on his knee. The way he tilts his head slightly or the way he shakes a little when he laughs at a joke made by the presenter. Then he shifts a little. Pulling his phone out of his pocket as it buzzes. He looks at it briefly before putting it not back into his pants pocket, but the inner chest pocket of his jacket. He doesn't get up. Not yet.

"He got a message," I whisper carefully.

"Koval."

"I would assume. Why isn't he moving for it?"

"Russo runs on his own time. He doesn't care that Koval is early. He'll wait for the fifteenth minute. Wait with him."

"Copy."

Back to radio silence. I keep an eye on my watch, waiting for the minutes to pass. Butterflies come to life in my stomach in anticipation. I notice Russo's foot tapping quickly. He glances around the room, a sign of his growing impatience. I wait him out as his anxious behavior gets stronger. Finally, at 8:13 P.M., Russo excuses himself to the washroom. He stands, finding his way up the stairs to the balconies overhead and into a hidden hallway to the left. I wait until 8:14 to do the same thing. Astrid takes the long way, going back through the main entrance and tackling the marble spiral stairs.

"Koval's waiting," Maisie informs us. "I've got him in my sights."

"Russo's on his way," I say, travelling the stairs as fast as I dare without looking suspicious. "I'm following. He's almost there."

"Copy."

"Allister, Colin. Positions." Astrid calls through, sounding a little out of breath.

"Ready for him."

"In position."

"Alright," I say. "Here he comes."

The sound of footsteps stops and I stop moving, pulling my pistol from my waistband. I inch forward, following Russo into the shadowy room. Then I hear the voices. They're distorted by the distance between us and I can't catch enough words to understand the conversation.

"Dear friend ... long ... been home."

Not enough.

I dig out the spare earpiece in my pocket and switch it to public, adding it to the comm line and giving it a gentle flick into the hallway. I hear their voices clearly through the ear piece.

"It's been a long time."

"Indeed."

"Last year, I believe we had a ... snag in affairs. I need to be sure that this will not happen again, Mr. Russo. Assure me of this." That must have been Koval.

"I can assure you, Petro. Trust me."

"Trust is a rare pleasure in this business, Mr. Russo. I'm not sure that's what I am giving to you."

"Well then, don't not believe me, if those words are easier for you to stomach."

"Your sarcasm is not doing you any favours, Mr. Russo. Watch that carefully. Today I am not a patient man."

Sebastián Russo chuckles slightly and I can picture him smiling condescendingly at the ground before he sucks in a breath and continues with his business. *"Always a such pleasure, Petro. Where's your happiness?"*

"Back home with my daughters. I'd like to return to them quickly."

"What is the rush?"

"It is my twins' tenth birthday tomorrow, Mirabella and Annalise. I'd rather not miss it."

"Such a family man."

"Russo."

"Of course. Let's proceed."

The two black market traders continue down the hallway, Koval in the lead. Russo turns to follow, but for a moment, he pauses and I catch my breath. He looks to the ground, just by his feet and notices the little clear shine of the ear piece. He chuckles a little and stomps on the tech, making the one in my ear scream with a lost signal. I bat it out of my ear canal and shake my head, my ear still ringing. I play with it for a moment, before putting it back in.

"Kole, Kole. Astrid. Come in, Kole. Come in."

"Astrid, Astrid. Kole. Clear, go ahead."

"What the hell was that?" Astrid asks.

"Russo saw the piece and stomped on it. He knows we're here."

"Then, we don't have any time to mess around. Converge on target. Take down Russo and neutralize Koval. Quickly."

"Copy."

I pick up the shattered pieces of the earpiece and slip them in my pocket on my way through the hallway once Russo and Koval are out of sight. Just in case. No evidence.

Just keep moving. Just keep moving.

I keep my pistol muzzle up and at the ready. A single gunshot rings out and makes the hair on the back of my neck stand up. I'd call for a safety check, but I don't want to give away anyone's positions. A hand plops out of a door frame, a slow pool of red blood collecting in the palm. I lower my gun in shock for just a second. I look around and then back at the hand. Around the base of the middle finger, there's a ring with no gemstone like the one Maisie had described.

It's Petro.

TWENTY- SIX

I stop short before the curved stairwell a few steps ahead. Did Russo go down the stairs or continue down the hallway? A foot connects with the small of my back and I lurch forward. I catch myself before falling down the stairs and spin around. I stare into the cold, wild eyes of Sebastián Russo. He grins wickedly, drunk with that powerful feeling that comes with pulling a trigger. I watch him carefully, our guns both aimed at each other, his ready for a head shot. I'm trained to deliver two to the chest and one to the head. I'm not about to change that now.

"Well," he snarls, licking a layer of sweat from his lip. "Here we are."

"Here we are," I say evenly. "I know you killed Petro Koval."

"Yes. I did," he admits proudly. "I'd tell you why, but you're not supposed to speak ill of the dead." He pauses. "It was impressive . . . your efforts to overtake me. Your only fault was that I, my new, young friend, have been in this business for longer than you have been breathing air."

"That's a long time," I say backhandedly.

"Indeed. Long enough to know that someone always tries to mess things up. Someone always tries to upend the plans. Always."

He narrows his eyes threateningly, looking even more like a snake than General Ryker. He looks almost too happy for this moment, like there's no greater joy than staring down someone from the right end of a gun.

We stay, locked in the stand-off. Petro's body lies a few feet away in the corner and I try my best not to look at him.

The twins' birthday is tomorrow. Mirabella and Annalise.

I'd rather not miss it.

I wince.

I'm sorry.

"Who was he really?" I flick my head to the motionless body. "Tell me."

"I suppose I could amuse you." Russo's grin flickers into something colder, viler and more twisted. I feel sick. "The knowledge will hurt no one when it dies along with you, my friend."

"Just tell me."

"Eager," he chuckles. I just need him to talk. About anyone. Anything. Just so I can stall until my backup arrives. If it's even on its way; the team could just as easily be searching a different corridor. "He was a Ukrainian family man. Very good man. Just trying to make a living and earn a few dollars so his daughters could go to good schools to start good lives. Although, it's hard to get a job with a past."

"What kind of past?"

"A pesky little twenty-year prison sentence for involuntary manslaughter." He grins like he knows something. "Between you and me, I don't think there was anything involuntary about it. Alas, the complications . . . you can only imagine . . . how they trailed behind him like a dog behind its owner. Made it hard for him to get any clean, white-collar job." Sebastián makes a motion with his brows, still enjoying this. I swallow hard.

A shadow flickers, but not by much. Just enough movement for me to notice it out of the corner of my eye. I tighten my grip on the handle of the pistol and think hard. I hope for Astrid to come bursting out of the clingy dark, but it's just another bulky man in a suit. The bouncer from the front doors. I narrow my eyes and scan over him, no awkward folds and bulges in his clothes. Nothing in his hands. He's unarmed. He grins at me, displaying yellowed teeth with a glitter of a gold crown in the front.

Unarmed and confident.

My fingers grow tacky on the hide of the gun handle. I'm losing control of the situation. I need to act. Now.

Without thinking of the consequences, I barrel towards Sebastián. I collide into him, hitting him hard and sending us both sprawling down the stairs. We tumble downwards, hitting every step, triggering starbursts of pain on the way down. Our yelps and groans match together like a song. I make it to the bottom first, rolling to a stop before staggering to my feet, a hand on my ribs. I already know I'll be black and blue in a day or two. The hallway we fell into is dark, the light barely enough to see by. Behind, white streams from the cracks in a door frame and the sounds of clanking and scraping of utensils mingle with fast and loud voices. It's the kitchen.

Russo gets himself up, spitting a jet of reddish phlegm at the floor before wiping his mouth and rolling his neck. I can hear his joints cracking and popping.

"Now," he inhales, sucking the air through his teeth. "That hurt."

"I know," I say, trying to be cheeky. I watch, almost in slow motion, as he picks up his gun from beside his foot and fires a shot. I duck before his finger gets on the trigger and the bullet flies over my head, burying itself in the door behind me. I reach forward with my legs, sweeping his out from underneath of him. He crashes hard on his back and I scramble for the kitchen door, ripping it open and sliding inside. I fix my jacket sleeves and straighten my collar. In the rush of the kitchen, busboys and waitresses move plates and platters, white hatted chefs scream at each other, and no one notices me. I grab an empty platter from an abandoned service trolley and try to blend in, keeping one eye on the door. An arm's length away, a bright red fire alarm lever catches the corner of my eye.

Finally, Sebastián throws himself through the door to the kitchen, and my arm shoots out, hand outstretched for the lever for the fire alarm. I slam it downwards, setting off a shrieking rhythmic whine that makes me grip my ears for a moment. The chefs and servers all disappear through the exit before Russo lets his bullets fly in rage, screaming and yelling at me. I take cover behind one of the solid counters as the sounds of bullets firing and expensive plates and glassware breaking compete with the alarm. I wince, feeling the sounds resonate in my brain painfully.

"COME OUT! COME OUT, LITTLE COWARD!" He calls to me as he comes further into the kitchen, impossibly louder than all the other sounds. The booming of footsteps from upstairs just adds to the choir as people try to evacuate the building to get away from the imaginary fire.

Get to safety.

No civilian casualties. No unnecessary deaths.

"YOU LITTLE COWARD! COME OUT WHERE I CAN SEE YOU!"

I keep my hand on my ribs, my chest rattling with each breath. I grimace and look to the swinging kitchen doors yawning wide open and practically begging me to run through them. I take a deep breathe, feeling a stab in the ribs, dropping to a crouch but not daring to move out of hiding just yet.

"I CAN SMELL THE PAAC FILTH ON YOU, BOY! BE A MAN AND FACE ME, YOU COWARD!"

I freeze. How does he know what PAAC is? How did he know that I'm from the organization?

"That's fine." He stops yelling, but sounds maniacal. His desperate and throaty voice sounds hungry. I listen carefully. "You like fire drills? I'll just have to smoke you out then, little coward. What do you think of that, huh?" I don't respond. I don't believe he'll actually set fire to the place, but there's no predicting a mad man with wounded pride.

"WHAT DO YOU THINK OF THAT, HUH?" he shrieks and I listen to the sounds of him throwing things and overturning trollies. I swallow hard and blink harder. Then, the orange-yellow glow and the crackle of newborn flames makes my hair stand on end. The room warms alarmingly fast and I can feel the sweat rise on my neck. The sprinklers hiss to life and rain down water, showering everything in the room. The stench of thick, wet smoke chokes me. I gag on the air.

I watch the door, still hearing it calling for my escape.

I reach into my pocket and pull out another clip and stick it in the pistol by my feet. It had fallen when I was ducking for cover from flying bullets. I quickly stand and fire a shot or two in defiance and hear him yell out painfully.

"YOU LITTLE COWARD!" he calls out, roaring even louder than before.

"That must've hurt!" I shout back to him and listen to his lopsided footsteps dragging closer and closer. When he appears around the counter, I chop at the back of his wrist and his gun flies out of his hand and out of reach. I notice the slow dribble of blood coming from his thigh.

My shot.

I jump out of the way to dodge a sloppy attempt at a strike, but go too far and slam backwards into a solid surface. Sebastián gets to his feet and his fist connects with my jaw. I stagger, falling to my knees. A second man appears and grabs me, keeping me down. I thrash and fight, trying to get loose, but his grip is like iron.

"Kole, I'd like you to meet Mr. Sawyer. He's a very good friend of mine," Russo growls, wiping the water from his brow. Russo recovers his pistol and squats in front of me, sticking the warm muzzle under my chin hard. I jerk my head up, trying to lessen the pressure and he only pushes harder. He grins at me.

"Such a valiant effort," he chuckles, looking even more like a madman with the water from sprinklers slowly trickling down the sides of his face. His suit clings to him and his hair is almost as wild as mine. "Such a ... heartfelt performance."

"You know about the Pacific Acting Authority Council." I spit, growing angry. "How?"

Sebastián just chuckles some more. "Look at you, brave little coward. You're the one with lead under your jaw and you still have the spirit to ask the questions. Marvelous."

"How?" I growl. The muzzle of the gun starts to cool. The water from the sprinklers still hisses down in sheets, soaking everything.

"Everyone knows them and their rot," he snarls, his lips curling up like a growling dog's. He shows his teeth, baring them when he speaks like an animal. "Their missions and their endless conquest for world domination wreathed in a peaceful package." When he speaks, he spits and I itch to wipe my face but Sawyer holds my arms firmly in place at my sides. I wince and try to loosen the grip. Still no use.

"World domination?" I echo.

He looks taken aback. "Oh, you brave little coward. Don't you know your precious organization's true intentions? But I guess lies are masked by truths, aren't they?"

"What are you talking about?" I snap, jumping at him a little. He chuckles again, like I'm amusing. Like I'm funny. I grit my teeth, feeling my anger boiling. I can feel water trickling into my vision, pulling locks of my hair down with it and making it difficult to see.

"I'm talking about your beloved purpose." He spits the last word out like it tastes bad. "Your muse. Your get up and go. The thing that drives you."

"You don't know anything about me," I snap.

"Oh, but I do. I really do. I know you. I know you so, so incredibly well," he says slowly, his voice like oil, leaking and oozing into my ears. I glare at him. He grins, open mouthed, at me. "I know you think you're doing the right thing. I know you want to make everyone back home happy. Your cohort, your leaders. Your *generals*.

I strain to jump at him, but am held back by Sawyer. The only sounds I can muster are angry grunts. I am so overcome with anger that I can't even form proper words.

"And now," Russo cocks his head to the side, grinning just a little wider. "I get to know how you die. Don't worry," he says. "I'll make it quick."

I stare him dead in the face, trying to look unbothered. Brave. *Brave little coward.*

I watch him get excited as he levels the gun with my forehead, ready to fire.

As soon as I close my eyes, all hell breaks loose in the galley. My eyes shoot open in time to watch Astrid slide into the chaos on her knees and collide with Russo, sending him sprawling. She pushes me out of the way, taking on Russo's bodyguard. Without a second thought, I turn around and stand, kicking the pistol away from Russo as he scrambles for it. There's a split in his bottom lip, staining his teeth red as the blood travels down his lower face. The water dilutes it, making it run off his chin.

Behind me the sounds of a fight continue while Russo gets to his feet slowly. I'll wait for him.

"PUT IT DOWN!" I hear Astrid roar. "PUT IT DOWN! PUT IT DOWN NOW!"

I turn only for a moment, but quickly wish I hadn't. The bulky man holds a small sphere in his hand. Astrid's eyes are alive with a new kind of fear and her gun is pointed directly at his forehead.

It's an explosive.

He has an explosive.

He's going to blow us all to Hell.

"Astrid—" I say, putting my hand out. "Just wait a—"

"PUT THE GRENADE DOWN!" She doesn't wait. The man shifts a little bit and I turn away, flinching as the sound of the gun drowns out everything else. Her face pales only for a moment before she wrangles her composure into place once again. I watch her. The man Russo called Mr. Sawyer is dead on the floor. She takes long powerful strides and kicks Russo square in the chest. He tips onto his back and she points the gun at his face again.

"Listen, answer all my questions truthfully and no one gets hurt. Your name is Sebastián Russo?"

"One and only," he spits.

"The man you shot. The man in the hallway upstairs. What was his name?"

"Petro Koval. But honestly, doll, in this business, it could have been anyone."

"Why was he here?"

"For the party! That's why I came, naturally. I could only assume the same for Koval. Of course, that's past tense. Now I have a different angle."

"Tell me the truth!" she growls, the gun wavering a little. "Why did Petro Koval come in all the way from Kiev just to meet you?" I'm starting to wonder why she's asking all these questions. We already know all the answers, but a blinking light shining through the fabric on the hip of her dress gives me the hint.

She's recording him. She's creating evidence.

"You've done your homework, sweetheart." He chuckles. "Petro was looking for a special, eh, birthday gift for his employer. He wanted to get out of the business, you see, and to do so, he needed to do one more transaction. Too bad that transaction ended up being his last."

"Back in Ukraine?"

"No, no."

"Where?"

"There are stocks all over this country, and the country next door. Honestly, darling. Keeping your supplies in your own home is like keeping your poison in your pantry. Absolutely stupid. And messy," he giggles. "Speaking of poison—" He drops something in his mouth. He cracks it with his teeth and takes in a sharp breath. I couldn't see it, but I could smell it. The bitter faint scent of almonds. He throws his head back, making himself swallow and coughs a little, white foam starting to bubble over his cracked lips. He gasps for air and falls flat on his back.

"Farewell ... sweetheart." He chokes and goes still, his eyes rolling back in his head. Astrid moves forwards and reaches into his pocket, pulling out a handful of chalky white pills.

"Cyanide," she says, staring at them. She rolls them around in her palm with her thumb. I spy a box of plastic bags across the kitchen and grab her one.

"Here. We'll take them back to the compound as evidence." I decide and she dumps them in. I look left to right. To the man with the bullet hole and then to the man dead by his own hand. I look up to the ceiling, remembering the body dead in the upstairs hall. I tighten my lips. This is a mess. I'm not sure if we can count this as a successful operation or not. I rub my neck.

"Astrid, Astrid, all crew," she calls into her earpiece. I get a double audio. "Clear. All return to the rendezvous point on the North end and await further orders. We're done here."

"Astrid," I say. "All good?"

"I'm fine."

"You don't look fine."

"Then stop looking," she snaps through a sigh, tightening her thigh holster through her dress. She looks extremely uncomfortable; both of us are soaking wet. "I did what I had to. Move on."

And with that, she moves on. She leaves before me and doesn't bother to wait. Out of the kitchen, up the stairs and out of view.

TWENTY-SEVEN

We had planned to take the scenic route home, down a long gravel road that winds between rolling hills and the cliffs that overlook the ocean. Even though it is dark out, it will be a nice drive back, smelling the sea and imagining the view.

PAAC has left two armoured cruisers at the point where the pavement ends outside the city. We were to switch from our alternative transport to standard vehicles. Amongst ourselves, we joked that not only did they want us in a safer vehicle, they didn't want to muddy up the city car; no scratches on the paint job.

Astrid and I took one and Allister, Maisie and Colin took the other.

"Alright," Allister says as we get in the cruisers. "We'll take Big Bertha. You guys get Rhonda."

"Rhonda?"

"Just go with it, man."

The moon hangs in the sky and I yawn, gripping the wheel while Astrid stares at the road ahead, probably thinking deep thoughts. Something catches my eye from her side, opposite of the ocean and the barriers on the edge of the cliff.

"What's that?" I inquire, just as something rolls down the hill.

"Swerve!" she yells, but I can't get out of the way in time. A boulder tumbles down the hill and slams with immense force into the side of the cruiser just behind Astrid's seat. She screams, ducking and covering her head from the falling glass. The vehicle careens off to the side and busts through the road barrier, bumping onto the stretch of greenery between the road and the cliff. The steering wheel moves under my hands, but the wheels don't respond. The brush and weeds disappear under the front bumper as we travel uncontrollably across the flat just before the cliff. The vehicle lifts slightly in the back, like it was hit with something solid underneath and the final bushes disappear under the tires. The view of the ocean over a craggy cliff face greets us with ill intention.

"No!" Astrid yells and starts to tug on the door handle. It won't release. "It won't open!"

"It's a safety feature," I pant, feeling the situation get to me. The water below is getting closer by the second. "Okay, okay." I breathe deeply through my nose, trying to calm myself before trying to calm Astrid. "It's okay. It's okay. We'll be fine." I nod. She looks at me like I have three heads, her eyes wide and mouth slightly agape.

She narrows her eyes and roars, "ARE YOU OUT OF YOUR MIND? WE ARE GOING TO—" Before she can finish, the car pushing itself seaward, stops with a jerk. I look backwards and Allister and Colin sit in the front seats of the other vehicle, the chain of a grappling hook secured to their front bumper guard.

"See. See?" I pant a little harder, not able to stop a lunatic smile from spreading on my face. "I told you we would be fine."

"Shut up."

The car lurches forward. This hook won't hold forever. If we want out, we have to move now and move fast.

"Doors are still locked," I say, gently jiggling the handle. We stare downward, facing the turbulent sea below. If we fall, there's no such thing as survival.

"I got it." Astrid unclips her seatbelt and holds herself up, gently easing herself near the dashboard. The car only sways slightly and I can hear the groaning and moaning of protest as the other vehicle strains to keep us safe. The noise doesn't sound reassuring. Astrid pulls a long rope out from underneath her seat. "Tie it around yourself like a harness. Over the shoulder and under the armpit. Not square around the waist." She shoves a comm set on her head and taps into it. "Colin, Colin. Come in, Colin."

The vehicle lurches a little farther to the sea.

"Colin, Colin. Come in, Colin," she calls desperately.

Farther.

"Colin, Colin! Fine! I'll do it myself," she growls and then pulls out her pistol and fires shots at the back windshield until cracks spiderweb through the glass. One more bullet spent and the thing shatters into millions of little glass pieces. She tries the comms again, looking at the other cruiser through the shattered window. "Colin, Colin. Come in, Colin."

She falls silent when he answers. I can hear fragments of his voice, but can't make out the words. She nods to herself.

"Be ready for a rope. I'm going to throw the line out the back window, so secure it to the rig. The hook isn't going to last much longer. We can't save the vehicle, but we can save ourselves. On my signal," she explains, the vehicle inching closer to a wreck. "Ready!"

The vehicle shudders and begins to fall in slow motion. Astrid pitches the rope out the window and grabs onto my shoulders. We hurry to get to the back window, but once we get out, we fall with it anyway. We plummet, holding our breath and praying until we are jolted to a halt. The vehicle keeps falling, eventually crashing into the sea below.

We pause in the air. Astrid clings to me, not secured by the rope.

"Climb. Climb up the rope." I grimace as the coarse hairs of the line dig into my palms and underarm. "Go." She starts going up, inching her way to the top and just as her white head of hair disappears over the cliff face, the rope begins to fail. I watch as a sharp rock jutting from the cliff starts to saw through the rope. I climb as fast as I can, hand over hand, inch by inch. But it's pointless and the rope finally snaps.

I hear Astrid's scream from the top of the cliff. "NO! KOLE!" The sound echoes off the rock face.

I panic, my fingers clutching the porous rock. I slide down the face, feeling the rock slice and bite at my arms, torso, and chest. It stings and I can feel the blood being drawn, but I still search for an outcropping. A foothold or anything to stop myself with.

When I hit it, and stop violently, the ball of my shoulder jars in its socket. I take a moment before looking up, starting to claw my way up the rock. I gather the rope and wrap it around myself, not wanting to lose it in case it is needed. I muscle up a hundred feet, fighting to the top. When I finally throw a hand over the edge, feeling the moist grass under my palms, I try not to take a sigh of relief. I don't want to jinx it. I use the last drops of my strength and force myself up with my legs and launch myself over the edge. I roll onto my back and stare up at the sky, panting hard and fast before pushing myself to my knees.

Astrid is already there beside me and wrapping her arms around me in an aggressive hug.

"I hate you so much," she whispers while she buries her face in my shoulder, sounding relieved.

"I know," I breathe, barely able to hold myself up and trying my best to ignore the aching of my muscles and the throbbing of my hands. All my fingernails are broken and oozing red. It feels disgusting. I try to touch her with just my palms, rather than my fingers, but then I realize that my palms are slashed and bleeding, too.

"Good going, man." Allister comes and pats me on the back. I grab his wrist, needed another person to steady me. "Epic plot twist. We thought you were a goner for sure." I appreciate he's trying to keep things light, but maybe some things were made to be dark. I put my forehead to Astrid's shoulder and just breathe.

Breathe.

You're okay. You're fine. You're alive.

Just breathe.

The ride back in the one surviving vehicle is rough. I look out the window, expecting the sea to be there, waiting to swallow me whole. This was a tough one. I think it will take me a while to shake off the fear. The roads are patchy, so Allister drives slowly. Astrid and Maisie sit in the back with me, Colin in the passenger seat. Astrid had found a first aid kit and is doing her best to clean the pebbles and dirt from my hands.

I hiss sharply when a piece of shredded skin catches on the gauze bandage and starts to bleed more. Astrid's eyes dart from my face to my hand as she loosens the bandage a little. Hydrogen peroxide drips between my fingers and splashes onto the floor of the vehicle. That stung the most.

"I'm sorry," she whispers.

"It's fine." I shake my head. "It really doesn't hurt that bad. I'm just being dramatic."

Allister looks at me in the rear-view and winks through a heavy yawn. Colin sits silently in the front seat, fiddling with the settings on a screen in his lap. The blue rays illuminate his face.

"Okay, Hero." She smiles softly.

TWENTY-EIGHT

It took a while to get back with Allister's abnormally slow driving. My muscles feel limp, like cooked spaghetti and they burned in some places while tingling aggressively in others.

I nod off, my head lolling back. I snap back awake and nod off again. The cycle of exhaustion keeps repeating.

The vehicle lurching to a stop woke me for the final time. I went bolt upright, before feeling a hand on my knee.

"We're here." Astrid yawns, speaking like she's bored and tired. She probably is. I roll my neck, feeling the knots of stress tighten with every movement. Astrid stands and helps me to my feet. I drape an arm over her shoulder, not trusting my own feet. Allister puts the vehicle in park and turns it off, pulling the keys from the ignition. We open the doors and step to the ground. The lights of the compound glow fiercely, like a beacon in the darkness. That is exactly what it represents to me in the moment. A beacon.

A beacon of hope and peace.

The doors of the entrance level crack and swing open. Professor Kingston and Professor Romanov appear in the frame and promptly close the distance between us. They seem a strange mix of concern and sternness, walking with purpose as Astrid keeps me from hitting the dirt face first. She barely struggles under my weight.

"9X." Kingston makes it to us first, Romanov only five and a half paces behind. "We saw one of your transport's tracking beacons die. We would have sent out another unit to provide for aid, but you made it back in time."

"We had a bit of a situation," I say, planting my feet and leaning away from Astrid.

"Would you care to elaborate?"

"The transport fell off a cliff!" Allister shouts. "Freak accident. Lost control of the steering and good bye Rhonda."

"Rhonda?"

"I wouldn't ask." I shake my head.

"Of course. Let's get you to the medic center." Kingston nods to Romanov who takes me firmly by the shoulder. Astrid moves to follow us. "Actually, Alpha. I would like to speak to you and your company."

"But—" I begin to protest.

"It will only take seconds."

"Sir, with all due respect, I would really—" I try to continue.

"Kole, please. Just take direction. Astrid will be with you within moments. You will survive without her guidance for five minutes," he snaps. I was about to protest, his words stinging, but I thought better of it.

Romanov steers me inside and down the hall to the medic center. I try my best not to look back at them. The Russian hadn't said a word since they met us on the asphalt and that was very uncharacteristic of him. His usual loud and unapologetic personality was stifled by something. I frown.

"Sir?" I ask. "Is something wrong?"

He grunts. "Nothing's wrong, Boyo. The world's just crazy, is all."

I frown deeper. He is acting weird. Weirder than normal. And that was concerning. Something must be really wrong for him to be bothered. "How fast can you prepare for a mission?"

"I need a little time."

"Give me specifics, Boyo."

"Maybe a week?"

"Five days."

"... How severe?"

"There's been an infiltration at an old base camp. It's too close for comfort as far as the old grand high council is concerned and they want it check out. The old camp is about fifty miles away."

"I'll run it by Astrid."

"No, no. Kingston is running it by her. You need to convince her, Boyo. This needs immediate attention, but because of the risk level, Fallon refuses to make it an order. Your Alpha can decline this mission," Romanov speaks sternly with thin lips.

"I understand, Sir. I'll get it done."

"Good."

———————

I had five days to heal. My skin had just scabbed over and the next day, we loaded the helicopter and were sailing just below the clouds. The quick push to initiate the mission made me nervous. Something was seriously wrong.

"Seven minutes until drop time," the pilot says over the intercom.

"Copy that, Red Four," Astrid answers, her voice sounding no differently over the line than in real life. "Unit 9X, prepare for deployment."

"Copy."

"Roger."

"Preparing for deployment as we speak, Alpha."

I stood, holding on to the overhead handles. I rock back and forth with the movement of the helicopter as if I was on a fishing boat taking on the rhythm of the sea, and try my best to hold onto my lunch.

The movement of the aircraft makes the weapons in my holsters bump against my leg. I had chosen guns from the armoury in the compound, slid them into my thigh holsters and strapped them in. I filled my empty pockets with clips and magazines from the aircraft's extra supplies, triple checking the make and size to be sure they fit the firearms. Bringing the wrong ammunition would put me on the list of official mission screw-ups.

"What's the play?" I ask, checking the clips on my vest that secure my parachute. It is not like I don't know the plan, but hearing Astrid repeat the instructions is calming.

"We get in. We grab what we need. We get out," Astrid summarizes, grabbing ammo and loading her own pockets. "It's simple."

"Sure. It sounds simple, but it's everything in between that we haven't hashed out that's gonna make all this not so simple," Allister mutters to himself. Astrid ignores him and I watch them exchange, or rather, not exchange. "What if we have company?"

"Then, we put out the cheese platter," she says sarcastically, loading a holster.

"You're funny. Truly. I mean that. But, seriously, how are we running this?"

"We'll go in. Maisie, Colin and you scout the perimeter in case anyone decides to pay us a surprise visit. Kole and I will go in and sweep the building and locate the targets. Colin, I want you to keep in contact with the chopper at all times. Everyone, keep your communication devices on and always connected to channel one. We don't know what's out there," she says, turning to stare out of the helicopter as the foggy forest races past in a hazy green blur. Once again, I can't read her.

"It'll be fine. We'll run it like a drill and be back before dinner." I nod, trying to be upbeat. "Total cakewalk."

"Okay."

"Drop in two."

"Copy that, Red Four." Astrid nods. "I want everyone ready in thirty seconds. No lags."

"Aye, aye, Captain," Allister shouts. She fights back a smile, I can see it trying to peek out.

"Alright," she says. "Let's do this."

Descending into the foggy forest was cinematic; it is nearly impossible to see through the thicket of the tree tops and the air holds the chill of early fall. We jump one at a time, about two seconds apart, plummeting towards the ground. I feel the wind whip my clothes around and tousle my hair before I rip the cord to deploy my parachute. We are to drop in, then meet at the rendezvous point half a mile from the building on the west side. We are cutting our timing close; it is only minutes before sundown. PAAC doesn't like active night missions; darkness adds unpredictability.

I crash through the tree top branches, scratching my arms and ripping my jacket in the process. The cuts sting, sharp and vibrant, but I have no major bleeding. Just the criss-crossed lines of bead trails, faint and hard to see in this light.

Not yet, anyway.

I open my arms, bracing myself to land, when my chute snags on trees. My harness yanks painfully, the straps digging through my clothing and into my skin. I groan a little and wince, suddenly forgetting the colony of scratches. I reach into my calf pocket and pull out a little two-inch knife and grip it tightly. Judging from the rest of the drop, it will shock my joints but nothing will break or fracture if I land square on my heels. The problem is then, of course, actually landing square on my heels.

I hold the little blade tighter and take a breath trying to calm myself. It's not the drop, it's the left-over rush of adrenaline that is still swimming in my bloodstream from jumping out of a helicopter from a high altitude.

I bunch the cords together and slash through them with the two-inch blade, beginning the drop. I almost make the landing, hitting solidly with one heel, but my balance is just a little off and I drop to my knees on final impact. It didn't hurt quite as much as I had expected.

I use the holographic goggles, pressing the button and having the holo-screen materialize before my eyes, bathing everything in the multiple greens of night vision. Although it's not quite dusk, deep shadows are created by the trees and foliage. I look around, listening for any sign of the others. Nothing. I am on my own, and that was fine. We have a solid plan that I have confidence in. That makes all the difference.

Five, six, seven minutes into the trek west to the rendezvous point and the forest began to come alive. Howls and screeches from animals unknown and the subtle rustle of leaves caught in a breeze. The creaking of old trees swaying under their own massive weight and the odd snap of a branch or the rustle in the underbrush as a small animal runs for cover from the night and its predators. It's peaceful and beautiful, but I never lower my gun.

I keep walking, my skin itching after accidently moving through a thick swarm of mosquitos. The sky has turned blue black, an inky soup freckled with silver stars. Through the goggles, I see the outline of the top half of a building looming in the distance. The beam of a flashlight slices through the blackness like a knife, startling me.

"Astrid?" It's the first name I thought to call.

"You blind, man?" Allister calls back. I can practically hear him smiling as he speaks. "I am not Astrid."

"The heck you ain't." I jest and grin as we near each other. "Where are the others?"

"Don't know. Haven't found them yet. I'm sure they're here somewhere." He shines his flashlight beam around them, illuminating a boulder or a rotting tree stump for half a second before rapidly moving on.

"Point it upwards," I say. "It'll work like a signal." Once he did, the response was almost immediate.

"Who's light is that over there?" Maisie calls, not too far away.

"Kole and Allister," I call back.

"Astrid and Colin are on your six." Colin's voice comes from behind us and I try not to jump. Even if I did a little, I hoped no one would see it in the dark. "So, the plan to get down here worked. What now?"

"You three take watch. Kole and I are going to sweep the building," Astrid says, switching on her own holographic goggles. We move in, slowly opening the front doors and exchanging grimaces at the long whine it gives in protest to the movement. We peer inside and it's clear that no one has been here in a very, very long time.

"Wow!" Astrid says, letting her gun drop to her side in a moment of shock. I lift mine up higher to compensate.

The walls are crawling with an interlacing network of leafy green vines. It is like a lost kingdom, a palace of vines and plants that no one has seen in thousands of years. We move through, finding new surprises. A small pool of water fed by the slow drip of a cracked pipe, the water trickling down the wall face and collecting, weighing down the floor tiles. Velvet purple flowers with neon yellow stamens that sway slightly in the draft we create as we pass.

"This is crazy. It's a jungle," I observe, looking around.

"I've got lights," Astrid calls somewhere behind me. I take off the holographic goggles and close my eyes, waiting for the light to seep through my eyelids instead of stabbing through my naked eye like a hot poker. The lights come on quickly, then a loud bang, like a gunshot makes them go out again. I open my eyes just to watch the glass rain down around me. I throw my arms over my head to shield my scalp.

"Kole! Watch out!" Astrid shouts and I don't know what she's talking about so I freeze and scan around, trying to find the danger. The white-haired girl barrels into me and slams me flat on the ground, knocking all the air from my lungs just as the hanging industrial light fixture crashes loudly to the ground behind us. The tinkling of cracking glass and the echo from the boom of impact ricochets all around us. Astrid rolls off, coming up smoothly on her feet and brushes herself off before offering me a hand. She has a slice on her arm, eating through her shirt and slashing down to the muscle.

"Thanks for that," I say, breathing heavily and looking at the wreck of glass and steel rings in a smashed pile on the floor. "That would've hurt."

"That would've killed," she insists. "And don't mention it. It's my job to keep my unit safe. First thing in the newspaper ad."

"That looks nasty." I nod to her arm, now slowly oozing blood. There's a piece of cloth hanging off a hook, probably from a tapestry or banner of some sort. I pull it down and wrap it tightly around the wound, creating pressure like Kingston had taught us. "There."

"Thanks."

"Anytime."

We continue, now on high alert and hands lingering near the opening of our holsters, trying not to get too comfortable. We have no idea what could be up the stairs or just around the next corner. It's best we stay ready for anything and everything. Stay alert and awake.

We turn the corner and are faced with a steel staircase leading upwards to the left and a hallway with many doors leading to the right "You take the hallways. I'll take the upper deck," Astrid offers.

"Deal."

"Five minutes. Move fast."

"Practically the fastest man alive." I wink at her and she punches me playfully in the corner of my chest. We split up and I comb through the rooms as I listen to her footsteps overhead. I move carefully, kicking doors open and checking out every shady corner, not wanting to miss a single thing before moving on to the next. As I near the end of the hallway, something catches my eye. A flash of red paint. On the wall is a large spray-painted emblem with words scribbled in the same paint underneath. Two capital Rs ringed by a circle with wings protruding from each side like it's about to leap from the wall and take flight at any moment.

The three words of a motto—*Outranked. Unequal. Unsatisfied*—are slashed messily beneath it. It's painfully similar to the PAAC motto and it sends shivers up my spine. Who is this? Whose emblem is this? Why is it here? I stare at it, trying to make sense of it all.

The sounds of quick footsteps from behind snaps me back to reality. I aim my firearm towards the shadowy figure standing still in the doorway. My hair stands on end. For a moment, I think the person is Astrid coming to find me, but this figure is too tall and lanky to be her. Definitely a male.

"Get on the ground!" I shout, pouring as much conviction into my voice as possible. The figure doesn't respond. He doesn't even move. "Get on the ground!" I shout again. Something moves in my peripheral vision, another figure darting across the floor by the wall. I adjust my stance to face them both. "Hands on your head and get on the ground! Now!" I'm shaken now. Between the freakish scurrying of the man on the floor and the aggressive stance of the one by the door, I am hoping Astrid is about to make a move.

In a flash, a third grabs me from behind, knocking the pistol from my hand. It clatters to the floor and arms clamp around my chest as I try to break free. I land a solid elbow to the soft mid-section of whoever has grabbed me, warranting a sharp grunt from them in return. I feel the stinging ache of a needle stabbing through the skin on my neck and I fight even harder, but soon it's all just wasted energy. The attackers shine flashlights, leading me down as I slump to floor. Two strong and burly guys drag a limp Astrid into the room, her head hanging with a curtain of her hair hiding her face and the toes of her boots scuffing the floor as they go.

"Astrid—" I force myself to make noise, but it only comes out as a murmur. "You can't ... Don't touch her."

I fall further to the floor, laying flat on my back now as the world gets hazy. A face appears in my tunnel of vision and looks down at me softly.

"Don't worry, Hero. We're not going to hurt you," he states. Through the haze I recognize him faintly. I squint just before the world falls to blackness and sleep.

It's him.

It's Jackson Alexander.

———

I'm not sure of where I am. I am moving, but not in a car or a truck. I can feel myself travelling, but without the bumpiness and roughness of rubber tires slapping a road. I force my eyes open and when I do, I'm staring at a sleeping Astrid, her chin on her chest and strands of her hair dancing in the slight wind. She's strapped into her chair, black ropes around her shoulders, and a seatbelt across her lap. I don't understand what's going on, but the sight of her makes me ease up a little. I don't know where Colin, Maisie or Allister are, but at least I still have her.

One of the guys comes back around and notices I am awake.

"Not time yet, Champ," he says and gently injects something, probably the same tranquilizer substance, into my bicep rather than my neck this time. "Go back to sleep."

After a short time, I nod off again, more peacefully this time.

———————

When I wake up for the second time, Astrid is the first thing I see. This time she's standing and staring out a light-filled window rather than sleeping and strapped to a chair. She has her arms crossed and I can't see her face. Her hair is down and she wears different clothes. A white, spaghetti-strap tank top and dark, tight-fitting blue jeans. I find myself in a bed, worn sheets over me. I push them off and try to stand. Before I get there, blood rushes to my head and I get hit with a wave of dizziness. I shake my head before trying again. Same result, but a little less intense.

Across the room, there is another bed, but it's neat and tidy. The patchwork quilt and the white pillows in perfect order. Even in captivity, Astrid had made her bed with military precision. The walls are old, log cabin in the woods style with the dark timbers and the white chinking. Astrid stands, still as a statue beside the window with billowing sheer white curtains hanging like wings.

"Where are we?" I ask, my voice raspy. I dig the heels of my palms into my eyes, seeing stars and trying to adjust before pulling them away again. Astrid looks back at me, no answer from her lips and ghosts in her eyes. She swallows hard, glancing down quickly.

"He calls it the Haven," she says with a tight voice. "But really, it feels like Hell."

TWENTY-NINE

It wasn't hell and he did call it the Haven. It was an old farmyard with a main house, a big old red barn, and a series of small outbuildings. We were on a grand tour, led by one of the burly guys who had brought us in. Tommy introduced himself like we were old friends, but I can't help but remember how rough he had been with Astrid. He carries his gun the entire time we are together, for the safety of the overall group, he claims. But I'm still not sure he is friendly.

We discover that the farmhouse is a medic center, a makeshift hospital where the kitchen dining table has been transformed into an operating table. The dining room is packed with crates and shelves for medical storage. We stop here and the nurse on duty cleans the gash in Astrid's arm and stitches the skin back together.

The big red barn serves as a central hall, a gathering place of sorts. The little outbuildings serve as barracks—sleeping space for everyone. This was the Haven.

Tommy takes us to the red barn and there we find a small group of misfits pouring over an expanse of a map. Astrid and I peer around for a moment. The place was exactly what a stereotypical barn would look like—rafters, stalls, and big dusty windows. The people in front of us start to notice us, one by one.

"Sky," one of them mumbles.

"Guys," Sky says, signalling the team to wrap up. She nods and steps away from the table. Everyone else begins to hurriedly roll up the maps before we can see them. I frown at that. Who are we going to tell? The man in the moon?

"Is this them?" she asks Tommy.

"It is."

"Very good," she answers, coming forward. She's shorter than I first thought, seeming to shrink as she comes closer. Maybe 5'1 or 5'2. Her hair is shaved to the scalp, just like dark peach fuzz. A tattoo climbs out of the collar of her shirt and winds up her neck and runs behind her ear. I can't quite make it out in the dim barn light. A scar slashes jaggedly through her right eyebrow and up to her center forehead. The thing I notice most about her though, is her left arm. It's shining brass and made of nuts and bolts and tubes and springs. A metal arm. I catch myself staring at it when she crosses her arms and sets her stance. I thought they only existed in action science fiction movies. But here it is. Here she is, attached to it and with complete control over it. It's incredible.

She extends her flesh hand for us to shake. "Hi." She greets us in a surprisingly low and raspy voice like she's been smoking all her life, "I'm Sky Lawson."

"Kole Danvers, Be—" I almost say Beta 9X but stop myself. She obviously doesn't care.

"Astrid Cardinal."

"You." Sky narrows her eyes when she shakes Astrid's hand and for a moment, I'm not sure how this will play out. Two strong women meeting face to face looks to me like a hard, scraping greeting between flint and steel. Sparks and gasoline. "Come with me."

She turns on her heel and powers to a pull-down set of stairs and climbs them up to a hay loft. I follow, not wanting to leave Astrid alone. Sky doesn't say anything, so it must be alright if I tag along. Up the stairs, what I expected to be a hay loft full of straw, is a fully functioning office and a desk with a wheelie chair turned with its back to us. The top of a head peeks out over it by about an inch.

"Jack. You have company," Sky calls and my heart rate spikes. The chair turns with a creak and slowly reveals someone I recognize.

"Hello, Astrid." Jackson Alexander says with a pained smile. Astrid looks frozen, like she doesn't know where to go from here. He looks exactly like his file; like he hasn't changed a bit from the day the picture was taken. The same eyes, same nose, same face shape. All just dusted in a light coat of grime and dirt.

"You coward!" Astrid cries out and lunges forwards. I get my arms out in time and grab her by the waist, reigning her back in before she can do anything she'll regret. "I thought you were dead!" Her voice breaks. "Maisie, Colin, Allister, I. We ... we all ... we all thought you were dead."

"I'm sorry," he apologizes. "Really. I didn't want it to happen like that."

"Did you even think of coming back for us? All this time you could've came back for us. Did you even think about that? Even once? You know once you're in PAAC there is no getting out. You know the only way out is to be rescued. Why didn't you rescue us?" she asks, her eyes misting. I still keep a hold of her just in case.

Better safe than sorry and I have the feeling that if I let go, Jackson Alexander is going to be very sorry.

"Astrid, it's not like that." He cocks his head. "Even if I wanted too, I couldn't without giving the Haven away. Besides, you're here now. You're out! You're free! You're finally here and you never have to go back."

"You say it like you've been waiting for me."

"I have," he says, nodding slightly. "Besides, why didn't you try to leave yourself?"

"That's not fair." She spits. "You know that. You know better than anyone that PAAC has such a tight leash on everyone that it is impossible to leave."

"It's hard. Not impossible," Jackson corrects her curtly.

She pauses, thinking on that for a moment. I suddenly feel like someone should be holding me back, or better yet, that I should let the white-haired girl loose on him. She shakes her head, taking a gentle step sideways away from me and turns to leave.

"Come on, Astrid!" Jackson calls down the stairs. "Where are you going?"

"To find my real friends," she hisses, continuing on down the stairs. Jackson turns his gaze to me. Sky turns to follow Astrid.

"So. You're him," he states, watching me like I'm a science experiment. "You're the new Beta 9X."

"You know me?"

"No, it's actually the fact that I don't know you at all is what gives it away." He smiles kindly. "Unless one of the others got replaced, too."

"No. You're right."

"Mm." He hums, reminding me scarily of General Fallon. "Take a seat, uh ... I'm sorry, but your name?"

"Kole. Kole Danvers."

"Kole." He rolls it off his tongue. "Please take a seat." I do, mostly because I don't want to be rude.

"What is this?" I blurt, not able to stop the words from leaving my lips, my curiosity spurring them onwards.

"What is what?" Jackson Alexander cocks his head at me.

"What is this ... place? This community?" I press.

"It's a family. Kids and teens from all over the area who needed a place to go. Who needed people, needed a *family*. Most of them are just randoms from bad situations and small failed homesteads but some of us are from PAAC," he explains, describing the ragtag establishment like it's some sort of resort.

"How long have you guys been here?" I frown.

"I've only been here for a year, since I got out. Sky started the rebellion about five years ago after she escaped from the PAAC compound herself—"

"Escaped? Why would she escape?" I frown even deeper, turning the expression into more of a scowl.

"She saw through them. She saw who they really are," Jackson says, looking deathly serious.

"Sky ... the girl with the metal arm?" I ask.

"That's her."

"What's that story?" I raise a brow. "How did she lose her arm?"

"PAAC mission gone horribly wrong. Her entire unit ended up dead and she was the only one to make it out. She mangled her arm in the conflict, had what was left amputated and then was supposed to be terminated." he explains. His expression doesn't change once, like he's told the story a thousand times. Maybe he has. "Well, she never told us how she escaped, but she got out somehow and started this. The Red Rebellion."

"And—"

"And she wants to get even. She wants to bring PAAC to its knees," he expresses. "She's about five years older than I am and has been working on this since she first got out. She's determined, I'll give her that. And she's not alone. Many of the terminated were not really terminated, and found their way here."

"Like you."

"You know about me?"

"Yes. I found your file. They said you were terminated." I frown. "But obviously ... that is ... wrong."

"Obviously."

"How?"

"PAAC's fatal flaw is pride. Let's just say they are so confident in their ability to control that they forget to lock all the doors at night. Lots of us escaped, like Peter Tarak. You might have known him, he's a fairly recent addition. Former Beta. You probably trained together."

"Peter is here? He's alive?" I ask quickly. Jackson nods slowly. I almost don't believe him. I saw his file, too. But I also saw Jackson's, and here he is. I guess PAAC's protocol isn't as successful as I thought.

"Yeah. He's doing well, too. Quite the comedian."

"Yes, he is," I say, looking at the floor. I nod, remembering the things Peter would say during Beta training when only Myrka and I were there to listen. The kind of outrageous randomness he would put forward. That was one of the things I missed most about him. Although it might be true that Peter is still alive somewhere, something about Jackson doesn't sit well with me. His charismatic, textbook superhero likeness has a few holes in it.

"But," I cock my head, "I still don't understand. Why didn't you go back for Astrid and the others?"

"It's complicated." Jackson sighs and I frown a little. It doesn't seem so complicated to me. Either he went back or he didn't with a reason for both.

"I'm sure I can keep up," I say, almost sarcastically.

He gives me a strange, searching look before nodding to himself slightly.

"Okay." He pauses, searching for words. "I didn't go back. I didn't go back because if I did, and I failed, she would've lost everything. Her entire life, her entire view of herself, is built off her accomplishments. Do you not think that if PAAC found her trying to run away, they wouldn't punish her?" He shakes his head at the desk table. "No. I couldn't take the risk. Besides, even if by some miracle if I did get her back here, she still would've changed."

"What do you mean?" I scoff, not believing it. Astrid is the kind of stubborn person who would refuse to change. She already knows who she is. Nothing could ever change who she is. Astrid is Astrid and that's it.

But Jackson seems to think otherwise. He looks at me, almost with sympathy for my lack of understanding and smiles kindly. "I mean, she would've lost everything if she came here. Even if she was free and away from PAAC and Ryker and everyone. If she could finally relax and just … just live, you know?"

"Why? What could this place possibly do to Astrid that PAAC hasn't already done?"

"PAAC gave her identity. We would've taken it away. You see, Kole. Astrid ... she wasn't the first female Alpha. Sky was."

THIRTY

Astrid wasn't the first female Alpha. I didn't believe it at first. But if PAAC had assigned me as Beta 9X and conveniently forgot to tell me that there was another not that long before me, why would PAAC gift Astrid the truth?

Because they liked Astrid more than they liked me, they were proud of her. Fallon saw her as a daughter and the other professors saw her as a work of art.

Or maybe they should all be winning Oscars for their performances.

Just one more fabrication from PAAC. Does it not bother them to tell us untruths as easily as they breathe air? To tell kids they are something other than they are, are someone other than who they are? To tell nothing but lies?

"Fake it until you make it. Confidence is confidence. Real or fake," one of the professors had said before a public speaking event.

Yes, but only until you find out the truth. Once you uncover that truth, everything you thought you've built crumbles away like a medieval castle on a time lapse.

The lies swirl and twist through my mind, making me question every single thing I think I know about myself. I wonder how Astrid must feel.

I freeze.

Does she know? Jackson refused to bring her here a year ago, trying to protect her. Why would that stop now? Why would finally seeing her after a year make him change his mind?

That's simple. It wouldn't.

That means this is yet another secret, and I'm in on it. I feel at liberty to share, but I don't know if I am brave enough to do so. I don't want to be the one to shoot her down or be within swinging distance when she does find out.

The camp was quaint and homey, but with that sense of dirty grit. A sense of plain and simple rebellion. Which was fitting, since they called themselves the Red Rebellion. Marching in the honour of revenge. It was their logo that I saw slashed on the wall in red paint at the jungle building; the double 'R' in the circle with wings.

Outranked. Unequal. Unsatisfied.

As the days wore on, I saw that everyone had a function, a job, a purpose suited to their interests and skills. I had thought Jackson was the leader, but when you think about it, he's just a Beta. Sky was the one who really wore the pants. She kept everyone in line. And Astrid stayed by her side for most of the time. Sky had been able to reason with her and bring her onto the team. I was surprised of how easily Astrid gave in. I hadn't seen the white-haired girl very much, she was always busy, learning or working for her keep. She was assigned to train the younger fighters, to make the hundred makeshift soldiers into a unit of mass destruction. I watched her one day, raking her new recruits over the coals in a bordered arena two square bales of hay high and filled with yellow sand.

"Always protect yourself. Your non-hitting hand should always be in this defensive position. Strong stances, a good base and a good grounding will inspire a good, solid hit. The better the hits, the shorter the fight," she says, displaying her own techniques. The PAAC compound's trademark techniques, even if they were just the basics.

Astrid still sports her blue jeans and white spaghetti strap tank that she found here, but her old black combat boots from the compound are laced up under the denim hems. Her white hair is still down, flowing freely to her shoulder blades, giving her a new, fresh look as it blows slightly in the wind and moves with her as she moves.

"Hey." Sky's rasp of a voice comes from my right side. She climbs up and sits beside me on the bales, her arm glinting in the sun. "She's pretty solid, eh? No wonder she was so hard to bring in. Tommy said she put up quite a fight."

"Yeah," I say. I want to talk about the Alpha situation. I'm sure she knows. Did Jackson tell her I know?

There's only one way to find out.

"So," I begin, sliding into the conversation clumsily. "First Alpha. That's impressive."

Sky shoots me a look quickly, narrowing her eyes. I watch her, trying to be calm, but the short girl is strangely intimidating.

"Jackson told me," I explain quickly. She scoffs.

"Of course, he did." She sighs and rubs her neck. "Astrid still doesn't know. I'd like to keep it that way for a little longer."

"For how much longer? She deserves to know."

"I'll tell her when it's time," Sky insists.

"When will that be?"

"Once she's done her job. She can't be distracted." In unison, we look out at Astrid and her trainees. They are moving better already and she has only worked with them for three sessions. The time might be coming sooner than Sky anticipates. "It's important that she does a good job."

"What do you need them for?" I ask, and she tenses. "You're not going to launch any attacks, are you?"

She pauses. "No. We're not ready yet for that kind of thing." That raises a serious red flag. Yet? They're not ready to launch an attack ... yet? Meaning that's an end goal?

"I thought peace was a core value here."

"Peace has to be earned and paid for. It's not something you get for Christmas wrapped in pretty paper with a bow and sitting under the tree. It's a struggle. Then once you win—that's when you get to call it peace." She frowns at me. "I thought PAAC would've made that clear. Maybe their core values have changed."

"If they ever had any at all," I scoff. Sky just looks ahead at her soldiers, not saying another word and drowning me in her silence.

Astrid moves on from hits to flip holds. She looks out to me and waves me over. Sky nods.

"Go. Help your girlfriend," she orders and I jump off the bales, plodding across the sand to Astrid. She grabs my wrist and moves me to where she wants me before continuing to teach.

"Don't fight me. Just go with it," she instructs, her chin almost on my shoulder, sending shivers through my spine and butterflies dancing wildly in my stomach at the thought of how close she is. I know Sky is still watching, but I don't really care.

"Flip holds aren't the most practical of maneuvers. They're showy and are only used in ideal opportunities," she says. "Mostly surprise attacks. If you're in a real face to face fight, don't try one of these. It won't do you any favours, trust me."

She moves away from me for a moment, setting up the fight as if we were really going at it. "Example one. Kole, chest kick," she says and I lift my leg as if I would be planting my foot in the center of her chest, only with half the speed I would actually use. She grabs my ankle and twists my leg, making me buckle and turn away from her with a little hop. "Now, I would probably pull this leg farther or sweep out his other knee, but I don't want to actually hurt him so just use your imaginations."

She lets my ankle go. As I stand up, turning around to face the trainees, I notice Sky walking away, en route to the barn. I frown at her back. Not entertaining enough for her, I guess. I help Astrid demonstrate a few more holds, flips, and maneuvers. Whatever she wants to do, we play out in slow motion for the crowd of trainees. The fake fighting is fun, except for the part when I am not sure what we are doing and accidentally get a real, full power punch to the face, warranting laughs and giggles from the audience and a sorry look and apology from Astrid. It hurts just as much as I thought it would.

The day was spent quickly and I didn't mind that in the slightest. Jackson is right, Astrid does seem different here. She seemed more relaxed. More at ease. More herself. It is cool to see her come into her own like that, and so fast.

We stay after the trainees have left, relaxing on the bales, and watching the sun creep closer to the horizon, the sky shifting and morphing, painted with splendid colours.

"Let's keep going," she says, jumping down from the bale and pulling her fists up loosely. She looks good, tired and dirty, but good. She takes a few fast steps back and pulls up her hair, tying it in place with the hair tie on her wrist. "No fake plays this time. Get serious."

"I'm serious. I'm completely serious."

She laughs a little and starts bouncing on her heels, coming closer with a grin.

"Serious as ever," I repeat.

"Hm." She giggles.

We don't do much sparring, rather we joke and pick at each other, while walking in a slow circle. Eventually, she loses the whole fighting spirit and just sits down in the sand. I gladly join her, dizzy from the circling. She sits still, peaceful with her eyes closed, with the sunset fading behind her. I try to think positively, but knowing what I know weighs on my mind like a thousand pounds.

I don't want to ruin this for her.

―――――――

After that initial night, we were each assigned to a barrack, mixed in with all the other people sharing a shed with bunks in it. The barracks are all close together, like a little village within the Haven. Boys and girls are separated. The quilted blankets smell musty. I can feel the plywood under the thin mattresses, which are just three sheets of foam stacked on top of each other. The furnace is body heat, and since heat rises and I am on the bottom bunk, the middle-of-the-night cold is something I'll have to get used to. Luckily, once the sun starts to come up, the entire place warms like a sauna.

Beside the barn and farmhouse, there is a makeshift pavilion, made of vertical logs with the bark still on and a pergola-style roof strung with lights like the ones at the PAAC anniversary dance. There are white folding tables and grey folding chairs set out under the lights and a long bar where all the food is laid out in a buffet. It was homey in a rustic, country living sort of way.

"Well. You look familiar." I hear someone drawl and I turn around. Peter Tarek stands with a plate of scrambled eggs and toast in his hand. I just stare at him for moment, not sure what to do. Less than a week ago, I was certain he was dead.

"Peter."

"Yeah, that's still my name." He grins. "It's good to see you man."

"Yeah," I say. "It's good to see you too."

"Sky told me you were kicking around somewhere. I thought it wasn't true, so I came to see for myself. I guess the old robot was right." Peter says with a kind smile. "How's Myrka?"

"She's ... she's good. Or she was good, I mean, the last time I saw her."

"Mm. Do you think she'll find a way out?"

I pause. Would she? She reminds me of a milder Astrid, and Astrid wouldn't have chosen to go out on her own, either. I don't know what she would do, honestly. But I am leaning towards her staying if she got the chance to choose.

So, I respond with a "We'll have to wait and see," not knowing what else to say. Peter just nods, and I think he's on the same thought track as I am.

"Speaking of Sky." He sucks in a breath. "After you finish your breakfast, she wants you in her office."

"Oh?"

"Yeah. It sounds urgent."

I follow the gravel and sand pathway to the red barn and enter through the sliding door that is already open. Sky and Jackson are sitting with the guys who were in the barn when we first showed up. They all look at me and I get serious déjà vu when Sky steps out in front to greet me.

"Kole," she calls. "There's something we need your help with."

I come closer. Sitting on the table are the same array of hand drawn maps that the group had tried to hide from me earlier. I frown when I look at them. They all depict the PAAC compound and its surrounding area.

"What is this about?"

"We need to know if our maps are accurate or not and you have the freshest memory on the compound's architecture." Jackson nods to the yellowed paper.

"Why not Astrid?"

"We can't distract her from her job. She is doing extremely important work as we speak. We added about fifty new students to her program and hope to expand even further. Most of the kids already here need to be retrained. She has much more combat knowledge than we do. She doesn't have time for maps in her busy schedule." Jackson rubs his top lip just like Astrid does when she's nervous or anxious.

"Besides," Sky adds, "she doesn't want anything to do with Alexander and he's an asset we can't afford to lose on this part of the plan."

I look at him. He looks at me and shrugs.

"I'm still confused."

"Okay," Sky says, like she's opening the room for questions.

"Why do you need the maps? I thought you guys said you were done with the system? With PAAC?" I frown. Sky just smiles at me. She shakes her head at the floor and rubs her neck as she comes forwards, putting that same hand on my shoulder and staring into my soul. Her metal hand weighs on my other shoulder. She smiles wider. She looks determined, ambitious. She looks dangerous.

"I don't think you understand what's been said. PACC is done with us, but we aren't done with them."

"You're insane!" I say loudly, almost shouting.

"Thank you." Sky grins, taking it the wrong way.

"No, that's not what I mean! You can't destroy PAAC! They will decimate the forces you take with you, and the ones that you leave behind will be hunted down and killed, and not just in a computer database this time."

"Not if we win." Jackson gets serious. I shake my head.

"No one is going to survive this. You have to call off all efforts, right now. This is suicide!"

"We've been planning for years, Kole," Jackson explains. "We're finally ready."

"You'll never be ready! You know the resources and the firepower they have. They will crash in like a category five hurricane and nothing will be left standing. You'll have to rebuild from nothing, that is if you even survive."

"We've done it before," Sky growls. "We've seen threats before."

"Not like this."

"ENOUGH!" Sky roars. "I've been waiting to take them down for five years! I will not give up this chance now! We have a plan and we are going to stick to the plan whether you are in favour of proceeding or not."

She may have the vote, but I refuse to back down without a fight. I set my stance.

"Call. Off. The attack. Right now."

"You don't have that authority. You're not a Beta anymore, you're not anything here. You're nothing. The bottom link on the food chain. You don't have the rank to tell me what to do, Kole," Sky rasps, getting more in my face. I glare at her from above. "You don't understand what's happening, you are just a child. All I need from you is help with the maps. If you don't cooperate, Astrid is going to know everything you don't want her to. That her identity, her version of herself is just a sugar-coated lie. Everything that will break her. I will tell her; I will tell her everything a lot sooner than I had planned to. Do you want that? Is that what you want, Kole?"

"'No." I swallow hard. Her change in tone and personality came at breakneck speed.

"I admire your drive, but know that you are not Alpha. You are not the leader. That's my job. Now, check the maps and report back. I want them done by midnight," she orders, before walking away, taking her entourage with her. Jackson pats my shoulder as he leaves.

"Don't worry 'bout it, man. She's just intense."

"I never picked up on that," I quip without any of the humor and all of the harshness. It's hard for me to forget that he still stands with her on her side of the field. I don't bother to watch them leave, keeping my back to the door, but listen to the footsteps fade away.

The maps, drawn of the individual wings with all their entrance and exit points, are arranged on the table like they are in real life.

North, south, east, and west all arranged in perfect pattern. There is no flaw that I can find and I wonder how many people have checked and double checked this over before me. I wonder how long they've been planning their launch.

The yellowed paper's edges are coarse and snagged. The paper itself has blotches and stains on it. As I review, my mind drifts. I can't believe that Sky is blackmailing me into this. Using Astrid as a grindstone to sharpen her own knives and then as a weapon against me? It takes serious effort to be that conniving. When I first arrived, standing in that balcony office for the first time, I thought Jackson was the one in charge. Now I see how wrong I was. Sky holds the reins, and she doesn't understand the word slack.

I pick up the pen Sky left on the table and grip the pen tightly. It has a gross grimy feel to it. Like a permanent coat of dust is clinging to it. I roll it in my hands, thinking about how badly I could ruin this attack with just this one pen.

THIRTY-ONE

Beyond the outbuildings of the haven is a little building with rusted tin walls. Based on the fragments of paint peeking through the red, you can tell that it was once painted sky blue. A single slant roof with an air hatch propped open by what looks like the handle of a broomstick. A little door that matches the barrack entryways, but no windows. I watch from a distance, until I hear a single voice spew a harsh sentence with some very colourful language. I move closer as a tall and willowy girl with long braided brunette hair busts through the door, coughing and hacking in between bursts of swearing.

She is wearing dirty jean overalls with a once-white shirt underneath. Heavy steel toed boots. Still coughing and waving away the air in front of her, she pulls her red bandana down from her mouth to hang loosely around her neck.

"Son of a gun," she berates herself. "How many times have I told you to watch those injectors, you idiot! I can't believe you blew another valve."

I smirk a little and move forward as white smoke billows out the air hatch from the roof. "Hi," I begin, extending a hand. "I'm Kole."

"Right," she says with a friendly grin, taking my hand and giving it a firm shake. She clears her throat. "Sky has you on cartography."

"Uh. Yeah." I try not to grimace at how uncool that sounds.

"Well, nice to meet you, Kole. I'm Alice. Red Rebellion chemical engineer."

"A chemical engineer?" I tilt my head.

"Well, kinda. I blow stuff up." She gives me a thumbs up and I study her. She's definitely different than any other girl, or person in general, that I've ever met. She has a raccoon eye mask of grime, probably smoke or cinders or something from the mini explosion she just created. I think her and Allister would get along great. "Yeah." She sucks in a breath, rocking back and forth on her feet. "It's a ... blast." She grins and winks at me. Now I'm certain Allister and this Alice girl would be friends.

"Ah ha." I smile a little at how much she reminds me of the Delta. "So, you pretty much just ... explode things all day?"

"That would be the ultimate dream, but sadly, no. It's my job to create the explosives. I only get to test a few of them. About one a batch. Just to see how everything would play out in real time, you know? Can't be taking faulty explosives into a battle." She nods as she talks. An alarm sounds from within her little lab, shrill and pulsing. I raise a brow.

"That sounds important."

"Eh, not really. It's supposed to signal if there's a threat of combustion, kind of like one of those carbon monoxide alarms, but it doesn't work too good." She sighs, looking back at the entryway as the smoke starts to subside. "Always ringing after the fireworks show, piece of junk."

"Sounds exciting," I say.

"I'd invite you in, but the air still holds the threat of lung cancer."

"Oh, it's okay."

"You should come back some time and I'll definitely show you around." She nods before untying her red bandana then retying it around her mouth and nose. She cocks her head to the side. "See you around, Kole. Have fun with those maps," she says before turning and walking back into her building. The sounds of banging and clanking metal on metal and the whoosh of a blowtorch follow her disappearance into the little lab shed. I laugh to myself and shake my head.

"I'll try."

Alice was an interesting character. She was different from anyone else in the Haven and it was obvious that she liked it that way. She wanted to be different, she wanted to be unique. She wanted to be something no one else could be; herself. It was refreshing.

But over the next several days, I don't see Alice—only the rows and rows of stacked hand-held explosives outside her door. It's daunting to just walk past. And in my mind, a sign of a foolish and dangerous strategy. Sky has had this attack planned for a long time, but I still think she's blind. Her rage over being injured and then ignored by PAAC has only grown since she's been away from them. She thinks PAAC stole her life, and she wants them to pay for it in blood.

In her drive for revenge, she has become ruthless and irrational and is going to lead Haven and its inhabitants to destruction.

The only person she'll take advice from is Jackson. So that's who I need to talk to. What he thinks is right and wrong and his view on ethics aren't quite as defined as Sky's. I am not quite sure what he wants. I don't know if he even knows what he wants. I need more time to figure him out. But I don't have that time.

I find him outside the sparring area, sitting on the bales watching Astrid work. That's all she does now ... work and train and work some more. He has an odd look in his eye. Almost like he's regretting or rethinking something. I approach him from the right side.

"Hey, man," I say, sliding up next to him.

"Hey." He gives me a polite nod. I'm about to start my speech, but he beats me to it. "I know she's being crazy and reckless. But, believe it or not, she knows what she's doing."

"Does she?" I wince. That's not the thought track I wanted to hear. "She's going to war against one of the most powerful forces on the pacific coast."

"I know. She knows." He sighs. "Although, she is moving faster than we agreed on."

"So shut her down," I say, desperately. "Jackson, you must shut her down. You're the only one she'll listen to anymore."

"But I want this, too," he argues, shaking his head. "I want to end this. For everyone."

"This isn't going to make it stop, Jackson." I look him square in the face. "It'll only make it worse. I'm all for standing up and fighting for things you believe in, but if we go up against them, gun to gun? There will be nothing left to believe in."

He pauses for a moment and I know I've gotten through to him. He's rolling over what I've said, his mind a rock tumbler, smoothing over and polishing each gem of an idea.

"She's never going to go for it." Jackson thinks aloud, rubbing the back of his neck. "She's hell bent on the attack."

"So, we slow her down."

"And how do you want to do that? Sabotage?"

"I was thinking more like work at a snail's pace, but I like your plan better," I admit, making him give me a lopsided look.

"That's treason. You know that right? Sabotage is treason."

"Yeah."

"Sky will do some serious damage if she catches you."

"Us." I nod at him, flicking my chin a little. "If she catches us."

"Most household chemicals are combustible, but to launch the explosion, you need a spark," Alice says, goggles strapped to her face and a matching pair making everything in my vision a murky yellow. A cylinder of flammable liquid sits on the table before us, giving off toxic fumes that can't be good for the lungs. She looks like a mad scientist, eccentric and brilliant. Her eyes are alive and she taps at the sides of the cylinder with her fingernails. It makes an odd sound, kind of hollow but also solid at the same time.

"Is this safe?"

"No, no it is not."

"Mm. Just checking."

"So, you have your everyday flammables, gasoline, stuff like that. But the actual explosion needs a little extra oomph. So, we have ... fulminated mercury. Good for big explosions. But, the problem with the mercury is the detonation. So, Sky helped me find a rare little gift called Azidoazide Azide, or C_2N_{14}. Extremely explosive with a small force detonation. Plant it, shoot it ... kaboom." She grins, looking manic and a bit frightening. "Here, put these on." She tosses me a pair of elbow length, banana yellow rubber gloves. I pull them on and my palms immediately begin to sweat.

Alice turns and slowly removes a cannister from a shelf. She unscrews the top slowly and I peer inside. Little red crystals like little shards of ruby—but much more dangerous than splinters of the real gemstone. They catch the light as she gently places a few handfuls of the C_2N_{14} inside into the cylinder of flammable liquid. She closes the cap on the cylinder and cannister and puts the C_2N_{14} carefully back on the shelf. Then she slashes a wonky cross on the side of the cannister, careful not to jostle the tube around.

"Alright then. Let's run the test."

Outside the shed, beyond her stacks of other scrapped projects and failed attempts, is an open field with scorch marks littering the grass. Alice makes her way across her testing field, and sets her pipe bomb on a muddy ramshackle table built out of spray-painted two-by-fours and plywood. She positions the bomb with the cross facing me and she runs back to the safety line.

"Care to do the honours?" She holds out a pistol for me to take. I do, unsure of how this is going to go. "Hit the cross on the dead center, or as close as possible. Take your aim, big shooter." I do, lining up the cross the best I can and firing only when I feel ready. The bullet screams through the air and slams into the cylinder. The thing erupts in a blaze of light, shooting splinters of the table and fragments of the cylinder through the air. The smoke clears after a minute, revealing newly scorched ground and a hole a foot or two down into the earth. We freeze, looking at the mess.

"Yeah. I think that'll work," she decides, with a nod. "Good work, Kole."

As the days go on, Jackson's and my plan of sabotage turns into nothing more than a glorious dream. Or at least that's what I thought.

One afternoon, he finds me in the open-air pavilion, a serious look on his face. Astrid sits on the bench opposite of mine, the first time we have sat together since Sky added the last batch of new recruits to her workload. We both watch him approach, curious.

"It's done," he says, eyeing me like he's clueing me in on something.

"Sorry?"

At just that moment, Sky walks into the pavilion, the furies of Hell following her like a thundering cloud. She peers around the pavilion, looking for someone. I get the sinking feeling that someone is me, the cartographer. I've been pouring over her maps, re-drawing the incorrect sections, and making notes on the inconsistencies.

Finally, she spies me in the cluster of people and makes a short job of cutting the gap between us.

"Danvers," she shouts. "The maps. Where are they?"

"I don't know," I answer.

Wherever Jackson put them.

I can't quite say it.

"What maps?" Astrid frowns. "I don't know about any maps." Sky raises her hand to silence her and my temperature rises. Astrid falls silent— like submission is actually in her nature and it makes me red in the face. Astrid shouldn't be taking orders from anyone but herself. She's the lead, not some second stringer.

"Once more. Danvers, where are my maps?"

"I told you 'I don't know,'" I insist, a little harsher than before. Jackson sits quietly the whole time. I stare into her eyes, feeling her rage wash over me like a ruthless wave. "I'm sorry."

I'm not sorry. Not really.

She glares at me with such hate.

The smashing of glass and Mom's scream. We huddle under a table as the shards rain down onto the linoleum flooring. I grimace and cower, feeling more afraid than I ever have in my life. Real rage lives in his voice and I've never seen him this bad before. The reeking scent of heavy alcohol is in the air. It's on his breath, in his clothes, in his skin. It's consumed him. The bottle of Johnnie Walker Black Label sits tipped on its side with the seven drops of whiskey that he missed glistening on the table cloth.

"It's okay. It's okay, baby. It'll be over soon," she whispers, tears on her face. "Just breathe. Just breathe, baby, just breathe."

It won't be over soon. It would still be hours until he gives up and decides to sleep it off.

I frown at myself. A memory, but not the kind I'm used to. All the others have been happy and enjoyable, but this was nothing like that. This one was dark and painful, but real all the same.

It'll be over soon.

"What's that look on your face for, Danvers?" Sky growls. "I WANT MY MAPS!"

"He doesn't know where they are," Jackson interjects, looking her dead in the eye.

"Do you?"

He pauses for a moment, looking to me then looking back to Sky. "I think we should go talk. Right now." The pavilion has gone quiet, all eyes and ears on our little scene. But Sky doesn't seem to care. When the pair exits, Astrid is left confused and out of the loop. But she doesn't ask any questions. She just scowls into her lunch, a bland and undressed garden salad. I watched her, waiting for her reaction to shift.

It did eventually, but not in the way I expected.

"I have training to do," she mutters lowly, then pushes her food away, gets up and leaves. And just like that, I sit alone at the table, warring with conflict.

———

The day came too soon. Nothing, not sabotage nor reasoning, made Sky change her mind. She was a storm set for the shore, and nothing could stop her. Astrid had trained a total of three hundred fighters for this day and stood tight lipped at Sky's command. She might show restraint, she might follow Sky's orders, but I know deep down, somewhere deep down inside, she really hates being so submissive. Alice has created her exploding masterpieces, made with the C_2N_{14} for long range detonation. Her exact words being "Plant it, shoot it, kaboom." With the amount of explosives she was delicately hauling into the old rickety truck boxes for transport, it looked like she was going to go crack open Fort Knox.

Even with Astrid's soldiers and Alice's explosive measures, I still wasn't sure this was a good idea. The odds still weren't on our side.

Sky found me lurking by the barracks when everyone was preparing. I was just watching, admittedly being a coward and hoping they'd leave me behind. Her eyes were alive with fire and she was wearing camo cargo pants, stocky black boots with spiked steel toes and a black Def-Leppard T-shirt. She had red paint slashed across one of her eyes and a giant gun strapped to her back with the muzzle in the air.

"Kole," she calls to me in her classic raspy voice that sounds like knives on rocks. "You'll miss the party from over there."

"Good thing I don't dance," I say, looking out at the business of preparing for the attack rather than looking straight at her.

"I'd like you to come," she pushes. "I think you'll finally understand what we are trying to do." I look down at her. She looks behind her and throws her head. Astrid, wearing her jeans and white tank top again, but this time with her hair up in a messy ponytail, turns to look in our direction. A red slash runs across her eye. "She'll appreciate you being there."

"It's sick. It is really sick, you know that?" I lift a brow.

"What is?"

"You using her as leverage against me." I shake my head before taking the first steps to the transports. "And what's even worse is how effectively it works." I follow the dirt path to the transport dock, where a circle of beat-up old trucks with the paint scratched away to nothing waits.

"I thought you weren't coming," Alice voices as I help her lift one of her crates. I cock my head, trying my best not to shoot Sky a dirty look.

"Change of heart, I guess."

"Mm. Well, glad to have you around, Kole," she says, although I don't think she quite believes me.

The bouncy ride wasn't quite like I thought it was going to be. Every mission ride we've had while with PAAC was, for the most part, silent. Everyone just taking that time to prepare, to try to map out their emotions and stifle them before the mission began. There is none of that today. All the emotions being felt are expressed in cries and screams and yells of excitement. It felt unorganized and disjointed.

I needed a plan.

One of the higher ups, a tall and stocky boy with rippling muscles, who follows Sky around as a personal bodyguard, stands at the front of the truck box, holding on to the cab roof and yelling encouragement. Sky, Jackson, Astrid, and Alice all pile into a truck with the odd patch of green paint here and there. I sit with Astrid's trained men, a gun in my lap. I know what it is. Generals with generals, soldiers with soldiers. To Sky, I'm nothing but an extra gun.

"What do we do?" The hype man booms, following the lines of a battle chant.

"We fight!"

"What are we fighting for?"

"To win!"

"When do we quit?"

"NEVER!"

THIRTY-TWO

The sky is dark. No stars. The moon hides beneath a plume of clouds. We can't see in the dark and we aren't allowed to use flashlights—in fear that we will give away our position. The convenience of the googles from our last compound mission is gone, the tech either lost or wrecked in travel.

Is this stealth necessary? As if PAAC is expecting an attack.

That's exactly why this just might work.

It's not going to work. We need to get Astrid somewhere safe.

Okay, Hero. Have fun with that.

"Troops! All eyes!" Sky shouts, climbing up on the tailgate of a truck. We parked the vehicles in a small clearing just far enough away from the compound that we would be lost in the darkness if someone were to look out the window. She points dead ahead to the glowing blue lights of the compound. "There is our enemy. They have torn us down and turned us into things we were not. They abused and mistreated, forced and punished. They played the parts of jury, judge, and executioner! They, they do not deserve our mercy!"

I look around at the intent eyes shining in the dark.

"They think they rule, but not anymore. Tonight, we take them head on. Tonight, we march into the lion's den. Tonight—" she stops yelling and pauses for a moment before saying her last piece at normal volume—"we set it on fire." The whoops and yells of excited fighters, sounding like the yipping of coyotes, follows her speech.

"She knows how to get a crowd going, I'll give her that," Peter admits, finding me in the dark. "You nervous?"

Am I nervous? Or am I just apprehensive?

"A little," I admit.

"Me too." He sighs heavily and rolls on to his feet. His face is creased with worry rather than nervousness; he's just downright scared.

"It'll be fine." I try to reassure him. A spooked soldier does us no good. "I'm sure it will be just fine. I mean, look at our numbers."

"Look at their numbers." He forces a nervous, bubbling laugh. "But, thanks for trying to make me feel better."

"Yeah."

The lines were drawn and we march in the dark. I grip my pistol and think about how useless it will be against the other side. Grisly scenarios play out in my head; none of them end well.

The land between the Red Rebellion trucks and the front doors of the compound is flat and marshy. The road was built around the marsh, but Sky is hell bent on going straight through to save time and energy.

We arrive, soaked to the knee from the murky water and we lay down in the grass. The search lights from the compound touch the ground, missing us hidden in the shadows. Sky gives the signal to go ahead and a handful of people dart forward, each armed with one of Alice's cylinders. They secure each cylinder upright and aimed at the building, and then dash back to the line of safety.

"We need to back up. Blast zone of twenty-five meters." I hear Alice whisper loudly somewhere down the line.

"Back it up! But stay low. Peel off in groups of five. Right wing and down. Move out," Sky orders and the groups start to peel off five by five until we are all in another line, just twenty-five meters farther back. "Snipers. Kneel up."

A body for each placed canister comes to a knee and, using a scope, aims their barrel at a package. The glow of night vision comes through the glass and splashes on their faces.

"Hold!" Sky starts to count down. I feel a moment of doubt and hustle to her side.

"Sky. Sky, just wait," I beg.

"Get back in line. Danvers. You've caused me enough headache. Ready aim!"

"But—"

"Light it up!" she yells even louder than all her other commands and the bullets scream through the air with distinctive bangs. The side of the building goes up in a fiery blitz before I can get another word out. The fire alarms and attack sirens burst to life, chirping and shrieking in two different, headache-summoning tones. It won't be long now until the soldiers come pouring out like ants from a mound flushed with water.

"Stand ready! Stand fast!" Sky bellows as more sirens join the choir. "Here it comes! Here it comes! Stand ready, stand fast!"

"What do we do?" someone hollers, sparking the beloved chant from the soldiers, crouched in rings, all guns locked on the new, fiery entrance. It's a mistake letting them come to us. Giving them time to organize. These precious wasted seconds.

"WE FIGHT!"

"What are we fighting for?"

"TO WIN!"

"When do we quit?"

"NEVER!"

"I SAID, WHEN DO WE QUIT?"

"NEVER!"

"NEVER GIVE IN!"

"NEVER SURRENDER!"

Sky takes a moment, putting her fist in the air, then takes advantage of the silence, speaking at normal volume, but still being heard over the screaming sirens and the cackling of the red orange flames clinging to the blast hole. She looks around at her troops, and for a maniacal second, she smiles.

"Advance!" she orders and her troops race through the fire.

THIRTY-THREE

Fire spreads through the wing. Flames lick at the entrance and claw to the roof just above it, sending thick black smoke billowing into the outdoors. Inside, was chaos. Complete and pure chaos. The Red Rebellion fighters had no order. They went rogue, each and every one of them struck out on their own to do as much damage as possible. I move through the smoke, staying low and looking around, playing defense rather than offense. I know these people. I refuse to be part of any active shooting.

Huddles of five, all dressed in black, move like an organized pack of wolves, hunting down the rogues. This is madness. For a moment, I thought that the rebellion's frenzy— bodies streaming everywhere, noises between shrill screaming and low, gruff yelling— might just overwhelm the PAAC soldiers. Maybe it would be too much for the units to handle. But that's just wishful thinking. The units are highly trained for exactly this type of scenario. They were created to control chaos.

"Rally behind me!" Sky shouts as she launches herself into the thick of it. She darts and dives and ducks around all the conflict, setting in with hard blows with the stock of her gun rather than taking anyone out. "Make for the control center! Make for the control center!" Her fighters converge, forming a human wedge and plow through the battle.

Maybe they did have some order after all.

The human wedge makes its way through the halls and I follow, seeing the familiar white blond of Astrid's hair in the throng of people. I move quickly, trying to beat them to the control center, hoping to turn them around.

I scramble up the stairs and slide into the control booth, a small outlook mounted on the wall overlooking the parking garage. The booth is usually used to keep track of what vehicles are being used or what repairs need to be made on specific transports. If the rebels get control of the space, they can use it as their base and take over PAAC room by room. Two big metal doors yawn open, practically inviting the rebels inside. I franticly push buttons to try to close them, but nothing is working.

The tip of the wedge meets the doorway and marches in just as a wave of PAAC soldiers line up. Fire opens and I almost cry out. People, kids, dropping left and right from the violence. I watch on in horror. The wedge narrows to a sliver and PAAC's line begins to fade away.

Next to my hands on the control board, there are several screens. The security cameras show the chaos in silent black and white, not only what is immediately before me, but the violence in other hallways and wings. Another full-strength wave of PAAC fighters is coming and then there will be nothing left of the rebellion. I panic. I frantically search, desperate to find something that would put some space between the two warring sides.

Just as the start of the second wave is roaring down the hallway towards the transport garage, appearing and disappearing out of different camera views, I see the blinking knob. It's in a glass case with a key hole at the base. I search around, not for the key, but for something heavy.

Think, Kole, think. Hurry up. They need you. Think!

There's a fire hatchet in a glass casing on the wall by the door. I grit my teeth and punch my fist through the glass. The casing shatters on my skin and I groan, feeling the little jagged teeth rip up my knuckles. I grab the hatchet and rip it out, shattering the rest of the glass. I lumber to the button, my hand slick with blood on the head end of the handle.

Swing!

I do, swinging the hatchet horizontally and breaking the glass box around the blinking knob. I look up from the control panel, a group of PAAC soldiers had entered the garage and I slam my good palm down on the button, cutting off all the other groups as the metal doors snap shut before anyone else can get through. The soldiers pause, looking backwards as their safety of backup melts away. The rebellion reacts like a cornered animal, cutting down any PAAC soldiers trapped in the room with them.

Except for one bullet. The single bang of the last shot rings out and the last standing soldier falls quickly, his last shot yet to hit its mark. And its mark is Astrid.

"NO!" I yell, but know that no one can hear me. Even if they could, what's to be done? Then Sky lunges, turning her back to Astrid and taking the bullet square in the stomach. Astrid turns to face Sky, her face tuning white. The controls around me began to go crazy. Someone is staging an override to disrupt the system. They are trying to bring PAAC down, not just in combat, but from the inside, sabotaging the technology. I scramble back down the stairs and run through the wreckage to Astrid and Sky, just as the doors start to shudder. I hit my knees as Sky forces her eyes open, gurgling and choking. She grimaces, showing us the red staining her teeth.

"Well, shoot, hey?" she forces out, speaking in all the colours of pain. "I wanted to say ... sorry." She looks lost. I put my hand on her stomach, creating pressure and feeling the warm red seep to my palm and spill over my fingers.

"You're okay. You're just fine," I insist.

"I know that," she says, forcing her lips to smile a little. "Hey, just know. You were right, Kole. Take care of them."

"You're not getting out of this that easy," I say, trying to be reassuring, but I sound more scared than she does.

"Kole. Take care of them," she says. "Please. For me."

I stare down at her. Someone who pushed me around and acted like a dictator was now telling me I was next to lead her rebellion. Telling me I was right.

"Okay." I nod, swallowing hard.

"Good," she breathes before looking to Astrid. "Girl, I have some bad news."

"I know," Astrid says, coming in closer, I reach for the gun on Astrid's hip but she stops me, looking me in the eyes. I see something I'd never thought I would see in her. She's accepted defeat.

"No. You don't. I'm sorry. You're not the first female Alpha. I was." She winces, shifting a little and coughing. A spot of blood beads her bottom lip. "But that doesn't make you any less. That is just a word used to describe someone. It's not your identity. You decided all that for yourself. All your strength, all your courage. Doesn't come from that word. That's all you."

"I don't understand, PAAC told me—"

"PAAC lies every time they open their mouths. Girl, listen to me," she says, now struggling to talk. "Don't worry, love. This won't change who you are unless you let it. Trust me." She wheezes and takes that peaceful last breath as her eyes gloss over.

She's gone.

"Astrid, get out of here," I say, looking to the doors. They inch open slowly and I can see the boots under the doorway. Countless.

"No," she says. "No, I'm not going anywhere."

"Astrid, please. Go."

"No! We stay together!" she insists, grabbing my wrists and putting them in the air.

"What are you doing?"

She looks at me with a kind of pain that I've never seen before. She's utterly and completely lost in her own skin. She's lost herself.

"They know us," she whispers before raising her own hands and the door opens and the soldiers come through, finding us on our knees, hands raised in a surrender, a fellow soldier's blood on our clothes.

"Hold your fire!" I hear someone shout. I hang my head. Surrender feels weird. It feels like a chill wrapping itself around you. The soldiers creep forward, keeping their guns aimed at us. It's like everything is moving in slow motion.

The soldiers reach us and force our hands behind our backs, using them as leverage to get us on our feet. My one wrist is pulled up sharply to between my shoulder blades and it burns a little in the shoulder. Astrid is treated similarly, but where I grimace, she doesn't make a face at all.

"Unit 9R, Wait. I'll take them to the heads," says a familiar voice.

Allister looks hardened, not how I am used to seeing him. He doesn't smile when he sees us, he doesn't even blink. He just frowns, and that frown doesn't go away as he pushes us down the hall, holding our wrists to our spines.

"Allister, please," Astrid says. He doesn't respond in words, only in snorts or grunts. "You don't have to do this." Another snort.

"Come on, man," I say, trying to chip into the silence. Allister breaks character only for a minute.

"Don't 'come on, man' me. You weren't the ones left to find your way back while you guys got to march off and plan this glorious rebellion," he hisses in my ear, putting a little slack on my twisted arm, inches away from letting me go completely.

"Was there anything glorious about that? About what just happened?" I snap back and he goes back to not responding. It was a cheap shot, but I'll take my hits where I can get them. I'm sure he's confused, that he thinks we just left him and tried to escape without him. If only I had the time and the privacy to tell him the truth. He takes us to the board room—the same room where Astrid had walked up to General Fallon and punched him in the nose—in front of all his council friends.

General Fallon.

I'd never thought I'd be back here. I'd never thought I'd have to deal with him again. I have no idea what to say, how to say it in a way that makes us not look so guilty. At the very least, saving Astrid from the guillotine. The doors open wide when Allister plants his foot in the slice between them and forces them open, marching in, us within his grasp.

"Allister Shepard. Delta 9X," he announces to the room with a straight face. "Targets retrieved."

"Well done. Please, Alpha, Beta, and Delta 9X, take a seat," Fallon says, motioning to the office chairs placed around the table. General Zhang, the ornery old man, peers at us through the video call screen. He squints and I wonder if he really can't see us or if that's just his usual disapproval shining through. The professors sit around the table, looking stern and grim.

We sit. Allister sits opposite us, almost like he's trying to distance himself from being associated with Astrid and myself.

"Delta 9X has told us what happened," Fallon says, looking at us softly. "Taken hostage in the chaos and confusion of a firefight. Being forced to act as foot soldiers to the unruly cause. Truly a trauma. I am so sorry we could not get to you two sooner." I look to Allister. He doesn't look at me, but at the seam in the table, picking at it with a fingernail. I frown. I didn't hear any words like *traitors* or *treason.* He had just snapped at me, thought I abandoned him after sharing plans about leaving in the past. He thought we left and joined Sky and the Red Rebellion willingly. I guess he told the council a different story. He saved us.

"Of course, we will have to assess the situation further," continues Fallon nodding first to Professor Marriott at his right and then making eye contact with Kingston and Ryker. "The protocol following a traumatic event is a leave of absence from the facility. We have a sister building. We will be sending you there for a mental evaluation and recuperation. Your unit members will go with you in hopes of rekindling your bonds."

I look around. Everyone's face is grim and Allister still doesn't pick up his head.

"Nonnegotiable I'm afraid." Fallon clucks his tongue, tapping a pen against the table. "Your mental health is a serious concern. Being forcibly taken and forced into fields of violence?" He shakes his head.

I frown at him.

"Completely horrific."

I watch him with a strange look on my face, like someone put a bad smell under my nose.

Completely horrific?

Completely phony.

"The toll, the damage if you will, that something like that has created will have to be dealt with. Unit 9X has weathered a lot. Let's repair that damage," Kingston interrupts Fallon, getting to the center of the issue. He could see I was on the fence. I tend to always listen to Kingston, and he knows that. I'm about to agree finally, when something in the hallway turns me away. A noise. A loud shrill shriek. It comes just once, but once is enough for everyone to realize something is happening. Something is, again, falling apart at the seams.

I stand and reach for the door, but it swings open in front of me. I jump back just in time for the oak not to clip my nose. Colin stares at me, backlit by the chaos of the hallway. He pants, looking around at the generals before settling on Fallon.

"General Fallon, Sir."

"Speak up, son."

"We have a problem with H-Con," he pants. My blood goes cold. "He's awake."

"Where is he?"

"I don't know, Sir. H-Con ... He's missing."

The room goes silent. They all obviously know about the project, H-Con7870. Why would they not? Fallon looks grim and his face is turning whiter and whiter by the second, taking on the next ghastly shade.

"Deploy all units," he orders. "And shoot on sight."

THIRTY-FOUR

We engage in the second battle of the day, but this time, it is an army against a single man.

Not a man. A humanoid. A humanoid with unknown strength and unlimited potential intelligence.

Essentially, a super soldier.

The sprint to get down the hall and to the armory is more of a fight than a race. All order is abandoned and people flood to the weapons room to get their firepower. The guns act like security blankets; H-Con could be just above us or right behind us, right around the next corner or hiding behind the last. The unknown threat makes us run that much faster to access tools to maximize our safety.

"Where's Maisie?" I ask as we round on the hallway, coming up on the armory doors.

"She's going to meet us there!" Allister shouts back. We had jumped in to help, not for PAAC as an organization, but for soldiers in the complex. I heard about H-Con from Colin. They need all the help they can get.

As we reach the armoury, a loud bang sounds and Professor Romanov is launched through the door and slams into the wall with a groan. He tries to get up, but slides back down the wall, his face contorting in pain.

"Professor Romanov!" I call and run to him. He looks over weakly and locks eyes with me.

"Get out," he exhales. "Get out of here."

Heavy footsteps and H-Con appears from the door. My eyes go wide. It towers over seven feet tall and walks with such strength that the floors shake. Its legs are thick and rippled with muscles, its biceps the size of my head. It zeroes in on Romanov.

"NO!" I yell out.

The monstrosity's attention doesn't waver. Astrid grits her teeth and clenches her fist and charges. I try to reach out to stop her but she's too fast. She hits a knee and then slides through on her side, wrapping her entire body around its feet, pulling one of its legs and kicking out the other. H-Con crashes to the floor with a giant, wall-shaking thud. Astrid scrambles out of the way so as not to be pinned down by the giant thing.

We all charge in, coming as backup to our Alpha. H-Con jumps up, as quickly as its mass allows. It picks Astrid up by her neck, her white blond hair swaying. She claws at its wrist, slamming her elbow down into its arm joint, trying to kick at its torso. Nothing gives. She gasps for air and I run faster. I jump, slamming both arms down on its elbow joint and let myself fall all the way to the floor to add weight. Its arm buckles and Astrid pries its cold fingers from her throat and falls on her knees, gasping and spluttering for air.

H-Con rounds on me, setting me as the new target as I scramble to my feet. It walks quickly, its hands curling into fists at its sides. I stay on my toes, making it easier to dodge its punches.

I weave right and left, moving around like a boxer. I can't get hit. One hit from this thing and I'm done. I keep moving, that thought of a one-hit fight in my mind.

Then it does something I'm not ready for.

Two arms fly forward to punch at me. I duck. I feel the air move beside my head and hear the sound of impacted flesh. Romanov is standing behind me with an arm outstretched in a simple, last-ditch block. Simple but effective. His skin where the fist hit him is red and already starting to welt slightly.

"I told you to get out of here," he snaps as H-Con drives a fist into his gut. Romanov stands for it, not going down a second time. He shoves me out of the way. "GET TO THE ARMORY! NOW!" he roars, pulling a large knife from his sheath tied around his thigh and slashing at the monster. He catches it on the hand, the arms, even once on the cheek, but it does nothing to deter it. We inch around the beast, following Romanov's orders. As I turn my back, I hear a blood curdling yell and turn around. H-Con presses Romanov against the wall and slowly forces the blade into his stomach until it is hilt deep. Blood bubbles and drips onto the floor. The professor looks my way, fighting to hold on to every drop of life left in him.

"Kole. Blood ..." he says, displaying the blood on his teeth. It flows past his lips and drips down his chin. The whites of his eyes turn a murky pink. "Wash it off ... hands, Boyo. Go," he says softly before his knees give out and he slides to the floor for the last time.

"NO!" I cry out as H-Con takes a step back. I move in to fight again, but Allister grabs me and turns me in the right direction, forcing me through the armory doors. They lock them behind me and I turn to smash my fist on them. " No! No, no!"

"Kole." Astrid puts a hand on my shoulder. "Kole, stop." I don't. I can't. "Kole. Stop." She wrenches my shoulder away from the door and locks me in with an icy stare. "He's gone." It's like a bucket of ice water splashing over my head. An instant chill. No mercy and no apology afterwards. "It's okay."

The armoury walls are covered in racks and shelves of multiple calibre guns and ammunition. The doors start to move, something slamming on them from the outside. That something being H-Con. The soldiers are pressed against the racks on the other side of the room, standing by. Their eyes are wide with fear, looking like the children they actually are. They shuffle anxiously as the doors whine and groan under the strain of the blows, their PAAC training inclinations overtaken by their powerful, natural fear. Astrid and I back up from the door and I notice even she looks a little uneasy. We are trapped. There is no way out and something is coming in. Something that wanted our heads.

"9X," Astrid barks, competing with panicked breathing and mild, closed-mouth shrieks. "Rally to me." She sets her gaze at the weapons rack near the doors and Maisie, Allister and Colin take the steps to come up beside us. Astrid moves quickly. She grabs the largest M16s from the racks, passing me a firearm. The metal is cool to the touch. It feels like a challenge. It feels like death. "Defensive position," she orders and kneels. I kneel beside her. Allister kneels behind me. Colin and Maisie stand in the back. We huddle together as a small wall in front of the rest of the compound soldiers, all too terrified to move.

"Astrid—"

"I know," she says. "I know." She looks around. "9X. Ready. Six to the chest, three to the head. Let's blow this monster back to whatever hole it crawled out of," she growls. The door starts to give, the hinges groaning and the timber rattling and splintering until a massive fist punches through. Behind the fist-sized hole, a face floats—looking almost amused.

"READY!" Astrid yells. "FIRE AT WILL!"

The door flies backwards, peeled off the hinges. Bullets scream and fly through the air, slamming into the monster, but not doing anything to slow the thing down. I grit my teeth and scream as I pin the trigger to the guard, feeding it lead until I have to re-load. Romanov's body in the hallway, slumped over, makes me even angrier. I'm focused to kill. Tears well up in my eyes, but I blink them away. No time for that.

The thing drops to a knee, then to another. H-Con is falling.

"HOLD ON TARGET!" Astrid roars over the gunfire. We continue, until it falls backward, its eyes open, but unseeing. The gunfire dies and we pause, not dropping our weapons but just waiting for movement. Everything is deafeningly silent. No one moves, not even H-Con. It's dead. We won.

We won.

David and Goliath.

We won.

We stay in formation as the herd of professors and generals leave their sheltered space and slowly come down the hallway. They look to Romanov's body on the floor in the hallway past the armory doors, then to H-Con slumped over backward on his knees. Then to us, a single unit in defensive formation, weapons still hot in our hands. Kingston moves first, going to check for a pulse that Romanov doesn't have. The knife hilt still juts out of his stomach gruesomely. I try not to look at it. It makes me sick. Ryker and Fallon move next, followed by Marriott. They come around H-Con carefully, seeing it ripped apart with bullet holes.

Fallon comes forwards, touching each of our shoulders, and we relax, standing at ease. We are all shining with nervous sweat, our arms shaking from the vibration and kickback of the guns. My heart still races like a thoroughbred at the Kentucky Derby.

———————

"Never," Fallon says from the podium, our unit standing slightly behind him, "in PAAC history, have we witnessed such bravery. Such courage. Such selflessness. The members of Unit 9X, Alpha Astrid Cardinal, Beta Kole Danvers, Delta Allister Shepard, Gamma Colin Dumont and Omega Maisie Greyer, have shown us exactly who they are as protectors and as PAAC soldiers. They stood in front of the threat like a shield for their peers, putting themselves in the line of danger for the cause." He looks back at us with a proud look. "Bravo, team. Bravo." He looks to the back wall again. "The Pacific Acting Authority Council wishes to bestow upon these extraordinary heroes the highest honor ever awarded to a soldier in history, never mind first year duty soldiers."

"A little much, isn't it?" Allister grins to me. I grin back, just happy he's not mad at me anymore. "Actually, it's just the right amount. Yeah, that's right. Worship me, peasants."

"For the members of Unit 9X, each will receive a medallion symbolizing strength, courage in battle, and composure in the line of fire," he says as Professor Kingston and General Ryker move down the line, clipping the medals onto the left side of our chests, just over the heart.

"Well done," Kingston says.

"Thank you, Sir." I nod. He winks, then shakes my hand and carries on.

"I give you your heroes. Unit 9X!" Fallon says. We stand before the crowd and they cheer and holler, some even going as far as standing for us. I notice Astrid beaming, her head held high. This is what she's dreamed of. No, not of being a hero, just being recognized for the work she does.

She could never have gotten this at the Haven.

Don't be like that.

Like what?

Like an asshole. Don't ruin this for her. She deserves it.

I know.

The council decided that a mental retreat would still be a good idea, even though we had proven we still work in perfect tune with one another. I'm glad; I want some time to think things over.

They had us on the next plane out. Their sister compound was less of an identical twin, and more of a total opposite. Where PAAC's walls are hard and white in buildings made of glass and steel, here are wooden cabins, painted stone walkways and fountains spewing chilled water with glittering coins in the basins. Greenery and gardens, shrubs, and trees. Everything natural and nothing cut back or obviously contained like the perfectly trimmed grass at the compound. It was like we were in a different country, on a different planet even. Not just a few hundred miles away. It was ... refreshing. I liked it.

A woman with long silvery grey hair flanked by a younger, brunette woman and a blond man greet us at the entrance of the largest building. They all sport the same white comfort clothing, almost like cotton pajamas. No logos, no tightness. A large glass dome sits off to the side, a small hallway attaching it to a larger building.

"Welcome to the Secura Institute," the older woman says with a kind smile. "I'm Willow Henley. This is Liza." She motions to the woman and then the blond man. "And Ben. Please, follow me." She turns, but her friends don't and we walk past them. They wear kind smiles and there is nothing insincere about them—not that I can tell, anyway, but my paranoia has been heightened in the last few weeks.

The grey-haired woman, Willow, leads us through the main doors of the building. Paintings, tapestries, and elegant marble sculptures on pedestals line the walls. People, all dressed in the same white pajama type clothing, walk past with kind smiles and joyful expressions. Laughter and the soft gurgle of running water from an indoor water feature layer like a musical addition to the ambient notes playing from a hidden speaker and the pleasant scent of vanilla and sandalwood incense. The atmosphere feels calm and peaceful, a stark contrast to what I'm used to.

This will take some adjusting.

"Here at the Secura Institute, you are safe," Willow says, continuing to lead us on a grand tour. "It's important for you to know that. We have to feel safe in order to heal. And everyone heals in their own time. We must remember, not everyone is in the same boat, but we are all in the same storm."

"I know that phrase." Maisie smiles. "Who said that?"

"I don't know," Willow admits.

"Wow." Allister cranes his neck to look around. "This really is weird." I was expecting the lady to snap, but she just looks at him with sympathetic eyes.

"Delta Allister Shepard. I have been informed of you. We have lots of work to do, you and I, don't we?" She cocks her head sweetly. "Lots of trauma to burn, and lots and lots of forgiveness to put out. We'll get there on your time. You are the clock to your own healing. Remember that, we don't move forward until you are one hundred and ten percent ready to."

"I don't know what you're talking about." Allister swallows hard, obviously lying. Willow just smiles kindly and nods.

"This way," she says, turning and walking down the hallway. She takes us to a warm, sunlit room with five beds, each covered with white and purple quilted blankets. "This is your room; I take it you are accustomed to sharing space. The Pacific Acting Authority Council likes to create close relationships between their unit members. I hope you enjoy the added colour. The PAAC compound is efficient, just a bit dull and drab." She smiles.

"Yeah, this will be perfect," Astrid assures her, nodding, and sliding back in to her role as Alpha. "Thank you."

Willow beams and nods. "I'll let you get then," she says. "When you are ready, feel free to explore on your own or come find me in the courtyard." She closes the door behind her with a gentle click. We all stare around the room and at each other. No one wants to speak after the mention of Allister having some kind of past trauma, but no one likes the silence either.

"What a place," Colin mutters, trying his best to smooth over the tension created by Willow's words, but just making things more awkward. Maybe we do need this retreat after all.

I take some time on my own, exploring as Willow said we could. I find myself in front of the indoor water feature fed by a waterfall coming down a wall of granite. A statue of a young woman with large wings folded over her shoulders, reaches down into the pool of water ... she looks gentle and peaceful. I look at it until something catches my eye. A butterfly floats through the air, orange and black. It lands on the tip of the finger of the sculpture that rests on a rock, dry of water. It flexes its wings slowly and climbs up to the elbow, just living peacefully. I watch it until another one comes and lands on the stone woman's winged shoulder.

I look in the direction from where the second butterfly had come, to an arched doorway closed with drapery. A butterfly flies from a breach in the curtains, this one a pale blue and white. I slip through the curtain and find myself in the glass dome I saw from the outside. It is filled with greenery and more water features. The space feels huge. I can't see from one end to the other. Red dirt paths wind through the space and I choose one just to see where it will lead.

"So, you found the terrarium." Willow appears from a corner on the path. She smiles and clasps her hands together. I look around at the beautiful place.

"Yeah. I guess I did."

"Hm." She smiles. "Walk with me, would you?"

I do, because it would be rude not to and because I have nothing better to do.

"So, you're the Beta, yes?" she asks, seemingly just making polite conversation.

"Yeah."

"Do you know what that means?" she asks.

"I've been thinking about it a little," I admit. "I think it means I make a good second place." I smile at the ground when she chuckles a little bit.

"I think it means a little more than that." She grins at me. "When I had my first visit to PAAC headquarters, long before you were the famous hero everyone talks about, the Betas always fascinated me. They were a real mix of everything. Some of them were more lost than anyone I've ever come across and some of them were very confident in the direction they knew they were supposed to go. Knew exactly who they were. I perceived them as having a kind of ... blind trust," she says.

"Blind trust?" I frown.

"Yeah. Thrown into a spot and told you have to both follow and lead by example means you have to trust the one whose advice you're passing on, hm? You have to be able to rely on the person you are mirroring your behavior after," she explains. "That takes real trust. To, essentially, leave it up to someone else as to how you're perceived by others has always been extremely brave to me."

"I never thought about it like that before," I admit.

"And do you think I'm wrong?"

I pause. "No. I don't. I think you're right."

"That wasn't a trick question." She smiles, just a little amused. "Just an invitation for conversation, but it further proves my point, doesn't it?"

"I guess it does," I say. "Can I ask you something?"

"About Allister?" she asks.

"Uh ... yeah." I say, frowning a little. She nods to the path as we walk another lap around the terrarium.

"I saw your face when I said something the first time. Allister was the only one not confused," she says. "Allister has had a tough life, Kole. He hides it well."

Yeah, very well. I had no idea.

"And the worst part of it is that he remembers absolutely everything."

"What do you mean by everything?"

"Kole, you know what I mean. He remembers. You remember, so does he," Willow says with a pained look like she can feel it for him. "He had trouble at home, ended up without a home at one point. He felt tragedy at such a young age. Life hasn't been kind to him in the slightest. I feel for him."

"He was homeless?" I say, my heart breaking a little bit. If only I'd known.

If only I'd known.

If only I had known then . . . what? I wouldn't have been able to help him.

I could've tried.

"He was. With two sisters, both younger than him, to care for."

I shake my head, aching for him.

"But you haven't had a fairy-tale story, either. Have you?" Willow sits down on a wooden bench on the side of the path. The humidity is starting to get to me. "I've heard your story as well. A broken home, your mother did what she could, but your father's drinking got in the way, didn't it?" She continues and I stare at her, trying to keep a handle on my emotions. I stare at the ground, just in case they spill out. "Eventually your mom gave in, resorting to drinking as well. Then, you were taken from the home that never really was a home."

"It was a home." I nod, clearing my throat. "It was a home at the start. It was my home."

"Where is your home now? The compound? The little camp where you were taken not so long ago? Do you know where your home is?" she asks.

I pause. I don't. I can't remember having a real home, just a place I happened to live. But I do have people. Allister, Colin, and Maisie. Astrid. My family. They're my home.

I shake my head. "My home isn't a place. It's people. That way it doesn't matter where we are."

"Very good, Kole. It takes people years to come to that kind of realization. I am very impressed. Well done, Kole. Well done." Willow smiles at me. A butterfly, another orange and black one, a monarch, flutters past on the breeze. I watch it as my throat tightens. I wasn't prepared for this today. Or maybe ever. Maybe that's what makes it so effective. I'd probably never be ready, but Willow didn't care. She knew it needed to come out.

"You and Allister. Maisie and Colin. Even Astrid. You are all broken in some way or another. In a way that needs to heal before you can really work together. Once you understand each other, and I mean in depth—truly understand why each of you are the way you are, why you do certain things—only then will everything fall into place. Trust me."

Trust me.

I've heard that so many times, but this time I actually listen. This time I actually trust.

"How do I do that?" I ask.

"I know you want to help your friends, it's a Beta thing. Natural instinct. The best way to help your unit is to just … listen."

"What if they don't want to talk?"

"Don't force it. They'll open up when they're ready." She points to a branch on a tree, with what look like leaves hanging from the underside. When I look closer, I see they are actually soon-to-be butterflies, each cocooned in a chrysalis, just starting to grow their wings. "Just like them."

We stare up at the little papery shelters and I finally understand the metaphorical butterfly garden and think about how it's the most beautiful figure of speech I've ever heard. I smile a little, just to myself and just because.

It feels good. It feels really good.

THIRTY-FIVE

The air is still and peaceful. This really does feel like a safe place. I think about what Willow said. We're all broken in some way. All these wounded people around me, aching in ways I don't realize. Hurting in ways I don't understand. It's a painful thought to go to sleep with, but still, sleep comes quickly.

A screaming match breaks out in the kitchen downstairs, just below my bedroom. A roar of voices echo through the air vents, twisting them and making it sound like howling. Snarling. I cover my ears but I can still hear. I hide under the sheets, but the angry sounds refuse to be ignored. I can feel all the rage collecting inside me like I'm a storm drain and the arguing is the collecting water.

"Please stop," I whimper to myself. "Please. Please stop it."

The screaming only grows louder. Angier. More aggressive. Then something shatters. Something crashes. A long shrill note rings out and I cry out loud.

"Stop it!"

The voices carry up the stairs.

"WHAT WOULD YOU DO WITHOUT ME? YOU CAN'T LIVE WITHOUT ME! WHO PAYS FOR YOU TO LIVE? WHO PAYS FOR YOUR CHILDREN TO LIVE?" Dad is really mad this time.

I can't even see him, but I start to get scared.

I can hear Mom in the kitchen. "I'd be better off than you think! I wouldn't have to clean up broken glass every night!" she yells right back.

"Please stop!" I cry out, with volume this time. "Stop it! Stop it! Please!"

Until finally, I can't take it anymore. I burst.

"STOP IT!" I scream louder than the other two voices and for a moment, they pause. The entire house is silent except for heavy breathing and grinding teeth.

"Please."

The morning comes with a breakfast of fresh fruits with vibrantly coloured skin, and honey on porridge. We eat together, as we would have at the compound. Everyone seems exhausted with puffy eyes and slouching shoulders. We are a rough looking group.

"Well," Astrid says, taking a sip from her cup before pushing it away. "I slept horribly."

"Ditto." Allister nods groggily. "Had a crazy real nightmare. Like, hyper realistic." He shakes his head, shaking out one of those early morning shivers. "Freaky."

"Mm," Astrid murmurs, reaching for more fruit.

"Do we have plans for today?" Colin asks, furrowing his brow. We all just look around the table at one another, assuming someone else had an idea for the day. "I guess not."

"Willow probably has something planned for us," Maisie chirps, nodding enthusiastically. "Some kind of team bonding exercise."

"Probably."

"She said something about a boat in the sea? Something about a storm, too?" Allister shakes his head, stabbing an apple slice flamboyantly with his butter knife. "I can't remember what she said exactly. In one ear, out the other." I watch him. I know he remembers. Not just what she said, but everything before that, too. What Willow said is very hard for me to ignore. I don't think she wants me to ignore it, either.

I can help him; I know I can.

If only he's willing to let me try. I can help all of them, if they let me.

Maisie was right. Willow did have something planned for us. A whole day of team bonding exercises that wouldn't work without complete trust. Little games, like leading someone who is blindfolded or perspective games that ended in laughter. It cleared the air like a warm breeze against a winter fog. It was refreshing.

The days went on and soon a week floated past. We all felt new, better. As Willow would have put it—healed. Our return to PAAC was starting to weigh on our minds.

"It doesn't have to be like this only at Secura," Willow says. The others, Ben and Liza, stand at her flanks, smiling as well. "Take this lightness with you. Hold it deep within and let it live forever."

Allister rolls his eyes good heartedly at the cheesiness. We all laugh a little out loud just because it's funny. Just because we can do that here.

"Thank you, Willow." Astrid nods. "Really. It's been great. We—"

A loud boom rocks the ground. I duck instinctively before seeing the thick black smoke billowing in the air. Shrapnel from the blast flies through the air and stings when it hits my skin. I grimace, shielding my face and eyes. Then, the sound of shattering glass as the butterfly terrarium falls apart panel by panel. The butterflies fly away, scrambling for safety in a cloud of colour.

"What was that?" Maisie says, hunched down beside me.

"I don't know."

I look down to my clothes, feeling something prick through the material. Sparkling red dust sticks to the white cotton like flies in honey, catching the light and twinkling. It looks hauntingly familiar.

C_2N_{14} residue.

Alice's explosive of choice.

"It's the Red Rebellion," I breathe. Astrid gives me a strange look.

"Did any of them survive the attack on PAAC?"

"They must have." I frown. "At least a few of them. Willow, we need to move now."

"There's an underground bunker across campus," she rambles, sounding panicked. Ben and Liza are still by her side, but looking a little less Zen.

"We'll go there then," Astrid decides.

"I'll lead," Willow offers and forges ahead. The path winds through the trees and forest that edges around the main clearing. The path is unkempt, but we continue running at full speed, winding around brambles and launching ourselves over fallen trees and large rocks. The stench of smoke is in my nostrils. It burns. The sound of gunshots make the hair on the back of my neck stand up. If they catch Astrid and I alive, they won't let us stay that way.

"Just ahead!" Willow calls, darting through the woods like a long-legged deer, graceful and strong. I follow more clumsily, but still make my way. Coming up on a concrete slab overgrown with lichen and fungi, we see safety. "It's right here! There's a trap door! Help me with it!"

Willow and I edge our fingers under the heavy slabs of cedar bolted together. Astrid comes to help us.

"One! Two! Three!" We groan and strain until we get the door open.

Three figures appear at the edge of the greenery. My blood chills. One of them shouts, pointing. Then all three of them start to run.

"Go," I say, gently pushing Willow towards the opening. She slides in. "Astrid, you next. Come on." She goes in and I hear them getting closer. They're close enough now that I can hear their boots crunching on the dead leaves littering the ground.

Out of time.

I know.

"Kole?" I hear. "Is that you?"

Once everyone else is inside, I kick out the support, letting the trap door fall without me inside and turn around slowly. Peter, Jackson and Alice stand, guns all pointed at my chest. I put my hands up and avert my eyes to their shoes.

"It's me," I say softly.

"We thought PAAC got you," Peter says, sounding almost happy.

"Why didn't you come back?" Jackson says flatly, unimpressed. "Sky left the rebellion to you, you know?"

"I know. She told me." I wince a little, looking farther to the ground. They still have their guns trained on me, so my hands stay in the air.

"What about Astrid?" Alice asks, almost hopeful. "Is she okay?" I freeze, before choosing the most strategic answer I can think of.

"She's gone. I'm sorry."

"That's too bad," Jackson says, his grip on his firearm loosening a little. The muzzle drops slightly. Alice and Peter relax their stance, their guns now pointed downward. Alice's mouth is drawn into a light line. I feel bad for lying, but I'm in too deep now.

"What happened with Sky?" Jackson asks, growing tight voiced and thin lipped just like Alice.

"I tried to save her. We. We tried to save her.

"We?"

"Astrid and I."

"Then you lost her?"

I nod slowly, keeping my eyes down. Better to shield the lie than to blow it. I still don't know what they're going to do about finding me alive. "I lost both of them. I'm sorry."

"I'm sure you did your best." Alice tries to sympathize. "But Kole … the rebellion is up in flames. We don't have any real leadership. It's turned totalitarian with Sky's old bodyguards trying to run the place. Kole, things are bad. There are no resources, barely any food and water. Sky's bodyguards have cut off all our shipments thinking that we can self-sustain."

"A single garden can't feed a whole town through winter," Peter interjects grimly. Looking at them now, they look more ragged than I remember. Cheekbones a little sharper and arms a little thinner. Not that there was much to shave off in the first place, the whole haven was a blend of slim and gangly kids. Now, they're on the edge of starvation.

"You have to come back. I know you are smart enough to bring us back," Alice pleads. I look up from the ground, staring her in the face. She wants me to come back? She wants me to lead the rebellion. I was born for second place. I was born for second-in-command. She obviously doesn't know me well.

"You want me ... to come back?"

"Yes. Please, Kole. Please come back. The youngest at the Haven are going to start dying from sickness without proper nutrition and we'll have no supplies to help them." I watch the three of them watching me. Their eyes are hopeful and they seem desperate. I think about the people in the bunker just below me. Each choice is followed by the sting of regret, but I have to finish what I started.

"I'm sorry," I sigh. "I can't."

"Then get out," Jackson snaps. "Get out of PAAC. You and Colin and Allister. Maisie. All of you. Get out. We'll wait for you." He gives me an affirming nod before his troop roll away back the way they came. I watch them disappear through the forest with a tight face, already feeling that regret. I turn, knocking on the trapdoor with a fist and standing back. It flies open and I slide inside, pulling it shut again with one final glance given to the smoke billowing in the distance.

Inside the bunker, I can't see anything. It's pitch black. A hand reaches out and pulls me through the murk. It's Astrid's. She leads me through the dark until a light appears at the end of a tunneled hallway. A faint orange glow comes from a collection of oil lamps and candles sitting in pools of melted wax. The members of the unit plus Willow, Ben and Liza all stand near the light, their faces illuminated. A punch comes out of left field and lands on my arm, hard.

"What the heck, Kole? Why did you do that?" Astrid snaps, brows furrowed and lips drawn tight in a frown. "What is the matter with you?"

"Don't start," I say. "Not now."

She gives me a lethal glare and I try not to show her that my soul is writing and withering inside.

"Who did you say they were?" Liza breaks the tension.

"The Red Rebellion," Astrid says without breaking eye contact with me. "Kole and I spent some time at their setup. They're trying to take PAAC down."

"Do they think that they will succeed like this?" Willow inquires.

"Yes," I sigh.

"Do they know—" Ben begins.

"Yes. They attacked the compound a week ago. It was an absolute slaughter fest. I'm surprised they had the organization to launch another assault, and this soon after," Astrid confides, looking at the others.

I look at the ground, confirming, "They know how strong PAAC is. They experienced it first hand. That's probably why they came here. Secura is still part of PAAC—"

"Partners. We're partners," Ben interjects, putting a finger up in the air.

"You're still in cahoots with the organization. That bond is what they're after, but they know Secura is more of a 'pen over the sword' kind of place. Peaceful and not likely to fight back. That's the only reason they attacked here."

"It's a bully scenario," Colin explains further. "Picking on someone clearly weaker because you know you can't take on the strong ones."

"How long will they stay?" Willow asks, her brows creased in worry.

I imagine she must be sick to her stomach. Everything she's worked so hard to build is at risk of destruction. The safety of her staff must also be weighing on her immensely. Her composure starts to fail.

"Until there's nothing left to destroy," Astrid says grimly. "They don't understand mercy."

Willow looks to the ground, putting a fist to her mouth. She goes white as a ghost, then flushes, looking like she's going to be sick. She swallows hard. I try not to watch her too intently, giving her as much space as she needs until she gathers herself again.

Finally, she straightens and says calmly, "Come with me." We follow her down another hallway wreathed in darkness and hidden by shadow.

"Being peaceful and isolated doesn't mean one is defenceless or naïve," Willow says as she forges ahead through the tunnels, oil lamp in hand. It smells like earth and potting soil. The tunnels are held up by beams and supports of different scrap woods; probably what was left over after creating the building on the surface. "Just up these stairs. Watch out when I open the hatch. We're going to get wet."

Wet?

Where are we going?

She unlatches the hatch and the trap door swings back violently as a torrential fall of water and copper coins rushes down at us, drenching us all. I shake myself off and follow her up the stairs. We come up in the basin of the faerie water feature in the main entry hall. The drapes are burning, flames licking and writhing on the fabric. Willow leads us in the opposite direction, off to the left and pushes a hidden button on the wooden wall. A section slides open and we slip through, making sure it closes behind us.

"We've been taking certain precautions. Being in the business of world revival and protection comes with certain ... hazards." Willow opens a door and pushes into the room. Racks of guns line the walls, strings of ammunition clips hang in sheets like material on display in a fabric store. I look around. The room seems very out of place in Secura. Extremely out of place. "We'll go on the offense. Peace may be forgotten for now, but let's not roll over and show our bellies so easily."

"What are you saying?" Liza frowns, looking almost as surprised by this room as we are. Maybe she didn't know it existed either.

"I'm saying, and excuse my harshness, let's give these ruffians what they came for. A fight."

"Don't shoot to kill. A few warning shots will send them off," Astrid says. "They're still gun shy."

"Noted."

We move out in the usual PAAC unit formation, using a hostage rescue strategy with the Secura leaders in the middle of the ranks, Astrid in the front and myself in the back. Astrid is right, we see a cluster of their forces, maybe four or five together at most and a few bullets over their heads make them scuttle back to their lines. We sweep the first floor, then the second. Climbing up circular stairs, I hope and pray that we won't meet anyone on the stairs.

The stench of the fire grows harsher, and an aggressive cloud of soot clings to the ceiling. In the hallway, Willow grabs a drape and Astrid pulls a knife from the folds of her clothes and slices the fabric. They cut it into strips and we tie the pieces around our mouths and noses to try to filter some of the smoke. But the cloth does nothing to aid the stinging of our eyes. I squint as we start to move downwards. I can feel the fire's effects as the flames leach the oxygen and replace it with smoke.

I'm starting to slow, getting drowsy. My limbs feel like they are made of lead. My lungs and eyes burn savagely. I can't get enough oxygen . . . asphyxiation. I heave a dry cough and feel wet on my lips. It tastes like copper.

My head spins as I stumble along, trying to keep up. I hear a loud shout and the air around me heats alarmingly quickly. A head of white hair moves in front of me and slams me to the ground, pinning me to the floor boards as a blast of flames comes from the window, heating the air above us. Astrid lets out a pained, guttural howl. I grind my teeth at the sound until it stops and someone doubles back to pick her up. It's Allister.

"Kole, we need to get her out of here. Now!" he shouts urgently. We pick her up, one on each side, listening to her short, painful, quiet cries. I get the first look at the extent of her injury and feel like I'm going to throw up. Her back, visible now that her clothing is burned away, is charred from shoulder blade to small. The skin, in various shades of red and pink, is tight and shiny and peels off in thin sheets without even being touched. Darkened in spots, almost black. It looks horrendous. Within hours, blisters filled with pus and fluid will cover her back like spots on a leopard.

"Let's go," I agree promptly. Astrid makes a growling sound as we start to move her through the hallways. I wince for her, not wanting to hurt her but knowing that we still need to get her out.

"Everyone else is already gone. I told them to go ahead," Allister says, looking around with glaring eyes. He's squinting too, being affected by the smoke. "We can't make her crawl through and the smoke is starting to lower. Move faster!"

We go as fast as Astrid will let us. We ask her multiple times if she wants to stop for a break, her forehead glistening with sweat and her face as white as a ghost, but each time she groans and shakes her head, forcing us onwards.

"We have to get to the terrarium. Highest roof, most oxygen," I pant. "Most of the windows are broken anyway, so we'll have lots of exit points." Sweat is dripping off all three of us like water melting from a glacier. The smoke only grows thicker.

We round the stairs and Astrid freezes, looking at them. "You got this," I spur her on. "I know you can do this."

"Doesn't matter ..." She groans, teeth held tight together. "If I can or I can't. I have to."

She throws herself down the first step and sucks in a fast breath. Each step she makes a new sound, but never stops, continuing on until her toes touch the ground level. She pants, her eyes closing and her walking stalled. We drag her through the room and through the drapes of the terrarium.

"Kole. The glass." Allister says, looking worriedly at the shining field.

"Doesn't matter." I shake my head. "It's the fastest way through."

As we enter, the rush of oxygen made my head go foggy, then clear again.

"Take a deep breath, Astrid. Deep breaths," I prompt. "We're almost there. We're almost there." I scan the outer shell of the terrarium. The structure's glass panels are all shattered from the first explosion. The triangular pane frames are big enough for us all to get through if we crouch, but it'll be painful for Astrid.

"There!" I shout, pointing to a random section, trying to give Astrid the feeling that I do, in fact, have a plan. We shuffle towards it. I feel little sharp pricks in the soles of my feet through my shoes as we stumble over the glass. Nearing escape, I can hear the shouts of people coming from all over. I can't tell if they are Secura or Rebellion. That scares me. We could be walking right into another capture by the Rebellion.

Allister shifts Astrid's weight to me and slides through one of the frames. He hisses a little and pulls his arm close to him, blood dripping in two paths of red down his bicep.

"Watch the corners. There are still little shards of glass in the frames!" He warns, turning around. "Come on, Astrid. Let's get out of here." He beckons to her and she folds at the waist just enough to get through. She hobbles through the frame, before hissing just like Allister. A line of blood appears on her right cheek. But she makes it, and when I get through, I pull the cloth off my face and tie it over the slice on Allister's arm as tight as I can make it. Professor Kingston would have been proud. Allister bleeds through the cloth, but not much. I think he'll be fine.

"Is anybody here?" Allister calls out as Astrid starts to grow weaker. She gets heavier as she starts to tire and her legs begin to fail her. "Anybody! Anybody, help!"

"Allister? Kole?" Colin and Liza appear around the corner of the building and rush to us. "We thought you got trapped inside!"

"Astrid's down. We need medical. Immediately." I cough a little, still tasting that coppery tang of blood, but licking it off my lips before anyone can see the colour. Astrid starts to sway on her weak feet.

"I have experience," Liza admits, raising her hand, and looking duty bound. "I was a battle field medic a few years ago."

"Okay," I respond, a little surprised. That was not the read I got from her. I'm grateful all the same.

"She's already blistering, which is a mixed sign. The skin is super tender, there's lots of hot fluids still trapped." She walks us through her process. Astrid twists and moves a little when Liza gently touches her blistering skin. Even the smallest touch makes her wince and strain. "She's in a lot of pain. Serious pain."

"What can we do for her?" Maisie asks, coming up behind me in that typical Maisie way.

"Get her somewhere with proper medical equipment. There's not much I can do here, and without any real supplies. This is a real hospital ER type case, not just a stitch and fix. Ask for some strong antibiotics. She'll be okay, I think. She'll have some scarring, but that's minor." Liza rambles, thinking out loud.

"Thank you," Allister says.

"Get your arm and her cheek checked out, too. Infection can be killer." She points at him, holding him frozen under her gaze. He nods submissively. "I'm holding you to that. Willow and Ben set out to contact General Fallon and General Ryker at the compound. They'll be here with forces soon to collect you and take Astrid to the medical ward." She pats Allister and I on the shoulder, and then Astrid on the hand. "You are very special people. I hope you understand that."

With that, the distant hum of a chopper in the distance fills me with immense relief. Then I collapsed.

THIRTY-SIX

I wake up in a hospital bed, staring at the ceiling. Splints are wrapped around my midsection so tightly it's almost painful.

Almost.

I put a hand to the coarse bandaging and try to sit, feeling a savage burning spreading like fire through the wrapped part of my body. I look around. Classic white walls. I'm at PAAC. Only one other hospital bed is occupied—the last bed in the row. I put my bare feet to the cool floor and sit on the edge of the mattress. I detach the wires that pin me to the heart monitors. The machine flat lines in a mechanical whine for a short time until I rip its cord from the wall, silencing it. I pull the IV pole close for support and stumble down the rows of white sheeted beds.

Astrid lays face down with her own monitor beeping steadily. A double strand of butterfly stitches holds the skin on her cheek together. I pull a chair to the bedside and watch. I watch the steady rise and fall of her chest as she breathes softly and noiselessly. I watch the stillness of her eyelids and her face. A bandage hides the marbled burns crisscrossed into the skin of her back. For the moment, she looks okay. Peaceful. Painless.

"It's a medically induced coma." Someone says from behind me. Professor Kingston in his black dress pants, shiny shoes and purple dress shirt stands between the rows of beds. "It was decided it was the best way for her to recover. This way she can heal painlessly."

I nod. It makes sense.

"She'll have substantial scarring, but I'm sure that's the least of her worries," he says coming closer, and pulling up a chair on the other side of the bed. "And for you, internal bleeding from some blunt force injury. Non-fatal."

I nod again. Kingston regards me carefully before finally speaking again.

"She means a lot to you. Doesn't she?" he asks, cocking his head.

"She's my Alpha." I shrug. "She means a lot to the whole team. We need her to operate."

Kingston just nods, like he's accepting the answer without fully believing it. As he should. It's only half the truth.

"I'll leave you with her." Kingston rises to stand, making his way to the door, polished shoes clacking on the tile before catching my attention one more time. "Oh, and Kole," he says. "No more adventures for a little while, okay? You need time to heal. Properly." He motions to his forehead and his abdomen. I nod, giving him a little smile. He leaves. I look back to the white-haired girl and her soft breathing. Tendrils of the burn marks peak out of the wrapping. Just enough to see the colour contrast in flesh. A taut and shiny fire engine red to a soft rose pink. I sit back in my chair, feeling the wood dig into my back. I cross my hands over my bandage and sit watch, letting some kind of distant relief settle in.

Even if it is just for tonight.

THIRTY-SEVEN

I visit her every day and every day she is still asleep. Always in the same position, face down. The only thing that changes is her bandages; nurses removing them and replacing them with new ones. One time, I catch them in the middle of the process, dabbing a minty smelling gel onto the open sores after all the water blisters had popped in a mess of fluids and infected pus. It looks horrible, but the nurse promises me it is healing.

"It has to get worse before it gets better," she says. I'm not sure how much worse it needs to get, this looks pretty bad.

I wasn't allowed to train or run any missions, so Unit 9X was without an Alpha and without a Beta. The team takes the free time, claiming they have decided not to move forward without us, but Allister lets me in on the real reason; they need a longer pause. I don't blame them. They deserve a break.

A week later, we receive the news that it is time to wake Astrid up, and we rush into the medical center. When we get there, she is already stirring. We come into the room just as she pitches herself to the side and vomits on the white tile flooring, making sounds that make my stomach churn. I try not to vomit myself and take care to come around the other side of the hospital bed. She moves herself back on the pillow, a nurse wiping her mouth with a napkin as Astrid pants.

"How do you feel now, honey?" The nurse tries for a smile.

"I feel horrible," Astrid groans. "Who hit me with a bus?"

"Natural response," the nurse chuckles. Another one scribbles something down on a notepad stuck to a clipboard, smiling to herself.

"Good to see you finally awake, lazy bones," Allister grins, putting a gentle hand on her shoulder, careful not to touch her burns.

"Hope you've been training. Once I spring this place, we're taking on the world." She grins a little. We all take a moment to appreciate her sense of humor. It's good to finally see her awake, eyes open and a smile on her face. She's probably still drowsy from the drugs they've been pumping into her system for the last few weeks. Still numb most likely, but once that changes, so will her smile. I'll just enjoy it for now.

Week by week, she makes progress. We take small walks to stretch out the muscles in her back and try to speed up the healing process. The skin is growing back, pink and healthy, but it is still too new and has to be sheltered from bacteria. The sharp stinging scent of antibiotic salve is becoming less potent the more time I spend in the medical center with Astrid.

"Well done," General Fallon and General Ryker find me in the training room. I am alone, working on a new combination of kicks and jabs. "Astrid's recovery is moving along quicker than imagined. I believe, in part, that is thanks to you."

"Not really, General," I wipe the sweat off my brow with my wrist. "I was just ..."

"Helping?" Fallon smirks. I scratch my lip.

"I guess that's the word."

"It sure is." He nods approvingly. "Kole, I just wanted to let you know how well you've been doing in your position. It's not easy being the Beta. You are doing a phenomenal job. I'm very proud."

"Thank you, Sir." I nod, trying to be appreciative but I still taste that bitter aftertaste that comes with everything the man does. "I'm trying my best."

"Your best is well above and beyond adequate." Fallon dips his head a little.

"When can we go back to active duty?" I ask, trying to change the subject.

"Always on the move, eh? Bravo, Kole. Good show. You can go back to active duty when both you and your Alpha are given the go-ahead from the head medical officers and Professor Kingston. If I were you, I'd rest as much as possible. There is a new flood of missions coming in from our scouts that need to be handled as soon as possible, and well, I'd like to assign them to 9X." He goes on about special assignments and some dangers, but I don't follow his words that closely. If we run the mission, then I will pay attention. Until then, I see it as wasted energy.

That night I thought about Secura. Willow. Ben and Liza. That led to the Red Rebellion and Jackson and Peter. Alice. Sky. The C_2N_{14} crystals that look like granulated rubies. Then, back to Secura. My thoughts were a playlist on repeat. A hamster wheel.

Then finally, my father.

Dad.

Something I'd stifled. I'd tried to forget because I didn't understand it. How could someone be that angry? Be that ... hurt?

I didn't understand it but I can't run from it anymore. My father was an alcoholic. That's something I wish I couldn't remember. Then, he pulled my mom in, drove her to drink as well. They spiralled downwards together and I was removed from the house. I haven't seen them since. The memories rush back so quickly and so painfully, like I'm breaking down a wall in my long-term memory bank. I shake my head, pressing the heels of my palms into my eyes until I see stars. Little bursts floating in the blackness behind my eyelids.

At this moment, for the first time in my entire life, I wish I was like everyone else. I wish I didn't remember anything at all.

Astrid improves and within the month, we are back on top. We take a week for test training, get our bills of health from the medical officer, and start anew. Being a favourite among the units meant it wasn't long before we had a new mission.

We stand in the equipment lab, picking over the table of gear. Romanov had worked on new pieces of weaponry. We looked at his work silently, not wanting to touch it or displace anything. I purse my lips, almost smiling when I notice the mangled chainsaw blade in the corner and a metal table sitting on its side with a large divot it its top surface. Someone was experimenting. A little scary, but I'm not surprised.

"It's a recovery," Astrid says, shattering the silence. "Just a routine operation. We don't need very much gear."

"What's the goal?" Colin asks, his fingers lingering on a clip.

"PAAC scouts found a few kids way outside the city limits. They're in a rough spot. Bad housing, hardly any food or resources. General Fallon wants to take them in and help them out."

"Well, bless his heart," Allister snorts.

"Mm." She makes a little noise and I'm not sure what it means, but she looks tense. "Alright. Let's go."

———————

Astrid looks nervous. She never looks nervous.

"What's going on?" I whisper, sitting beside her on the transport helicopter. She throws me a look that could've set ice on fire. She rolls her shoulders and her neck. I watch her hand clench and unclench, leaving little angry halfmoon impressions in the flesh of her palms. The cloth of her shirt hides her neck and makes her jawline sharper. Her porcelain skin seems to glow in the light of the chopper and her hair is done up in her signature Viking reverse braid. Her legs are crossed like a lady and she is tense and rigid. I swallow hard.

Get it together, Danvers. Get it together. This is not the time.

"You can talk to me," I pry a little at her titanium armour. She inhales deeply through her nose, staring at the exit sign across the chopper with her icy gaze.

"My parents died on a mission like this," she says, shaking her head slightly and looking down at her hands in her lap. "A recovery mission. I don't really remember it but the records say that the locals staged an ambush and took out the entire unit in minutes. There was nothing they could do."

"Astrid." I suddenly feel like the biggest jerk on the planet. "I'm so sorry."

"It's fine," she says. I can practically see her shutting down again. "Happened a long time ago."

"I ..." I'm about to say something to fix it. Something that will instantly make everything alright but the AI voice steals my moment.

"Please rise and prepare for deployment."

She stands without hesitation and leaves me sitting, staring at the wall by myself. There's a gun rack by the sliding door and I pull a standard black .38 calibre pistol from the steel grids and tuck it in the empty holster strapped on my thigh. I didn't think I would need another pistol but Astrid's story made me change my mind. I feel its weight immediately. I feel eyes on me and turn, seeing Astrid with her eyes narrowed at me.

"Just in case."

"Hm."

Not minutes later, I stand with Maisie, Allister, Colin, and Astrid with a parachute pack strapped to my back. The weight makes me feel like I'll fall over backward and I lean forward to compensate. Astrid hands out the ear pieces. She touches the conference button on hers to speak directly into our ears rather than shouting over the wind.

"We'll drop and relocate. There's a supply shed at the center of the drop zone. I want everyone accounted for before we move in. I'll go first. Standard procedure, so wait and drop at two second intervals. See you losers on the ground," Astrid says and I catch the charm of her smile before she steps out fearlessly and lets herself be taken by the wind. One by one, they all dropped off until only Allister and I were left in the helicopter.

"Kole!" Allister grins like a wild man. "You're next, brother! See you on the other side!"

"I was gonna say that!" I laugh.

"Stop stalling, man! Just shut up and jump!"

I stand still, grinning.

"I'll push you out myself," he warns and gives me a playful shove towards the door.

Just getting near the opening makes my heartrate spike so high that I become nauseous. Trying not to remember my last jump when I was caught by the trees, I swallow hard and step out, taking the plunge. In a single adrenaline supercharged rush, I go weightless. Like a piece of paper being thrown by the wind, I rock from side to side. I starfish, spreading my arms and legs until I break through the low misting clouds to stare at the green of the grassy hillside, wonderfully tree-free. I pull the cord on the chute and it deploys, lurching me upwards painfully before I am rewarded with a peaceful, scenic downwards float.

Once both my feet are on the ground, I make my way east, towards the rendezvous point at the supply shed in the field's center. It's less of a shed and more of an old warehouse with a paneled window ceiling and warped tin walls. Rows of wooden shelves hold cans, jars and plastic containers of unlabeled liquids. The air smells of dust and gasoline. A pipe coming out of the wall produces a steady drip of murky water that collects in a little bowl in the concrete floor. A divot carved by the persistence of erosion. My hand floats to the gun on my thigh as I examine the place.

"Oh, yeah." I hear Allister from behind me. He passes me, looking around without a care in the world. His hair is dishevelled from the wind and is almost standing straight up. I can only image what mine looks like at the moment. "I could hang here. Maybe get a beanbag chair. Some Christmas lights, you know, the little ones that change colour and all."

"It's probably radioactive," Colin says, leading the girls inside. Maisie's strawberry hair is down and ragged while Astrid's white tresses are still firmly tucked in a braid. Only a few strands gone awry.

"Nah, man." Allister shakes his head. "A little moldy, maybe, but not radioactive."

"Alright, let's get to work," Astrid brings our attention back to the mission, pulling out a new black drawstring bag the size of a brick from her pack. From it she produces five pairs of green-lensed goggles.

"The holographic goggles." I grin, taking mine. "Barnes' invention."

"Mm hm."

"Heat vision?" Allister grins idiotically. "I forgot all this cool stuff was even on here! Dang! Ryker's giving us the goods, huh?"

"Actually, Fallon sent them," Colin says, blinking his eyes furiously to adjust his vision. "His name was on the release form." Again, competition between Colin and Allister sparks and I find myself enjoying the solid familiarity it brings to our dynamic.

"Alright, we'll go in teams. Colin you are with me. Allister, Maisie and Kole will be together. Stay on the comm line and stay alert. If one of you finds the three kids, or any of them, secure them before you notify the teams. Recovery is priority number one." Astrid nods her head. "Alright. Let's hit it."

We spend as least half an hour searching the disaster of the warehouse before we dig up a clue. We didn't know if the three kids were still living here or if they had moved on. Then, we found it. A little sock with its purple and yellow stars all faded and a giant hole in the heel. Next to it sits an open can of sauce and noodles with a spoon stuck in it.

"No mold." Maisie performs the smell test, turning the can in the light. "This would rot real fast here, too, with all the humidity. Probably opened this morning or last night. The spoon handle isn't as cold as the chair."

"Body heat."

"Mm hm."

Then we hear the footsteps, bare feet slapping the concrete. A clatter of an avalanche of paint cans makes me jump out of my skin. I turn to see three little white ghosts, frozen in the mess of tin.

"Hey," I say, pouring a kind of gentleness into my voice. I don't want to scare them away. "Hey, guys. I'm Kole and these are my—"

"We know who you are!" the oldest snaps. He's a boy of maybe eight or nine with chestnut hair and piercing eyes. He clutches the younger ones close to him, a girl with stringy blonde hair tumbling like a curtain to hide her face. The other is a male version of her with shorter hair and wild eyebrows. They look about the same age. They must be twins. He dips his chin a little, taking a step back. "You're the bad guys."

Why does everyone keep saying that?

"Oh. Oh, no sweetheart. We're not the bad guys." Maisie tries for a smile. "We're the good guys. We're here to help. We can get you clean clothes, a comfy bed, good food and some clean water. What do you think about that?" The younger ones look desperate, trembling fingers and runny noses. The oldest shakes his head.

"No!" he cries out. "Just go *away!*"

He takes the others by their hands and runs, dragging them along after him. They leave the warehouse through the yawning doors and bank for the treeline.

"If they get to that treeline, they'll be gone," I say.

"Got it." Maisie after them, disappearing through the opening almost as fast as the trio had. Allister stays in the warehouse in case they double back and I jog out into the greens, waiting for the play to begin.

"They split up! Repeat, they split up!" Maisie says in my ear. "Little girl secure, but the other two are nowhere to be seen."

"Eyes peeled, people." Astrid's voice comes through like a lighthouse in storm. Steady and strong. "They can't live here on their own for much longer." Then, everything goes quiet as we plunge into a game of hide and seek. I stand in the middle of the field, waist deep in spear grass. I close my eyes and listen. Sea gulls and the rustling of plants. Quick breathing.

There.

I open my eyes and zero in on a small patch where the grass was being held down by something heavy. Just a little patch, about the size of a crouching child. But then, the quick, panicked rustling of movement catches my attention as the oldest boy runs past me. I lunge to grab him, but miss. I chase after him as the grass begins to thin and leads away to the craggy rock of the cliff face.

"Young boy. Center field!" I say into my ear piece, on the doorstep of frantic panic. "In pursuit of the oldest."

"I got it!" Allister replies.

The transition between soft dirt and hard rock shocks my ankles, but there's nothing to slow me down and I bridge the gap before throwing my arms around the kid, trapping him close to my chest.

"*Let. Me. Go!*" he hisses, thrashing like a wild animal, screaming and shrieking so loud I feel his voice resonating in my ears. I grit my teeth and hold on tighter to the wriggling weasel of a boy. In a flash, his head connects with my chin and I see stars as the pain rattles along my jaw. He gets out of my grasp and tears down the rock flat. I follow, but am too far behind to catch up.

"No!" I shout. "Wait!"

But it's all for naught. I make the mistake of blinking once and he disappears over the edge of the cliff.

I scramble after him and come to a screeching halt before the rock drops off, leaving way to the jagged rocks and vicious sea pounding on the roughs. There is no sign of the boy, only the swirling white caps and gleam of the wet, salted black rocks looking like the serrated teeth of a monster's jaw. My chest pounds as I watch, hope, for a sign that in some miraculous turn of events that he survived.

I feel Maisie's hands on my shoulders and she steers me from the cliffside and into the sympathetic gaze of the unit. Astrid holds the young girl on her hip, nose buried into the crook of her neck and Allister keeps his hands on the shoulders of the other boy. No one knows what to say.

"Fallon's been notified," Astrid says, tight-lipped. "He knows we're done here." I nod. It's the only thing I can think to do.

"Hey—" Maisie starts, but her voice is cut off by a loud noise in the sky. The roar of helicopter blades beating themselves a path through the misty clouds steals my attention. It lands, a black metal beast on the coastal field. Teams of men emerge from the aircraft, ducking before coming to speak with us.

Only, they don't say a word. Instead, they pull the children from both Astrid and Allister.

"Hey!" I say, but can't do anything. I'm outranked. Moving against officers above my status would mean serious trouble for 9X. "Go easy on them. They're just kids. You'll hurt them." My words mean nothing. They force the kids roughly into the helicopter and leave us to wait for the next transport— just as the rain takes its cue to unleash its unforgiving cold on us.

THIRTY-EIGHT

I drive my bare knuckles into the punching bag, pummelling the material. The snap of my fists on the leather reflects the sound of my slowly mellowing anger. I can still smell the salt and rain of the air on the coast. I can still feel the crack of pain from the headbutt to the chin. The slip of the fabric as the boy slid away. I grit my teeth and punch harder, craving the feeling of my skin splitting on impact.

"You should really tape your knuckles." Astrid sits, leaning back on her hands on the sparring platform. She sits above me, looking down as I work. "Split skin is painful, but I guess that's probably what you're after. Right? Little distraction?"

"Maybe."

She studies me before sighing a little and standing up slowly and carefully, working knots from her shoulders while keeping her fragile skin in mind. I watch her. "Come on, get up here," she says. "I want to kick your butt properly."

The one light that is still alive in the training room shines its golden rays down on the circle where I was about to die. I hoisted myself up and into the spotlight. She pulls her fists up, starting to move around slowly in a new, intimidating strategy.

"Take it easy on me, eh?" A smile crests my lips. She scoffs. I decide to amuse her, letting her win. She won't be moving like she normally does, as she is still on the mend from her burns. I'll let her win. Maybe it'll help her.

"You wish," she jests.

She turns quickly, rotating at the hip and lands a kick to my ribs before I can even think to react. It didn't hurt much, so I know she's not trying to completely mangle me. It gives me some hope for survival.

"Fists up," she scolds. "Get serious, Danvers. You look like you're made of spaghetti."

"What?" I grin. She comes in again and grabs my wrist, tweaking it and forcing me down to a knee before letting go and sauntering away, confident in her own superior skill.

"See?" she says, smiling now. "Limp noodle."

"Oh, yeah?" I grin and sweep my leg, taking her out at the ankles. She gets her elbows back and softens her fall a little bit, but can't do anything once I plant my hands on her arms, holding her down to the mat. My breath catches in my throat when she laughs. Actually laughs, not just a little giggle, but a real, good, heart healthy laugh. In that moment, I want to tell her everything I shouldn't. What I can remember. What I've seen and what I know. Maybe it would impress her. Maybe it would make her hate me. Then, I get the need for something else.

I crane my neck down and kiss her ever so softly, breathing in her sweet and smoky scent. The perfect blend of feminine flare and roughness. It's intoxicating. Addicting. But when I pull away, it's like the stopper for those secrets is thrown away and they all come out in one long and exploding sentence.

"I have to tell you something," I pant. I let her up, sitting back. "I have these dreams, like things that have happened to me."

"Everyone has dreams, Kole," she says, her smile undying and I'd like to believe it was me who put it there.

"Not like this. I mean, like, *vision* type dreams. Memories. I know I sound insane, but I know I'm right," I ramble, desperate for her to understand. "I think ... I think I can remember a life outside of the compound. *Before* PAAC."

She frowns. "That's impossible," she insists, "There isn't a life outside PAAC. It's just the compound. Always has been." I run my hands over my head, hearing my pulse in my head like a snare drum pounding along to a song.

"I know! I know it is! But, please, I swear I can remember," I blurt. "There was a woman with dark brown hair and she smelled like lemonade and sunshine and they were trying to take me away from her. We had this giant dog, like a cross between a mastiff and a great Dane or something. I think we called her Bailey and she loved to play fetch, although she never actually brought the stick back. She'd swim in the lake by our old house with the faded grey siding. There was a little girl, too. My little sister. She had blonde hair, like my dad. He was really tall like me and he liked to sing to make us feel better when we were sad even though he is actually really bad at it ..." I pause for air, scanning her face. I can't read her. "You don't believe me. Do you?"

She hesitates. I'm scared of her answer.

"I do believe you." She decides finally. I look up at her, feeling a little hope. "And that's what scares me."

That night, I didn't dream of the people I told Astrid about.

Instead, I dreamed of *her*.

We were back at the warehouse, but without all the dust and clutter. The window pane ceiling was the only thing separating us from the perfect blue sky with calm wisps of clouds floating past the beauty of the golden sun. The salty scent of the sea had turned into the sweet smell of the forests. It was entirely new, but entirely familiar at the same impossible time.

In this dream, I walked into the warehouse, seeing it completely empty with just Astrid standing in the very middle of it, alone. I smile, embracing how excited my heart is instead of trying to ignore it.

"Kole." She beams. She sounds like she's underwater. "I have something to tell you, too." She smiles and for the for the first time I allow myself to think of her not just as pretty. She's beautiful. And when she doesn't look like she wants to kill me, she might even be gorgeous.

"You do?" I say, coming closer. She nods, taking me into a hug. That should've been the first warning sign. Astrid doesn't give out hugs like that. She doesn't hug at all.

"Yeah," she whispers in my ear. I can feel her breath on my neck. "I wanted to tell you ..." She takes a step back, breaking our connection and I watch a shadow pass over her face. "That you, Kole, put us all in danger." Her mood changes and the light in her eyes is replaced with a cold, sadistic malice. She lands a hard, full fronted kick to the center of my chest. I feel it rattle my ribs and send echoing starbursts of pain clawing through my chest cavity.

I wake before I hit the ground, jolted back to real life with no warning. I put a hand to my head, rubbing my eyes before opening the sliding divider to enter the real world. My unit is already dressed and gone, so I follow suit, heading to the Beta training level for classes before I win myself a tardy.

The winding hallways are less of a maze with every step I travel through them. I walk through the pristine corridors in a slick uniform with a real sense of purpose on my shoulders. With our unit having fought its way to the top, my chest swells with pride at all the hard work we've put in.

But all that melts away when I see the familiar blonde hair, wild eyebrows, and sparkling eyes of the twins from the cliffside. A gaggle of younger trainees travel in an organized pack up the hallway. I stop them in their tracks. They halt without a word of complaint, waiting for me to make the next move.

"Uh, hi." I murmur to the twins. "How are you guys?"

"Okay, Sir." Their little voices answer in unison. I nodded a little.

Sir. I don't like that.

"Hey, listen. I am really sorry about your big brother, okay. So, so sorry." I say, then hesitate at their looks of confusion.

"Big brother?" The little girl squeaks in a high-pitched voice, reminding me of a chipmunk.

"We don't have a big brother. We aren't even related, Sir." The boy shakes his head. "It's just us."

I swear the sun fell out of the sky as I looked at the two kids. Just the other day, they were so heartbroken they did not have the strength to even speak and now they can't even remember the loss of what made them so devastated in the first place. What's worse, they can't even remember they are related, much less siblings. They really believe they are just kids who happen to be marching in the same line as everyone else. Like everyone else. Sirens echo in my head. Something isn't right. Something is horribly wrong.

Something is horribly wrong.

"Kole Danvers." The gruff voice of General Ryker makes me freeze. "Is this your first tardy, soldier?"

"Yes, Sir." I say, turning to look as his beady eyes narrowed to slits like those of a venomous snake. "Won't happen again, Sir."

"It better not, soldier. Now, get to your class. I assume you were expected there five minutes ago," he snarls. "Fallon won't be pleased."

"Yes, Sir. Sorry, Sir," I say, facing the siblings. They look up at me with such confusion, I don't doubt they have no idea what I was talking about. The sirens scream louder. Something is wrong. And it's Ryker's fault.

"Get going, son," he says, walking away in his locked, square-hipped way down the hall before taking a corner. I step aside to let the cloud of soon-to-be soldiers pass and I count to five in my head.

One.

The painful reek of antiseptic.

Two

Cold, white walls.

Three.

My mother's smile glowing in my dream. The shattered liquor bottles on the floor. Red wine droplets splashed on the walls. Crying.

Four

Real Astrid's smile. Her laugh. Her scent. Simply *her.*

Five.

Simply. *Her.*

I open my eyes and surge ahead, following Ryker's every step. He leads me, unknowingly, down a new corridor with a keycode access; I wouldn't be able to slip through if he hadn't an oddly flamboyant habit of flinging open every door he opened with gusto. I soft-toe it over the shiny tiles, following him like a cat burglar. I slip through another restricted-access door and flatten myself to the wall beside an interior window. I hear voices. Unfamiliar, but with Ryker's joining the choir.

"Hello, Doctor Mulhallen," Ryker says, his voice slightly muffled through the glass. "Certainly punctual, indeed."

There's another entry, but I don't dare go through it. I'm in deep enough.

"I'd rather have my time wasted sooner than later," a woman's voice says bluntly. I can't see her, but I imagine her as a shorter woman with eyes piercing with intelligence. The drifting scent of rose and vanilla on the air could only be her, unless Ryker had taken to smelling half decently in the past five minutes. "Wouldn't you agree ...?"

"Ryker, Doctor. General Ryker. And I would agree entirely."

"So, tell me, *General*," She says the word carefully, picking around it like it's a poisonous flower. "Your operation. Five-year-old, six-year-old children. Do you have to take them so young?"

"Ah, Professor Mulhallen, think of them as fine wines. There is a moment in which they are between the threshold of maximum delight and souring into vinegar. This is the age at which our programs are the most effective. We take the children from places people would never even know they're missing. It's a natural resource that the world willingly gives up. Orphans, troubled youths. All molded into the perfect, obedient soldiers. We have to edit a few things, granted, but that comes with the territory as I'm sure you understand. Harvesting the young—"

"Can we please refrain from using the term *harvest*, General Ryker? They are still human beings. Children even."

"My apologies, Doctor, but I hope you can see where I'm coming from?"

"Unfortunately." The woman sighs audibly. "How do you know your ... methods are effective?"

"The serum you mean?" Ryker.

"If that's how you do it, then yes. How does it function?"

I tense. She's asking all the right questions.

"It works as a coating, targeting all cells related to the specific memory and glossing them over with a stubborn solution so they cannot be absorbed by the brain. Rather than being recollected as a solid memory, the memory pieces just bounce off and the brain harvests no old information. It's the fastest and most secure way to pick and choose memories, should an incident ever occur."

"An incident, General?" Doctor Mulhallen delves into it. "What would that look like?"

"A defect." My blood chills. "In those cases, we erase the existing memories of the defect from the minds of the unit members and then replace the missing rank. Standard procedure."

"This has happened before, General? You can imagine I would regret investing in an unstable program."

"Only once or twice, I assure you. It's very rare that the serum doesn't take." I think of the file after file of terminations, they are not all that rare. "Nature tends to be stubborn if it isn't held with a tight rein. You see, the human brain is made to adapt. Engineered, if you will, to evolve. There are a few genetic anomalies that destroy the serum rather than embrace it, but they are easy to weed out from the others."

I take an instinctive step backwards, pushing harder against the wall. I can feel my face paling and my stomach turning while my mind races. My chest heaves, nostrils flare and I feel light headed.

"And the defects are disposed of properly?" Mulhallen asks.

"I see to it myself."

I turn to run, but don't see the cart being wheeled out in front of me. I slam into it, metal to flesh and vials crash to the floor in a mess of glass. I shove the cart out of the way and leap over the mess, bolting down the hallway and out the door. Passing the whiteboard in the general's staffing room on my hurried and frantic way out, an assemblance of five words was the only thing I took notice of.

Fire drill. Tomorrow 1:25 P.M.

———————

I don't follow Ryker's orders and I don't attend class. I make a beeline for the 9X dorm and lock myself in until the rest of my unit trickles in to find me. To both my pleasure and my disappointment, Astrid is the first one to come in. I rise from my chair quickly once I see her.

"Astrid!"

"Kole!" she accuses, narrowing her eyes. "What are you doing here? Beta training doesn't end for another half hour!"

"Trust me," I breathe, taking her shoulders. She watches me, the lights of confusion and concern playing together in her eyes. "Trust me, it's okay."

"Trust you about what, Kole?" she says. "Calm down before you say anything else."

"It's Ryker, the system, everything is corrupt!" I shout, feeling oddly excited because I was right. I was right about everything. "And I knew it! I *knew* it!"

"Hey, what's going on?" Allister, Maisie, and Colin travel through in their trio, in time to hear my outburst. "Jesus, Kole. You on something wack? What did you take?"

"Allister," Maisie scolds.

"Kole," Astrid warns, putting a gentle hand to my neck. "Focus. What are you talking about?"

"I overheard Ryker talking to an investor. Some ... Doctor Mulhallen." I swallow hard.

Colin's eyes light up. "Marylin Mulhallen?" he asks. "She's here?"

"Who is she?"

Colin snorts, like it's something really quite funny. "Not an investor. She's the high and mighty founder of Eva-Corp."

"What's Eva-Corp?"

"They run humanitarian missions all over the globe. Natural disaster clean-up, housing, water missions. If you can name it and it's for the good of people, they pretty much own the market. I'm surprised you've never heard of her. She's a huge name. And, honestly, I'm not surprised she'd be interested in PAAC, considering the work we do."

"Right. Okay." Astrid waves him down to silence again. "Carry on."

"They were talking PAAC operations, but they sound different through a general's perspective. We are not people to them, we're subjects. Lab rats. *Things*. They took us from our real homes and wiped our memories. They have been manipulating us ever since. They took all of our choices away from us and they clouded our vision and made us believe they were good!"

"How?" Allister pops a brow, folding his arms skeptically over his chest. I can see his brain working on the possibilities, though.

"He called it a serum. Like an injectable."

"Routine vaccinations." Maisie's face goes slack.

"What?"

"Before . . . when we were little . . ." Astrid mutters, looking around like she's waiting for something. "We would get routine vaccinations. Then . . . then they decided we were all . . ."

"Immune." Colin frowns.

I have hazy memories of different illness vaccines. Small pox, HPV. Ones you wouldn't question. But now I question everything. Astrid just shakes her head, trying hard not believe any of it.

"Kole. Listen to yourself! This is impossible!" Allister says, his joking nature all but gone.

"Is it?" I point at him. I look at Astrid. Her face is blank. She knows. "Can any one of you, other than Allister, remember anything before this compound? No? Because they took your memories and they aren't about to give them back! You remember those kids on the cliffside?"

"How could we forget, Kole." Maisie whispers, hugging herself.

"Okay. I ran into the brother and the sister this morning," I say and they all look like they're expecting some good news. I swallow hard, sorry to disappoint. "They don't even remember having a brother. They were standing right beside each other and didn't remember one another, either. PAAC destroyed all their memories with this serum and they're going to turn them into soldiers just like us. These kids are going to think that they are doing the right thing, because just like us, they know nothing else. *We know nothing else.*" My voice shakes and my heart shakes harder as I watch the faces of my comrades, my family, fall as they realize the truth. I know it's the horrible, terrible truth and there's nothing we can do about something that's already done.

It wasn't two seconds later that the calm Delta Allister Shepard has my shirt collar twisted tight in his clenched fist and my back against the wall.

"Why am I different?" he whispers, pain brimming in his eyes.

"I am too. It didn't work on us. I don't know why. It just didn't, but take it as a gift."

"I don't want to remember my past as a *gift*, Kole. It was a nightmare!" he growls. I take hold of his wrist, trying to get myself a little more oxygen. "We stole for them? We stole *children* for them? Just so they could have a few more soldiers for their army? A few more guns? And we didn't say anything?" His voice cracks and rises, while his eyes start to water. "We didn't even question ... that ... that what we were doing was wrong. *I* didn't even question it."

"It's not your fault," I whisper. "You didn't know."

"But I could have asked," he growls and for a moment, I think he is going to punch me, but then the fabric of my shirt slips from his fist and he takes a few wobbly steps back, before flopping down on a chair with his head in his hands. I reach out for Astrid's shoulder, feeling the cloth of her shirt under my fingertips.

"It's none of our faults," I say, looking around. "But it will be if we stand by and watch it happen. Someone has to stop it and we're the only ones left who want to stand against them. We have to stop Ryker."

"Right. But how do we do that?" Maisie asks, sitting on the arm of Allister's chair and holding his white-knuckled hand. She rubs circles on his shoulder as he stares at the ground. "There's only five of us and Ryker has access to every unit in the compound, and all its resources."

"But what if you go higher?"

"Higher?"

"There's gotta be someone higher up on the food chain than Ryker. There's always a bigger boss." I think out loud. "Always someone more powerful."

"Like the General of War, ranking higher than just General," Colin says. I point to him.

"Exactly."

"I'm on it." He slides into his computer desk, typing furiously.

"Kole, please, just listen to yourself," Astrid says and it's only then I realize I'm still hanging on to her shoulder. The moment I let go, I feel like a leaf shaking in the wind. "We can't go to war against the compound. The Rebellion had more resources and soldiers and even they couldn't do it. Look at us, Kole. We couldn't even keep three kids safe."

I shake my head. "We don't have to go to war. Not really. All we have to do is make one strong case and the whole program will shut down." She stares at me and I know she's judging me. I've seen that look so many times that if someone asked me to sketch it on a piece of paper, it would be uncanny. I watch her face, made completely of stone until she shakes her head ever so slightly.

"Kole Danvers," she says. "You are the craziest person I have ever met." She holds out her hand and I'd be lying if I said I didn't flinch a little, thinking she was going to hit me. I take her hand to shake and I can see the smirk trying to creep out at the corner of her mouth. "So, what's the plan. Before I change my mind."

Fire drill. Tomorrow 1:25 P.M.

"Alright. Here's what we're gonna do."

THIRTY-NINE

Getting the supplies was easy. The simple white lie of a training exercise and we were granted the ear pieces for communication. Colin had a ghost drive, untraceable and undetectable. All I had to do was copy and transfer the files. That night, the night before the day of the drill, Colin and I sat at his computer while he sorted through lines of code and computer demands that made my head spin. He looked for a way in, a digital map to ensure that we could hack into the system without being discovered, and having a way to tell if we were being followed or not.

"Alright," he says finally. "We're in. I can see heat signatures through the entire building."

"Good job, man," I say as the plan starts coming together.

Morning comes. We go about our regular training schedules and converge in our common room at 1 P.M. At the sound of the fire alarm, screaming through every speaker in the compound, I look at Astrid and wink. Except for Colin, we file out of the dorm, fighting the flow of the crowd. We branch off into an empty hallway. The plan is for Colin to keep us on the screen, guiding us through. We break off into partners, Allister and Maisie taking the corridor on the left while Astrid and I prowl to the right.

"Alright, Colin. We're a go," I whisper into the ear piece, trailing just behind Astrid as she scans every inch of the hallway.

"I can see you, copy to both groups. Keep going. You're alone." Colin's voice crackles only slightly.

"Lima Charlie." Maisie's voice joins the party.

We come down the hall silently, the ghost drive in my pocket feeling like a ten-pound weight. If this didn't work, PAAC would win. That would mean so many other kids would be forced into an unnatural life, like we were. I couldn't let that happen. This had to work.

The hallways we had chosen complete a circle, branching off from the main hall at equal points and slowly curving to meet at the control room where all the classified files are stored. The white walls drag on, feeling painfully familiar.

"What else do you remember? About your mom?" Astrid whispers, two fingers to her comm to disable it temporarily.

"Little things." I copy her trick, still looking around but moving faster now. This fire drill won't last forever and this is an odd time to ask about my memories.

"Like?"

"Uh ... she wore this necklace, a gold chain with a little cross for a pendant. Dad and I got it for her for Christmas one year."

"What else?"

"She never took off her wedding ring. No matter how bad things got. She never took it off once. She always insisted on making homemade birthday cakes instead of just getting a generic vanilla one from a bakery. Thought it tasted better homemade with love," I say softly.

"Did it?" she asks. I give her a confused look. "Taste better homemade?"

"Yeah," I say. "It did, but I could just be biased."

"I'll trust you not to be." She sighs as she speaks. "I've never actually celebrated my birthday. Here it's ... just another day."

"When is it?" Kole asks.

"August ninth." She smiles at me. "Yours?"

"November twenty-sixth," I exclaim. "We are almost twins!"

"That isn't even close!"

"Close enough."

"They're not close at all!" She laughs.

"Just roll with me here!" I grin. "I'm saying, when we get out, we'll have to celebrate them together." She smiles at me and I would be an absolute fool not to smile back.

It was a strange thing to talk about as we creep closer to the information we need to destroy this place, but it passes time quickly. I find it stranger still that something you would think so little of at the time is one of the things that you remember most. Like the exact way Mom would stand at the kitchen island and fuss over every little detail on one of her cakes until she was satisfied that it was good enough. She was talented, too. People came to her for a cake as often as they went to the bakery because when she made them, it made that birthday feel special.

Like driving with Dad when I was small, sitting on his lap and thinking I was doing all the work with my little hands on the wheel. It something that just the two of us shared. No mom, no little sister. Just us. Rolling along the dirt roads in summer with the windows rolled down, trying to make a windstorm in the cab, and thinking that the road would never end. *Praying* that the road would never end. Dirt roads and barbed wire fences all around as roadblocks. Rare patches of pavement. There were days in the compound when I wished I was a normal Beta, obedient and oblivious. But only when the pain of everything I didn't want to remember came back. Not today. Today I wouldn't change a thing about what I remember and what I have forgotten. I'm lucky in a sense. At least I know who I am.

"Kole?" I hear, snapping me from my thoughts. "Are you there?" Colin talks in my ear. Astrid waves her hand in front of my face.

"He's here," she says.

"Kole and Astrid, one more little corner in the hallway and you'll see a door. Allister and Maisie have other people on their tail and need to peel off to hide. You'll need to move fast if this is going to work."

"Got it," I say and we run the rest of the hall. Colin is right, but the door comes sooner than I had expected, ending our sprint in an abrupt halt. I place a hand on the door and the entire place drowns in darkness. Then emergency lights begin to flash red.

"Colin?" Astrid asks, a strain to her voice. My eyes adjust from the constant change from darkness, to red hue, to darkness, to red . . .

"Looks like they're practicing all protocols today."

"Yeah? What's this one?" I grit my teeth, anxiety building and threatening to landslide.

"Lock down drill. Keep going."

And we do, pushing open the door. A figure with his back to us makes my heart plummet to my stomach. He's standing at the computer, typing furiously on the key board, his work appearing on the large overhead screen fastened to the wall. He's *deleting* all the files we need.

"Hey!" I call and the man turns around. I am staring into the stone-cold face of General Ryker. "What are you doing?" The light flashes off his face, illuminating every white line and scar. The unmistakable dull glint in his eye appears and disappears. Did he catch wind of what we were going to do? Why would he have a reason to erase vital PAAC files? He should be running fire drills and lock down protocols with everyone else.

"You don't understand this, kid! You don't understand anything about it! Get back to your dorm!" he growls throatily. For a moment, I am afraid of him. He looks wild and ragged like some kind of wild beast that escaped the zoo. "I mean it! Get out of here!"

Astrid pulls up her fists, moving in quickly. She gets around him, being smaller and more agile, kicking him in the side and sending him lurching my way. I drive a punch into his kidneys with a grunt of effort, this time hitting to injure. Ryker drops to a knee, pain written all over his face and Astrid pulls the hair tie from her braid before forcing Ryker's hands back and securing him expertly.

The struggle is short and I am glad. I suspect the only reason we got him down was because he wasn't prepared for us to actually confront him. To actually attack. Even in those few minutes, we violated so many rules, our ranks would be stripped from us and we would be left at the bottom. But those ranks mean nothing to me now. Once, they certainly did. Now, I couldn't care less.

I jam the ghost drive into the USB port while Astrid keeps General Ryker restrained. Even without the files Ryker deleted, there are still thousands and thousands of icons and folders to sift through.

"Colin. How much time do we have?" I say, breaking radio silence.

"Uh …" I hear furious typing on the other end. "Maybe five minutes or so."

"Great," I growl under my breath.

"What's going on?" Allister breaks in.

"There are too many files to sort through and not enough time. I'm bringing them all," I explain hurriedly, searching for a 'select all' option.

"Whatever you are doing, Kole, do it fast. You got company coming your way. The heat signatures in the hallway are off the charts."

Great.

The pressure makes me shake and I start to make mistakes, delaying the finicky process even more.

"Kole!"

"Don't yell at me! You're freaking me out!"

"Kole!"

"Dude!"

"They are right on top of you! Get out of there! Now! You have a limited window! Take it now! Forget the files."

"No. If we don't get these files, we have nothing against them. We need them," I insist desperately. "Astrid, watch the doors." I point across the room. Her face is tight, but she nods anyway and takes the orders, even if they are from a Beta. I'd be lying if I said I didn't feel good about it. I turn back to the screens.

"Where do we go, Colin. Which hallway is the least crowded?" A burst of empty static. I freeze, putting my hand to my ear.

"Colin?" I beckon, looking at Astrid. Her face goes slack. "Colin, Colin. Come in, Colin."

"You don't understand anything!" Ryker howls again from his spot on the floor. Astrid pulls his shoulders back and he winces. I wheel on him.

"Stop *saying* that! What don't we understand?" I shout. "We don't understand that you are a murderer? That you're stealing kids to put in this great army? Brainwashing them? Taking their memories? Their entire *identities*?"

"There is more at play than just that," he says. Astrid tweaks his wrist from behind his back. I can tell from the contortion of pain on his face.

"Spill," she whispers calmly.

"PAAC was corrupt from the beginning," Ryker groans. "I didn't realize how bad it was until I got higher clearance and was allowed into the labs. I couldn't do anything against the doctors and officers when it came to the creation of the units, but when Fallon started ordering the termination of defects ..." He shakes his head at the ground before looking at me, pinning me down with a harsh gaze. "The only reason you're still here is because I deleted all your damaged files and replaced them with acceptable data."

I frown, confused.

"What?"

"Your examinations, the mental one specifically. If Fallon would have seen the real results, that you were resistant to the memory protocol, you would've been terminated on the spot, and all your friends' memories of your existence would've been wiped within the hour."

"Those vaccinations weren't really vaccinations," I say, my voice shaking. "Were they?"

"No. They weren't. Disguised mRNA serum, to interrupt your past memories and freeze them. As your cells reproduced, your new DNA kept past memories at bay. It's the easiest way to administer them on a mass level without raising questions about what the injections were for."

"And what about—"

"Jackson Alexander?" he asks. I go to stone. He supresses a grin. "Yeah, I know you found him in the files that night in the Gamma labs. I also know you found him alive. Jackson was caught in his exams, like you would've been if I hadn't intervened first. Fallon took him, thinking he got rid of him and then administered another vaccine to anyone with significant contact with him. Your girlfriend here . . . well, let's just say she wasn't always your girlfriend."

I look at her. She looks at me. I already knew, but I was trying to forget. Astrid's eyes hold more conflict than I've ever seen. I'm not even mad that at one point she was interested in someone other than me. I'm mad that they would take him away from her.

"Sick. I know," Ryker says softly, something not in his nature. "And it'll only get worse as time goes on. He'll make more allies and new technological advancements."

"You said Fallon thought he got rid of Alexander ... what do you mean?"

"I helped him escape. And others. Jackson Alexander, Peter Tarek. Someone named Alice and another named Sky. I assume you've met some of them. I can't count how many I have helped get out," he says, watching me.

"How did you do it without getting caught?"

"I had to be stern and gruff and cruel to fit in with Fallon's posse. I wanted the killing to end. All the challenges like the Tournament of Valor and the exams. Everything is designed to expose the defects. To weed them out from the rest. One big game of cat and mouse. All they have to do is sit and wait. All they have to do is watch for the signs."

"Why do I remember him?" Astrid asks.

"Remember who?"

"Jackson Alexander."

Ryker sighs. "Because I knew that would have been one of the worst things PAAC had ever done. Your entire unit remembers him because of a placebo. I switched out the memory wipe with a harmless solution. Essentially, you forgot him on your own. I've tried hard to bring PAAC down, but it's impossible to even get them on their knees. It's a futile effort, really. It'll continue to go on."

"No," I say finally. "It won't. We're going to stop this. We're going to stop all of this." I put a hand to my ear, trying to sort through an incoming burst of static. "Dammit, Colin! Get this under control!"

"I've been . . . leave . . . base . . . compromised!" His mangled words come in between the attacks of static that scrape on the inside of my skull, worming their way in through my ear holes. Distant shouts and yelling act as background music and my hair stands on end as the door on the other side of the room flies open, letting uniformed men spill in. One holds Maisie with just a simple twist of her arm. She's bleeding and her entire left shirt sleeve has been ripped from the shoulder seem. It takes two men to hold Allister, one on each arm and he still struggles against them. He's bleeding, a steady line coming from his split lip and more bleeding from an oozing gash on his forehead. Even though they have been caught, they didn't come easily. But, it's not the rough state of my comrades that make my stomach tie itself in a knot. It's the last man through the doorway.

"General Fallon." Astrid stands straight up to face him.

"Wonderful work, 9X," he says, the words rolling from the tongue of the beast. "I'll take it from here." The lights flash again and it's the first time I notice the pistol clenched in his white-knuckled fist. For a man of such masculinity, the weapon looks strange and unnatural in his hand. I move slowly, swiping the ghost drive from the port and slipping it back in my pocket, unsure of how much data I have in my hands.

"Kole, son, why don't you move away from the circuit board and join your friends over there?" Fallon says, trying for a calm demeanour. But I can see it crumbling like a sand castle being ripped apart by the surf. I set my jaw and stand fast, clenching my fists. Fallon's gun hand shakes in silent rage.

"I'm sorry, Sir," I say, doing a better job at staying calm than he is. "I can't do that."

"Do as I say, boy. I don't want to make a mess." He warns venomously. "Blood stains are tricky to get out after they set in." I swallow hard, staring down the barrel of the gun. I slowly raise my hands in surrender, but move in no other way.

"I'm sorry, Sir," I say.

"No, Kole! Fight!" Ryker shouts from the floor, Astrid crouches beside him with an officer's hand on the back of her neck. That makes me angry. He shouldn't be touching her. Fallon turns and for an earthshattering moment, the clap of thunder from the gun is the only thing I can hear. My ears ring, I selfishly scan over every inch of Astrid, searching for the bullet wound before recognizing the blooming flower of blood in the very center of Ryker's chest. The reek of burnt gunpowder hangs in the air like a choking cloud, then begins to mingle with the unmistakably coppery metallic scent of blood.

He shot him.

Astrid springs forward, pressing a palm to the man's chest while struggling against the officer holding her back.

"You're crazy!" she shouts at Fallon, whose eyes make me leery of what he'll do next.

He enjoyed that.

Of course he did. He's been waiting to do it for years.

Of course, he has.

"You sick, twisted man!" she screams. I couldn't have said it better myself. Trails of blood ooze out between her fingers, staining her hands and skin the same daunting colour as the flashing lights, still playing their part in the confusion. Her face wrinkles like she's about to cry and I watch the rare tears fall from her cheeks under the breath of a light sob. Ryker died somewhere between the flashing lights and the ragged breaths and I couldn't help but think he was one of the lucky ones.

"Now," Fallon pants. "I trust you all will come quietly?"

"Not on your life," Allister snarls and receives a heavy blow to the gut from one of the other soldiers, folding him at the middle.

"Alpha?" Fallon cocks his head at Astrid. She stands slowly, staring at him dead on. "Isn't it your job to command your unit? Or should I call you in to the council for treason as well?" The late general's blood drips from her knuckles and I get the feeling it's not the last red I'll see today.

"Go ahead. It won't do you any good, General."

"Why's that, sweetheart?"

"I'm not the Alpha anymore," she says, looking me in the eye. "Not really."

Fallon sighs. "Alright then." He pulls his gun up again and it's like time slows down right before my eyes. The roar of the pulled trigger competes with the blood rushing in my head and I imagine the bullet traveling through the air, carving its path towards me. Out of the corner of my vision, I watch Maisie wrench her arm free and dodge the outstretched arms trying to grab her. She dives, hitting the ground, painting the floor with a scarlet streak as she slides across the tile. I put a foot on either side of her, guarding the Omega from Fallon as Astrid slides to Maisie's side and turns her on her back.

"Maisie," she says quickly, pressing her hands in CPR fashion to Maisie's abdomen as the petite girl sucks in a fast breath. Astrid's voice is breathy and shaking. I know it's bad. "Maisie, hold on. It's okay. You're okay."

"How *insistent* are you that all your friends die before you?" Fallon snarls at me, still hiding behind his gun. "How *desperate* are you to be the hero of this story that you'll let every single one of them die for you? You are the only defect! This carnage is unnecessary. C'mon, Kole! What are you doing? You could save them! You could save them all!" He licks the sweat off his top lip. I freeze.

He doesn't know about Allister.

Let's keep it that way.

"Can you help her?" I ask.

"There is still plenty of time for her, my boy."

"If you help her . . . " I tremble everywhere. "If you help Maisie, I'll go with you."

"Deal," Fallon says, snapping his fingers and his men surge forwards. "I'm so glad you finally came to your daft senses, Kole. You're *learning*. I am so proud." They take my wrists and pin them to the flat of my back and force me out of the room.

I fight to make sure they don't anyone else. "Take me last. Take me last, or I won't go." Fallon looks at me and sighs, wiping his brow.

"You are in no position to edit the deal, Kole. Give it up." He grins. The officers stoop to collect Astrid in the same fashion, but she fights to stay with her Omega. They practically lift her off the ground and force her to her feet, shoving her out the door after me. She never stops struggling.

The last vision I have of the 9X Omega was her pale face and blue lips, lying on her back with the bloodied fabric of her shirt clinging to her stomach. It was terrifying.

FORTY

The room is white with a single table, also white, and two chairs at either end. One side had two straps built into the surface. It takes only five seconds for the officers to push me into the chair and secure my wrists to the table. The table is so shiny and perfectly glossed that I can see my reflection staring back at me. Wide bags under my eyes, alive with ghosts. One eye is bloodshot and ringed with abraded skin from when the guard purposely shoved me hard into a corner on the way here. My hair is ragged and disheveled. My lips are dry and cracked, bits of dried blood on my chin and under my nose like a craggy river. My head feels like it is stuffed with cotton, but I have never had clearer thoughts in my life. I have never had a clearer idea of what I was supposed to do. How I was supposed to do it.

I had to kill Fallon. I had to kill the man sitting across from me.

"Well, Kole," he says like the classic old Fallon, tricking everyone with a trustworthy smile and that feel-good sympathy. "I never would have imagined in a million years that we would be sitting here in such a ... situation."

"How's Maisie?"

"Expected to make a full recovery. Thanks to your bent pride," he says with a kind smile. The kindness feels like the flat side of a knife on my throat. Dancing dangerously close to the cutting edge, now that I've seen his true colours. He sighs. "This isn't easy for me either, Kole. Please try to understand that."

"It's not?" I say, feigning surprise. I know he's lying. That's all he does.

"Of course, it's not. You were like a son to me, Kole."

I slam my fists on the table with what little movement I'm allowed and enjoy seeing him jump. "Don't compare me to family," I hiss. "I have one. One that I'm going to find and go back to. One that you *took* from me."

"Kole. I know your situation. Don't lie to yourself. You don't want to go back. You are better off staying here with us. It's easier that way."

"Easy?" I snarl. "What about any of this is easy?"

"I can see that you are angry, but the time for anger has passed," he says, folding his hands on the table in front of him. I wonder what he sees in the reflection. A hero? A monster? Maybe the perfect mashup of both. Or does he even care enough to look? "I have questions for you to answer and it would be in your best interest to do so, quickly, and honestly. Not to mention Maisie's. The plug is still pullable, you know. How much do you know?"

"I know one plus one is two. Two plus two is four," I say blandly.

"Maisie," he warns. I draw my lips tight.

"Alphabetically or chronologically?" I toss my head.

"Whichever way you prefer." I watch the vein pulsate in his forehead.

"I know the truth," I say and he narrows his eyes.

"Do tell."

"I know about the vaccinations, what they do and how they work. How you are manipulating the mRNA and DNA of your soldiers. I know about the kidnapping, child soldiers, manipulations. The thousands of terminations. I know you are hunting defects. I know enough to destroy the entire operation," I threaten, my voice level and challenging. He nods to himself before standing up and making his way to the door.

"Your intellect never ceases to surprise to me, Kole. Truly. But, of course, in order to quote," he sneers, drawing quote marks in the air, "destroy the operation ... you'll have to tell someone first. And here? In this room? I see no one viable to tell." He smiles wickedly at me. "I'll have you know your entire unit has been cleared for termination. You have until tomorrow evening. Sleep well, Beta. Oh, and . . . operation ..." he says, once more drawing in the air, "is not the correct word."

"Oh?"

"No. I think the term *empire* suits us much better. Don't you?"

The sound of the door closing was louder than a gunshot.

——————

The second time they sent me a visitor, it was a bittersweetly familiar face.

"Hello, Kole," Myrka greets me, her hands folded in front of her. She wears the usual black sleeveless turtleneck and slim fit pants, the PAAC emblem on the right breast pocket. Her long, raven-black hair is pulled into a tight ponytail and her eyes are sad.

"Myrka. It's good to see you," I say, nodding a little to be polite. "How's training?"

"We begin our basic leadership courses tomorrow. They're supposed to be pretty fun," she admits, looking everywhere but my eyes.

"Did Fallon send you?" I ask, thinking about how I'll be erased from her memory by tomorrow's sunrise. Why are they making her suffer like this? She has nothing to do with anything.

He knows it hurts. He's just kicking you while you're down.

"He did," she nods weakly, tears welling up in her eyes. "He thought it would be best if a friend broke the news."

"What news, Myrka? What happened?"

"It's Maisie," she whispers and my heart plummets into my stomach. "She's gone."

"When?" I clear my throat, trying to shake off the constricted feeling that comes from crying.

"Last night." She dabs at the salty water droplets on her cheek. Her voice is tight. "They said she didn't feel any pain with all the morphine and everything."

"Was she alone?"

"I'm so sorry, Kole."

"Was she alone?" I insist a little harsher than I mean to. Myrka pauses and looks to the tiling between her combat boots.

"Yes. Yes, she was alone."

"I should have been there," I say bitterly, clenching and unclenching my fists. "At least to make sure she wasn't afraid."

"Kole ..." Myrka comes forwards and puts a hand on my shoulder. "We both know Maisie wasn't really afraid of anything."

"Everyone's afraid of something."

Myrka stands for a moment, her eyes misting ever so slightly. She looks like she wants to say something more, but an invisible tether stops her. Fallon is playing one hell of a hard game.

"I should go," she whispers, barely loud enough for me to hear. I nod numbly. "I'm sorry, Kole. I really am."

"I know."

A single tear falls and leaves a glistening puddle on the floor the size of a dime. I watch the light play in it as she opens the door and exits, leaving me alone with my monstrous thoughts. They chase each other, making so much white noise it begins to sound like a thundering parade, making my head throb. But one thought is louder than the others; a chanting anthem telling me it's all Fallon's fault. The pounding belief doesn't falter or quiet in the slightest. I wish it would stop. But Fallon started this. He started it when he began hunting defects and eliminating anyone outside his margins of perfection. Anyone who is different.

But Unit 9X isn't different. It's just me.

And Allister.

No one discovered him when Jackson was caught. He would have been fine.

He would have been fine if I hadn't shown up.

I put my head in my hands. I should have made sure to only bargain myself, not the whole unit. They could have continued living. *Maisie* would still be smiling and laughing.

Or would she? Would there be any possible way that they would remember all of this, or even any of it any of it? Maybe they would get little glimpses and scattered fragments in dreams like I do, but would they recognize what they are seeing? Without Ryker around to administer a placebo, would PAAC wipe their memories entirely? Thinking about all these "what ifs" and "maybes" is just wasting time.

Seconds pass into minutes and minutes crawl into hours. Before I know it, two stone-faced officers stand in the light of the door frame, the PAAC emblem glowing against the black of their uniforms. I can see their holsters are full, meaning they are armed and prepared for a confrontation. Of course, they would be. Fallon forgets nothing.

"It's time," one says, without emotion. Once I stand, they unshackle my wrists from the table. They bind my hands, but in front of me this time, probably because I don't struggle. They know a broken spirit when they see one. Their hands come down on my shoulders and they escort me down the pristine hallway to the lab doors at the end.

As I walk, I think of everything and everyone that has led to this moment. Astrid and Allister. Maisie, Colin. Willow, Ben and Liza at Secura. The confrontation with Sebastián Russo and how pretty Astrid looked in that lavender dress. Then, how scary she was after she pulled that trigger to kill for the first time. I think about Sky and Alice, Jackson, and Peter at the Red Rebellion. The famous C_2N_{14} that looked like powdered rubies floating like lethal flakes of glittering red snow from the sky. The mapping job in the old barn and Astrid's training lessons. The pavilion and Alice's little wooden science lab for concocting explosives. A smile slips out just for a moment.

We walk in silence until the echo of a gunshot rings out, crisp and short. For a moment, I think it's in my head. A flash of another memory from the day before, but I know it's happening in real time when one of the officers flinches and pulls out his own pistol. The other slumps against the wall, leaving a streak of red on the paint.

I take the situation as an opportunity, kicking out the back of the standing officer's knees and swinging my bound hands like a mallet. I feel the crackling of cartilage and the warm spurt of blood as the back of my hand connects with his nose. He groans and falls to the floor, putting a hand to his face and curling into the fetal position.

My face splits into a crazed smile when Allister and Colin jog out from behind a corner, Allister holding the pistol.

"Jesus, Kole," Allister snorts. "You look awful."

"Yeah, well, it wasn't exactly a five-star stay." I grunt as Colin slips the restraints from my wrists. I shake out that pinched feeling before taking a full holster that Allister hands me and strapping it to my thigh. The weight feels almost comfortable and a new sense of security washes over me like a fresh thunderstorm in a drought and I drink it in.

"I'm gonna leave a complaint at the office." Allister grins idiotically.

"Besides," I flick my head at the two. "You guys don't look so hot, either." Colin's usually combed hair is wild and he has dark bags under his eyes. His hands shake like an old man's and he looks around nervously. He's got a split lip and he's favouring his left leg. Allister has a black eye and bruises all over his face. Slashes and trails of blood on his forehead, shoulders, and neck. A wild look to his eyes like he just got off a thrill ride at a carnival. Their clothes are ripped and wrinkled and all three of us stand barefoot in the hallway, the cold tiles warming under the soles of our feet. The guards had taken our socks and shoes when we were detained in case we had any concealed weapons. Besides the rugged looks and their obvious exhaustion etched into every line of their faces, I was happier to see them than I had ever been.

"Where's Astrid?" I ask, my smile quickly fading.

"They took her first," Colin says. "You could hear her kicking and screaming all the way down the hallway. Kole, I'm sorry to tell you, but Maisie—"

"I know." I cut him off, swallowing hard. "Fallon sent a distraction in to tell me."

The sound of smashing glass and pained screaming comes from behind the lab doors.

"There's our girl." Allister grins. A round of gunfire makes my blood rush even louder and Allister quickly puts a hand to my shoulder. Without another word, another glance, another breath even, the three of us bolt down the hall toward the struggle. On entrance, it's chaos. Gurneys and tables are overturned, the lights are shot out. Paper and glass litter the floor and I can feel little shards underfoot. Bullets fly from one side and pierce the wall beyond, leaving little smoking holes in the drywall. I catch a flash of white hair from behind a table and duck, moving quickly and sliding in beside Astrid. She is hiding from the gunfire, using an overturned table as a shield.

"Well, it's about time," she mumbles as Allister and Colin clumsily slide in beside us. "What took you guys so long?"

"Colin couldn't get his makeup right." Allister grins. Colin backhands him on the shoulder. "Just be happy we're here, princess," he says, and gives her shoulder a light squeeze. "So, what's the plan? We can't hide out here forever."

The labs have two doors, one on either side, both opening up to staircases that lead to the Delta flight training school and then to the helipad on the roof. I inch over to the side of the table, as close as I dare, and fire a few bullets. The shooting quiets for a moment, as our opponents realize we can hit them too, before it starts back up again like a choir of death.

"Okay," I say. "Here's what we do. Allister and Colin get to the helipad and fire up a chopper. We can get out that way."

"I'll fly." Allister's hand shoots into the air. "I volunteer."

"We're all gonna die," Astrid taunts.

"Nah, sister." Allister grins. "I was top of the class in the flight portion of Delta training. I got this. And if we do crash, it'll be the most epic, glorious way to go out in all of history."

"Ah. Right. Now I'm reassured."

"You're welcome."

"Guys," Colin hisses. "We're literally under heavy fire. Focus."

"Right, sorry, man. Kole, continue, bro."

"We can't all get out at once, we will have no fall back. You guys go first, Astrid and I will stay here. We'll destroy the lab and get out on the other staircase. Wait for us. We'll meet on you on the helipad," I say, wincing at the disarray of the plan. "Okay. Go!" I yell and Allister and Colin disappear up the closest stairwell as Astrid and I pop up over the table and open fire.

"This is a horrible plan!" Astrid yells, gritting her teeth but still firing off rounds.

"I know! I was just trying to make sure they got out! I'm sorry!" I call back.

"Don't be! I love it!"

A racing heat stings my shoulder and I drop behind the table again, afraid that I've been hit. Astrid follows me, inspecting the little gathering of blood on the shirt.

"Just a graze," she says finally. "We have to move. They have a lot more ammunition than us. They can sit over there and fight all day long. We don't have time for that."

"No. We don't."

"So, now what, Hero? We run for it?" she says with a little shake of her head, a little smile playing on her lips. For a moment, I can't hear the gunfire anymore.

"We'll die." I raise a brow. "We'll sneak around, use the tables as cover. We have to get to the stairwell for this to work. Otherwise, they'll be able to see our tactic and cut us off at the helipad. Or at the top of the stairs, whichever comes first."

"You mean the stairs right beside them?"

"That's the one."

"This is dumb. Like, really, really dumb."

"I know."

"We really are going to die. Like, for real this time."

"I know."

"But we don't really have any other options."

"I know."

She sighs, shaking her head. "Okay. On your count."

"Three," I say, skipping over one and two. We get up and move, firing rounds over the edges of the overturned tables in an attempt to drive them back, but they keep firing at us. I slide in behind another, closer table, getting a better angle and taking down three of the seven officers closest to the stairwell entry. Astrid pulls in front of me, picking off two more. We move like we're playing a game of leapfrog. We make ground faster than I had expected.

The last gunman drops to a knee and we make a break for it, hitting the stairs and climbing as fast as possible.

When we make it to the top of the stairwell and to the Delta flight training classroom, a single shot rings out. Astrid falls forwards and hits the ground quickly behind a double-faced bookshelf. She clamps a hand to her side.

"Ahhh," she hisses, sucking in a breath.

"You're hit?"

"Yeah."

"Come on out, Kole," Fallon calls, sounding as ragged as we look. "You know she's wounded. Leave her and come out."

"We have to get you out of here," I whisper, putting a hand on her leg and turning, peering at Fallon through the cracks in the book spines. He's starting to move around the desks. "Can you run?"

"Probably," she says grimacing. "But I'm not going to leave you if that's what you're trying to say."

"Astrid, please," I beg, desperate to at least save her.

"Forget about it."

"If I cover you, can you get to the door and to the helipad? There should be medical supplies in the chopper."

"I can get there, yeah, but what about you?" She shakes her head. "I can't just leave you here with him. He's gonna kill you."

"You'll have to."

"You're kidding, right?" she hisses at me, eyes flashing. "Kole. Did you hear me? He's going to kill you."

"Not if I get him first." I raise a brow. Her hands grab my shirt collar and brings my face close to hers. She looks angry.

"This is not the time to be the hero," she growls. "New plan."

"Alright. I'll cover you while you get to the door. I'll backtrack and take the long way around through the compound. You guys bring the chopper around and meet me on the north side."

"That's better," she says and closes the distance, her kissing me this time instead of me kissing her. When she pulls away, everything is in HD and I feel like I could run a marathon. "Ready?" she asks, struggling to her feet. I help her up and nod. In sync, I come around the edge of the bookcase and taunt Fallon into a firefight as Astrid's shadow dashes past the floor. She gets to the stairs before my clip runs dry. I throw my gun at the twisted man and dive back behind the bookcase before covering my head and tearing back down the stairs. The sounds of his thundering footsteps coming after encourages me to go faster.

My chest screams with every panting breath and I throw my shoulder into the revolving lab doors and sprint down the hall, hanging a sharp left to follow my way to the north stair systems. I can still smell Astrid's smoky sweet scent lingering in the back of my nose and I smile crazily before I make another run.

We might actually make it.

I might actually make it.

Eventually, I'm sure I've lost him and slow to a run rather than an all-out mad dash, before entering the north side and climbing a flight of stairs. When I reach to push open the door at the top, it opens for me, revealing the flaming mouth of a monstrous inferno chewing up the room beyond. The pressure builds and the flames erupt through the doorway in a massive explosion, shoving me down the stairs hard. I roll and stagger to my feet, cradling my midsection as the flames leap down the stairs, following me like little red demons. I take a new turn and land in the control room, the place still trashed from the earlier fight that had led to Ryker's death.

I fall behind the counter despite my efforts to stay on my feet, exhaustion taking over. I cough into my fist and watch the scarlet dance with the saliva in my palm.

"Great," I rasp, watching the colours play together. The rusty taste of the blood infects my mouth, thick and choking.

I'm hurt.

I'm hurt bad.

The sound of feet on the stairs makes me jump. Heavy footsteps come in time with my heartbeat and I wipe my hands on my pants, swallowing down the taste of copper and biting back the craving to retch.

"I know you're here," Fallon's whisper precedes him into the room. Only his voice and the crackling of the fire can be heard. "Come on out."

I notice a little black sphere with a shiny metal pin on the ground. A handheld. Ryker or one of Fallon's team must have dropped it in the earlier fight. The pin was still in the safety lever. I wipe the blood from my lips and crawl onto my stomach, reaching for the device.

"I'm impressed, really." Fallon chuckles a little. "You stayed undetected for a long time. If we weren't on opposite sides of the coin, I'd even be proud." I stretch as far as physically possible, ignoring the screaming of my injuries and the blood dripping off my lips as I grit my teeth and try harder.

"But I guess you can't take all the credit for your escapes, can you?" Fallon continues as my fingers graze the pin. "How long were you conspiring with our dear General Ryker, rest his precious soul? How long did he foster you under his wing? Or did you even know? That seems to be a recurring theme. Your . . . blissful ignorance."

I snatch the pin from the little handheld and lob it across the room just as Fallon rounds the corner of the counter and aims the barrel of his gun between my eyes. He sways slightly, a smile curling on his lips from sick, joyous pride and he cocks his head.

"Well. I'm sure you and Ryker will be seeing each other very soon," he says and I slump backwards, pulling my hand out in front of me and brandishing the silver lynch pin hanging off my middle finger.

"Will we?" I pant with more breath than voice and the room erupts in a fiery chaos.

The next thing I remember, my ears are ringing.

They ring so horribly that I slam my palms to my head in a desperate attempt to stem the noise. The steady scream makes me groan. But I am alive, probably dying, but still alive at the moment. I prop myself up on my elbows and army crawl through the mess of glass and debris to the door. I prop it open and take the stairs on my hands and knees, coughing and hacking. I manage to stand and stagger through the door at the top of the stairs, the red exit sign glaring at me in the emergency light. The building would have long been evacuated by now.

Nudging the door open with my shoulder, I take a deep drink of the chilled night air as it whispers over my sweaty skin. It tousles my hair and makes it hard to walk in a straight line on my weak, wobbling legs. I've made it to the helipad, but the sight of the empty roof makes my heart drop. There's no helicopter in sight and if one was coming, I should be able to hear the rotary blades churning the clouds that float past the blinking stars.

The door slams open behind me. I turn to see the relentless husk of a man, his skin marbled with the colours of burnt flesh ranging from medium rare to very well done. His clothes are singed and blackened and there's a heavy limp to his step. When he speaks, his voice is throaty and desperate. Rough and gravelly.

"You think you are *so. Clever?*" he growls. "Don't you?"

I turn back around. He's got me cornered.

Trapped.

"There is nowhere, *nowhere*, to go!" he cries, confirming my thoughts. The heat from the fire on the floor below makes the roof beneath me shudder. Soon, this whole thing is coming down. I can hear the flames roaring and the support beams warping and bending. All the noises are deafening. Then, all at once, the noise is overtaken by the sharp crack of splitting concrete and a fracture line appears only yards ahead of me. My breath hitches and I stumble toward it before the fracture turns into a chasm. It's my only chance of escape. I have to cross it.

What are you going to do when you get across?

Let's see when I get there.

The flames reach upwards and the fire is growing alarmingly fast. I transform my stumbling into a stiff-legged run before pitching myself across the slash. I feel my knees give out, buckling, and I fall hard on the other side just as the face of a helicopter breaks through the clouds. I smile a little, putting my head down with my forehead on the concrete. I feel a little safer, finally, like maybe we will make it after all.

A heavy thump hits the ground and hands grapple at my ankles. I turn quickly, seeing Fallon's scarred face only for a moment before he is ripped away. I watch him and a flash of white hair tumble a few feet away before I put my head back on the concrete, feeling exhaustion take over in turbulent waves. Through the pulsating starbursts of pain racing through my head, I can make out the struggle. Astrid and General Fallon fight in a whirlwind of maneuvers like only two soldiers can. Parrying and striking, evading, and blocking only to reset and try again and again. Finally, Astrid makes her move in a series of kicks to the chest, forcing him backwards and closer to the edge with every hit. He stands on the edge, balancing desperately and trying not to fall.

"You won't kill me," I hear him say. "I raised you. I'm practically your father!"

A lingering bout of silence.

"Be careful who you trust, General Fallon. Salt and sugar look the same," she growls, hostility curling off her lips. I pick myself up, holding the back of my hand to my bleeding lips just in time to see Astrid pull her elbow back and drive her fist straight into Fallon's nose, setting off a crackling of cartilage. He stumbles backwards before disappearing over the edge, falling prey to the flames.

The building begins to shriek and shudder and the supports weaken ominously.

"Astrid!" I call out, now on my feet. "Come on! We don't have much time!" She stands absolutely still, transfixed by the flames. Not even the howling wind can make her sway as she watches the smoke curl into the black air in wispy breaths. "Astrid! Let's go!"

She turns around, catching me off guard with the ghosts of tears in her eyes.

"Go without me!" she yells over the wind.

"What? No! There's nothing left for you here!"

"I can't leave! I don't belong anywhere else!" she says, her chest heaving, desperation sticking to every word. I move to her, taking her shoulders in my hands and feeling her shaking.

"Astrid, if there's anywhere you don't belong, it's here. They aren't your family. This isn't your home. They took you away from that. They took away your everything. They turned you into something you were never meant to be."

"But . . . I don't know anything else." I could see the game of tug-of-war raging behind her eyes. I smile softly, trying to chip away at her fears. "Everything I've worked for, built, made, done. It's all . . ." She looks back at the fissure. "It's all on fire," she whispers.

"So, we'll start over. Build and make new things. A new life."

"Kole—"

"Astrid. We have to move. Please."

She turns and regains control of herself, squaring her shoulders. We board the helicopter with Allister in the pilot's seat and fly away from the inferno, into the complete wilderness of the world we know nothing about. I watch the flames lick the sky before I fall away into nothingness.

"Kole." A soft hand on my arm wakes me up. I open my eyes and my head feels like it's been stuffed with cotton. When I try to sit up, I feel like tendrils of electricity are curling through my abdomen. I put a hand to it. "Hey. How do you feel?" Astrid's face appears in the haze. The daylight streaming through the windows is strange compared to the darkness of last night. It already feels like it was eons ago.

"Like I got hit by a bus," I mumble. My lips barely work.

"Well, you're still breathing," Allister puts a hand on my knee. "Glad to see you made it. Welcome back, sleeping beauty."

"Where are we?" I ask, propping myself up with my elbow and looking out the open door at the field of green with little clusters of trees here and there. A patchwork quilt of fields held together with seams of barbed wire fences.

"Home," Astrid says and I look at her. She's smiling wider than I've ever seen before. "We're home."

ACKNOWLEDGEMENTS

I want to thank Jeanne Martinson and everyone at Wood Dragon Books. I have learned so much through this process.

Thank you to Callum Jagger, for the amazing cover design.

Thank you to my family—Mom, Dad, Danica, Jackson—for listening to my every up and down for the past two years regarding the project.

Thank you to writer Terry Wolfe for his encouragement.

Thank you to my teachers—especially Mrs. Keller and Ms. Nelson—for being incredibly supportive.

Thank you to the many community members of Wood Mountain and Glentworth who have been so interested in my progress in realizing "The Amnesia Project."

Finally, to my many friends, who have been such great support.

ABOUT THE AUTHOR

Payton Todd has been writing short stories all her life, but the Amnesia Project is her first novel. The original draft of the novel was written when she was fifteen years old, after winning Wood Dragon Books' Young Author Competition.

She lives in Wood Mountain, Saskatchewan, Canada with her parents, sister, brother and dog on a cattle ranch. When she's not writing, she spends her time shooting archery competitively, playing volleyball, and learning new songs on her guitar.